PRAISE FOR ARTHUR NERS

"A *Trainspotting* without drugs, New York..."
—Hal Sirowitz, author of *Mother Said*

"For those who remember that the eighties were as much about destitute grit as they were about the decadent glitz described in the novels of Bret Easton Ellis and Jay McInerney, this book will come as a fast-paced reminder."
—*Time Out*

"Touted as the bottled essence of early eighties East Village living, *THE FUCK-UP* is, refreshingly, nothing nearly so limited.... A cult favorite, I'd say it's ready to become a legitimate religion."
—*Smug Magazine*

"Having 'grown to tolerate all of New York's degradations,' Arthur Nersesian's main character is irresistibly charming, funny, and real. Nersesian's writing, reminding me at times of John Patrick Shanley and Gogol, is beautiful, especially when it is about women and love. *THE FUCK-UP* is a terrific success."
—Jennifer Belle, author of *Going Down*

"Not since *The Catcher in the Rye,* or John Knowles' *A Separate Peace,* have I read such a beautifully written book. . . . Nersesian's powerful, sure-footed narrative alone is so believably human in its poignancy. . . . Nersesian mixes 'F' trains, lumpy couches, SoHo lofts, dive bars, lonely divorcees, porn theaters, posh brownstones, embezzling employers, ritzy Hard Rock Cafe parties, deceitful, would-be kept starlets, bathroom-stall poetry, free Mercedes-Benzes, and even Mormons. Whew! I couldn't put this book down."
—*Grid Magazine*

"Fantastically alluring! I cannot recommend this book highly enough!"
—*Flipside*

Also by Arthur Nersesian

East Village Tetralogy (four plays)
Tremors & Faultlines: Photopoems of San Francisco (poems)
Manhattan Loverboy (novel)
New York Complaints (poems)
Tompkins Square & Other Ill-Fated Riots (poems)

CK-UP

Arthur Nersesian

POCKET BOOKS

NEW YORK LONDON TORONTO SYDNEY TOKYO SINGAPORE

This book is a work of fiction. Names, characters, places and incidents are products of the author's imagination or are used fictitiously. Any resemblance to actual events or locales or persons, living or dead, is entirely coincidental.

Portions of this book have appeared in the *Portable Lower East Side*. Previously published by Akashic Books

POCKET BOOKS, a division of Simon & Schuster Inc.
1230 Avenue of the Americas, New York, NY 10020

Copyright © 1991, 1997 by Arthur Nersesian

MTV Music Television and all related titles, logos, and characters are trademarks of MTV Networks, a division of Viacom International Inc.

ISBN: 0-671-02763-8

First MTV Books/Pocket Books trade paperback printing May 1999

10   9   8

POCKET and colophon are registered trademarks of Simon & Schuster Inc.

Art Direction: Tracy Boychuk, Deklah Polansky
Graphic design: Deklah Polansky
© MTV Networks. All rights reserved.
Cover photography: Jason Stang and Clay Stang

Printed in the U.S.A.

TO JOHNNY TEMPLE

ACKNOWLEDGMENTS

I would like to thank those who helped bring this edition into print:

Patrick Nersesian
Kim Kowalski
Jennifer Belle
John Talbot
Laurie Horowitz
Zeke Weiner
Greer Kessel Hendricks
Eduardo Braniff
Kristen Harris

ONE

Perhaps the price of comfort is that life passes more rapidly. But for anyone who has lived in uneasiness, even for a short, memorable duration, it's a trade-off that will gladly be made. When I was in my teens, I made an appraisal of how comfortable my life could turn out when I became the age I am now. Because of a mechanical failure, the prediction was inexact. Things reversed. I ended up living somewhere I once avoided, with a woman whom I genuinely once disliked.

Recently we celebrated our seventh anniversary together with a decent dinner and a not dreadful film. I got out of work early that evening and took the

F train to Forty-second Street. I crossed Fifth Avenue toward the Main Branch of the Public Library, but paused in the middle of the crosswalk. It was filling up with the evening rush hour crowd: men in trench coats, secretaries in tennis shoes, cabs in the crosswalk, cars honking, leviathan buses zooming inches, braking, zooming again, and bike messengers slicing through it all. The last time I was in that spot, seven years ago, there wasn't a person in sight.

Seven years ago that day, as dawn rose, I remember standing in roughly the same spot watching as the traffic signals hanging over each intersection slowly turned yellow then red. Cars zoomed forward, headlights still on, staying ahead of the changing lights; at dusk they could make it all the way down without a single red light.

At rush hour, the entire avenue was gridlocked. But I could still faintly make out the small white crown of the Washington Square Arch at the very end. The anniversary of my relationship coincided with that dawning, and although that morning marked something that eluded celebration, it couldn't be forgotten either.

Something honked at me, so I crossed the street, reboarded the packed F train, and returned to Brooklyn for the anniversary dinner.

Before I got canned from my first job, back in the early eighties, I had relations with a waitress who subsequently became a girlfriend. I was a prep cook, at one of those West Village singles dives, and I think the boss was jealous over Sarah; she was one of the last waitresses there whom he hadn't screwed. She lived in the East Village, near the Saint Mark's Cinema, which is currently the site for the Gap. Soon after my dismissal from my prep cook job, I moved in with her. It was about a week after my new-found residency, while passing the Saint Mark's Cinema, that I noticed a sign written in a distressingly angular cursive. It read: "WE NEAD USHER!" I entered the theater and had a quick dialogue with Stan, the manager on duty, who hired me on the spot and wanted me to start that evening.

The only lasting memory of that virgin shift was the ejection of a wino. Pepe, the owner, quickly pointed to a bum as he was barging through the back door. Trying to impress the boss on the first day, I ran toward him and unintentionally locked elbows; we swung about in a one-hundred-and-eighty-degree turn, as if in a square dance. When I broke loose, he propelled himself back out into the night with his own momentum. After the incident occurred, Pepe embarrassed me by mentioning that while we were spinning around he couldn't tell who was who. The derelict possessed my basic features: my age—twenty-two; my height—five feet, ten inches; and my weight—a hundred and fifty-five pounds. By the time the first year of ushering had come to a close, I was the longest surviving employee. Pepe had fired everyone.

One night, toward the end of that summer, for want of anything better to do, I jotted down a misconduct list composed of all that I had witnessed there: seven reported pocket-pickings, four robberies, one slashing (it barely broke the skin), and a pistol drawn (it wasn't fired). I couldn't begin to count the unnatural acts and unreported molestations. Despite these offenses, the most heinous crime in the myopic eyes of Pepe was smoking.

I took as many weekday matinee shifts as possible. These we called "lawnchair shifts" because the audience was largely composed of neglected old folks who took advantage of the pre-five o'clock senior-citizen rates. At the opening of the shift, each usher was issued a flashlight, and since we weren't allowed to leave the auditorium—that was what Pepe called the theater—I'd read by flashlight.

So that was my day: opening the theater with the manager, helping the geriatrics into their fold-out seats, starting the film, making sure the image was good and that no one was smoking or being too enthusiastic. Then I would read. During the intermission I would mop the lobby, clean out the ashtrays, tour the aisles—politely awakening all the dozing grandparents just to make sure they hadn't died—and when the film started, I would read again. Only once did I try to wake someone up and fail. He was a nice old guy that would shake a lot, and it seemed sad that his long life had come to an end in the middle of *Turk 182*. After a year, I had read *The Education of Henry Adams*, *The Autobiography of Lincoln Steffens*, and the first four books of *Remembrance of Things Past*, all with the films of 1982 as a backdrop. I didn't even realize how much subconscious seepage had occurred until some time later when I was watching a rerun of *On Golden Pond*—I kept conjuring up strange images of young Henry Adams studying in Heidelberg.

The Saint Mark's was a second-run house. The patrons were basically from the neighborhood, and so were the employees. When Pepe first took over the theater in the early seventies, the neighborhood was different; it was rougher but things were cheaper. By '82, the East Village, at least as far east as Second Avenue, where the theater was located, had become gentrified.

Perhaps because the neighborhood was becoming ritzier and Pepe was elevating the performance standard, or perhaps because one gets disgusted with minimum wage quickly, there was a large turnover rate. After two months, enough Angels were fired to populate a heaven. Two Jesuses were also dismissed: one was apparently too "brusque," the other was "obtuse," according to the ever idiosyncratic Pepe. When someone was fired for an Anglican reason, he was usually fired by Pepe. He did most of the firing, and I always wondered where he got his language. Then one Sunday I watched "Masterpiece Theatre" and heard Alec Guinness call someone "opaque." The next day, someone else was fired with the same word. No one ever knew what the words meant and they were either too proud or too lazy to look them up, so they submitted quickly and retreated back eastward.

By the close of my first year at the theater, Pepe had slowly replaced the Puerto Rican locals with NYU students. It was during the NYU drive that a freshman from the film school was hired. Her name was Eunice. Like me she was from the Midwest, I think Indiana—and I was in love. She was from the America beyond the oceanic Hudson. She had apple cheeks and spoke with a twang. Sarah, on the other hand, was strictly New York, right down to her Eastern European via Lower East Side roots. Eunice was accommodating; she would laugh at my jokes, or smile when she caught me staring at her. She was a Red Delicious transformed into an Ivory Snow girl. She had a natural innocence, a kind of perpetual virgin quality, as if she didn't know of the demon genitals that secretly dwell between the legs of all, waiting to spring.

At first she balked at my advances but she didn't make me feel like the deceitful swine that I was. She knew I had a girlfriend and she didn't dismiss me because of it. By the first month of our acquaintance we were dating frequently. These dates were usually long cold walks lined with progressively luring questions posed by me. At times she would giggle dismissively. During the walks I would lose myself and ask questions that would reach out like oily fingers into concealed and tender areas of her past. As much as love meant striving, an always-approaching-yet-never-reaching titillation, I was for the first time in love.

This was during Sarah's final month in college. She was vigorously battling incompletes, preparing for that last barrage of finals, and scouting around for a graduate school. She was grateful for my mysterious absences and quickly accepted that I was working late. That January unraveled into thirty-one long days, and each of the evenings stretched far and thin like taffy. The art of courtship is a patient one, and I was getting an indelible chill from the many strolls. My own limited Midwestern experiences broke the ritual of dating into two stages: the initial part was taking the girl to some kind of spectacle—like a movie or roller-skating. This was the ice-breaking stage, where a passing of time would allow a familiarity, an understanding of priorities, incidental touching, the cultivation of ease. The second part was trickier. It usually required the use of some enclosure, a car or an apartment, and some kind of narcotic was helpful. The point was getting laid. At best, it was a seamless series of subtleties. But Eunice was far-sighted and conditions were never very good. She could see the dark brambles beyond the sunlit pathway, so usually all she would politely allow were those damned walks. One evening, after a particularly tedious promenade that left me feeling painfully raw and primitive, I told her what I wanted. She sweetly and neatly explained that she would not compromise, indicated that it was late, and suggested that perhaps I had better look elsewhere. Both of us in a huff, I left her in the lobby of her dormitory.

At home that night, I felt as swollen and feverish as a blister. Lying next to the sleeping Sarah, I turned and twisted. I was beaten but not defeated. The next morning Sarah was at school early and I spent the day rallying myself for that night's assault. In a week's time, though, the unexpected occurred: Sarah graduated. I took the day off to watch the commencement, and then after congratulating her with a big kiss I rushed to work to pick up Eunice for our nightly walk. Sarah's sudden freedom gave her an added awareness, though. For the first time, she wondered about my nightly delirious state and the extra care I had recently invested in my attire. I learned later that she had followed me one night and spied on me and Eunice slurping on a soda, two straws in the same cup. When I returned home that night, exhausted and frustrated, I lay quietly next to Sarah, who was probably playing possum. She was not confrontational and apparently didn't know how to approach me. The next day, I awoke late and Sarah was already up.

"I want to talk with you," she quietly muttered.

"'Bout what?" I asked as I quickly tugged on last night's clothes.

"About us." Her voice remained hushed and her eyes were fixed to the ground.

"Later," I replied as I raced out the door. It was a Tuesday and the only day when Eunice and I worked together. After opening the theater, the people came in and the show started. The day manager was working upstairs so I was able to sneak out to the candy stand and talk with her.

"Why are your clothes so wrinkled?" she asked me. I explained that I hadn't had time to change from the previous night.

"But it's more than that." She reached out and took a pinch of the fabric, "I've noticed this about everything you wear."

"What?"

"All your clothes are old."

"Well, how am I supposed to buy a wardrobe on minimum wage?"

"Minimum wage? How long have you been working here?"

"Almost a year."

"I think that's longer than anyone else."

"It is," I assured her.

"Well, you should get a raise."

"I probably should but this isn't a real job."

"Well, if you can't even afford to buy clothes, then you should find a real job. Clothes are a necessity."

"All right," I replied to close the issue, "I'll ask for a raise." And then we changed the subject and talked until the manager came back downstairs. I went back into the theater and forgot about the conversation until the intermission, when Pepe walked into the theater. He was about to vanish into his office when Eunice yelled over the counter to him, "The usher would like to speak to you."

After a year of working there, the only communication Pepe and I ever had was an occasional nod. I found him petty and undeserving, and he probably didn't notice me at all. Suddenly there he was, looking at me, attention undivided.

"Come on up."

I followed him up to his office. He offered me the seat across from him.

"What's up?"

"Well, Pep," I began nervously, wondering if I should bring it up, "I just finished a year of working here."

"Yeah, so I worked here for years, what else is new?"

"Well, you own the place."

"What are you getting at?"

"Well, I was wondering about a raise?"

"A raise? You mean a monetary raise?"

"Sure."

"I've never given a raise before. This isn't that kind of job, kid. It's minimum wage; the President gives you a raise here."

"Well, I was wondering, under these circumstances, if you might give me one."

"Look, kid, I wouldn't want anyone making a career out of this. How can I put this—it's the kind of job one takes when going through troubled times. Nestor, for example, he just got out of Riker's Island—in fact he's here on a work-release program, and Neville was just released from Bellevue."

"Yeah, but both of those guys were fired. In fact, most of them were fired, and you can rely on me to be here during the rough times."

Pepe nodded his head, pursed his lips, and looked out the window a moment. "This comes as a complete surprise to me, kid. But all right, I'm experimental, maybe it'll supply incentive." As he said this, he typed figures into the old-style calculator on his desk, and finally, pushing a tally button, he calculated. "I'll give you a raise of twelve point eight cents an hour, take it or leave it."

I thanked him and then the phone rang. How the hell he came up with twelve point eight I'll never guess, but without saying goodbye to me or hello to the phone, he held the phone to his ear and silently started feeding figures into that calculator in the center of his desk. As I returned to my post in the theater, I figured that now I could buy a Snickers candy bar every three and a quarter hours without having to dig into my preestablished income. When I proudly told Eunice how I had won my twelve point eight cent increase, she sneered and said that I had mishandled it.

"What do you mean? Twelve point eight cents?" I responded. "What do you call that?"

"What the hell can you do with twelve cents?"

"What was I supposed to do?"

"You should've threatened to quit." She went on to say that I was spineless and needed to learn to be more assertive.

"More assertive?"

"That's right," she said, and then revealed a bit of herself. "Back home in Gary, the Mormons taught a person to have fortitude when they were in the right."

"Well I'm sorry but there were no Mormons upstairs in Pepe's office to help me with this one."

"Well, you might consider joining a church," she remarked. When I smiled, she added, "Oh go ahead and snicker, but it could build a little character."

"Fuck you," I replied and marched back into the theater, where I felt like a moron. As the film played I thought about Sarah. She would exert a calm pressure when she wanted to improve my quality of life; additionally she would have sex with me. I had turned into an infidel with Eunice. After the film ended and I performed my usherly duties, I apologized to Eunice. She too said she was sorry.

"Listen, this is hard to explain, but this relationship is causing me a lot of hostility and anxiety. I'm doing things that I wouldn't normally do, so I think that we shouldn't see each other anymore."

"What?" She looked concerned.

"I can't deal with this anymore."

"You're just feeling bad now, that's all."

"No, I feel used, I feel like you're getting what you want and I'm not getting anything."

"And what exactly am I getting?"

"I'm like...a hungry dog that's following you everywhere and you won't feed me but you won't let me starve either."

She said she was sorry for the undeliberate grief she had caused and agreed that we probably shouldn't see each other any longer. After work, for the first time in a month, I went right home, but all was dark. I didn't know it, but I was too late. Sarah left a note; her brother had picked her up and brought her back to her parents' house on Long Island for the holidays. That night I did laundry, took a shower, and after a low-calorie meal and a little TV, I went to bed.

Eunice called me the next day to announce that she had just got her airline tickets and she was going back to Gary, Indiana, for winter break. She asked if we could meet somewhere before she left. I said no, curtly wished her a happy life, and hung up.

During the next few days, I got increasingly lonely. Pepe noticed me whenever we passed in the theater. He would scowl. I think he wanted me to work more for my raise. The twelve point eight cents an hour didn't seem to have much effect on my life. It seemed to affect his life more. Then I learned that the two box office girls who had worked almost as long as me had also asked and were reluctantly granted raises; now it was costing him thirty six and a quarter cents per hour and it was coming out of his personal income. After work that night, a friend offered me complimentary tickets to the Ritz Christmas party. I didn't care much for places like that, but I didn't want to be alone for Christmas. So after a turkey hero I got spruced up and went.

While waiting to get into the Ritz, I wondered what possible dance halls the place could have been. I was once waiting for a friend in front of the Saint, which I later learned once housed the old Fillmore East. An old hippie stopped in front of me with a surprised look of recognition. He started making a bunch of frantic and overexcited gestures. When he caught my attention, he asked me if I worked there. Before I could reply he sighed and pointed inside the place.

"One night," he took the liberty of saying, "I took more acid right in there than anyone else anywhere, ever!"

The Ritz had peaked about a year before and now it was on the decline, but so was I. Area, the Saint, Danceteria and the Palladium had divided its clientele. The club phenomenon seemed to be a three-way synthesis between concert halls of the late sixties, dance halls of the forties, and singles bars of the seventies. Someone, probably the late Steve Rubell, pieced together these cultural Portosans: Scrub some massive old toilet of a place, bait it with a bit of glamour, Andy Warhol protégés set the vortex spinning with initially coveted, now annoying, comps. Once the masses dropped in, trapped and floating, they were flushed down with exorbitantly priced drinks. By the late eighties, Area, the Saint, and Danceteria would be out of business.

That night there seemed few alternatives. After a half an hour of watching music videos and drinking beer, I made a pass at one of the many chubby Jersey girls bouncing around on the dance floor. Another bland band was strumming its heart out without exciting anyone. I was about to leave when I noticed a guy in his mid-forties get onto the center of the dance floor wearing a John Travolta white suit, complete with vest—a dated image of how "youth" was presumed to look. Dancing with him was a young girl in a flimsy evening gown. As I inspected closely, I couldn't believe my fucking eyes—Eunice! I slowly moved closer. They were dancing tightly pressed, his hands playing along her back, slowly resting down on the cheeks of her buttocks. Wild conjecture and reckless speculation started structuring.

Could this be a paternal figure who had changed her diapers years ago, perhaps a much older stepbrother from a previous marriage who wrestled with her when she was a sexless adolescent? A kissing cousin or a cuddling uncle? For a moment they slipped into a splash of light, and the contrast of his olive-leathery skin against her milky lightness completely obliterated the relativity theory. Perhaps it was a neighbor or a landlord or some avuncular figure who was gay as a gooseberry. But in a moment they were kissing and his orbiting hands were wildly grazing around her body. What the fuck was going on?

I had no right to be jealous, but I hated Yuletide deception. I stormed out. With all the cash in my pocket, which came to the entire twelve point eight cent bonus multiplied by the week, I was able to afford two quarts of Budweiser. I returned home, downed both bottles, and became victimized by a drunk-abusive imagination: Eunice was probably soothed by his paternal pontifications, intoxicated with tropical drinks, the tab was on him. He probably feigned an excuse to stop over at his house. Once there, she'd lay down while he waited in a distant shadow for sleep to snare her. Her clothes would slowly, mysteriously be zipped, clipped, and slipped off her body. Soon she would be lying exposed, legs half parted, on his bed, deceptively king-sized since even his wife no longer slept with him, enticed by new sheets for the occasion. Eunice's doll-like eyes slowly blinking, a melody in her mind, an easily earned grin, attention nodding, fading.

Stay here tonight. Home is far. The walk, dangerous. The night, cold. Sure, she replies, as if with a slumber party companion. His wife—the menace—away for the holidays, an annual Florida getaway ritual. His slithering and forked tongue moving up and down the PG-13 parts of that luscious body. Wait till she's asleep. He's barely restraining, knowing full well this is the last time he'll drain the goblet, a valediction to the vagina. Beyond this—memories. When her liquor-naive body can resist no more, and the chasm of slumber finally gulps her, he leers. First, just a veiny, reptilian hand stroking along those sacred miniature curls. A gourmand enjoys his banquet slowly, sumptuously. But starvation collapses pacing, hot, flushed thoughts race: if passion were reason, *erectus ergo sum*!

Middle-aged, unilateral copulation; grunt/rasped breaths, a semi-erect display, a monsoon of sweat, his nose beginning to itch and run, palpitations, a free hand grants a nipple's tweak, lips stroked, reactions reaped, but...but...premature sputterings, flounderings, a disheartening sperm count, hyperventilation...sleep.

Sarah awoke me the next morning. I was naked and shivering. The blanket had fallen to the floor. Sarah had come home earlier than expected. "I couldn't take the parents." Apparently everything her mother served was garnished with guilt.

I was glad to be back with Sarah. Despite the holiday break, though, she was still heavily embroiled in school matters and the hunt for a good graduate school. I sensed something was wrong when at one point I tried to kiss her, and she pushed me away and said, "Not now."

"What's the matter?" I asked.

"Why are you such a mess?"

"I'm always a mess. You should be concerned when I'm not a mess."

"I suppose," she replied in a small and distant voice.

The only affection I could offer Sarah seemed generated from my hostility to Eunice. At one organic moment I hugged and kissed Sarah, but she remained distant and finally she lapsed into silence. I attributed it to her being worn thin by the parents. She needed to be left alone a while. It was already five o'clock, the sun had set—a cold day was now bleak. I was scheduled to work that night. I kissed her, changed my clothes, and went off to the theater.

When I got there, everyone seemed unusually kind. The candy girl couldn't offer me enough popcorn. The manager on duty, a new guy with whom I got along well, realized that I was tired and allowed me to sit in the lobby and relax. I wasn't curious about the kindness; I assumed that it was fate's compensation for all the recent misdealings. I didn't anticipate that it was all just pity for what was to come. After the movie, I went into Pepe's office, where he sat like a fat cat eyeing me.

The evening's intake of cash was in the box on the desk between us. He put the box in a desk drawer. I figured I had been working here for a year now and perhaps he felt it was time to offer me a manager's position. Staring down at other items that were sprawled along his desktop, he started speaking. "This isn't easy, because you were here longer than just about anyone else, but I'm going to have to release you."

"Huh?"

"One of the patrons complained that you were... duplicitous."

"Duplicitous?!!"

"Uhhh, yeah."

"Spare me that S.A.T. crap! I went to college!"

"Fine, the fact is I don't like you."

"Why?"

"You started a bad habit. People are asking for raises. Whenever I turn someone down, they bring up your name. I've got to put an end to this. Simple as that."

"You can't do this. I'll take you to the fucking labor relations board."

"Go ahead, you don't belong to a union; this is only a minimum wage job."

"I gave you a year of my life. I've always been on time, courteous. What kind of a person are you!"

Silently he ushered me to his office door where he handed me an envelope. "This is what we owe you."

Canned! It was the second job that I had been fired from and I felt guilty.

As I walked home, I pieced together details and realized that he had waited until after the holidays to fire me because he knew that nobody else would work on Christmas day for just minimum wage.

When I arrived home, Sarah wasn't there. By the time I finished soaking in a bath while watching TV, it was midnight. Sarah still wasn't home. Since I was wide awake and was mulling over being fired, I dressed and decided to go out for a beer. In the East Village most of the bars had started out as Eastern European hangouts, but more and more they became alcoholic cafeterias due to the growing influx of students. By the mid-eighties, the last of the Iron Curtain refugees in most of these neighborhood pubs were just the bartenders.

As I peeked into the many area bars like the Verkhovina and the Blue and

Gold looking for a familiar face, it struck me how time had passed. All of the old crowd had moved on. After stopping here and there, I arrived at the Holiday Lounge on Saint Mark's Place. It was brimming with children who paid for overpriced drinks with their parent's money. By the time I had shoved through them to the rear, I felt ancient. Just as I was about to head back home, I caught sight of a chunky punk in a leather jacket. He was sitting in a booth kissing some girl who was lying horizontally along the bench with her head lying idly across his fat lap. When I positioned around to look at her, my heart quit—it was Sarah! I grabbed his collar and yanked him up.

"What the fuck is your problem?" he yelled.

"I'm her husband!" I hollered. When I tried to pull her upright, she remained drunk and limp.

"What the fuck are you doing?" I shouted, shaking her to gain some degree of sobriety.

"What the fuck am I doing?" She leered. "The same thing you've been doing for the past month."

"What?"

"Humping that candy girl, you fucker." And she slapped me full in the face and stormed out. I felt my skin turn into goose pimples and walked past the prepubescents, who looked back at me, the twenty-three-year-old cuckold. I slowly walked home, chewing my bottom lip to a pulp as I juggled half-lies and half-truths seeking a plausible reconciliation.

When I got home, Sarah had heaped all my clothes in the hall and left a sign taped to the outside of the door: "If you try to come in, I'll call the police."

I collected everything off the floor: some books, three T-shirts, five pairs of underpants, an out-of-style suit and a pair of polished dress shoes. With that big ball in my arms, I headed down First Avenue to the F train on Houston Street.

TWO

The F train stopped at the Carroll Street station in Brooklyn. Once again, I was off to stay with Helmsley. His apartment was the only place I could go without having to ask permission; I had his key. Neither of us had any immediate family, so we were brother orphans.

He also happened to be one of the most intelligent and determined people I had ever known: he was one of the youngest people ever to attain a professorship at Bryn Mawr. I later learned that he was also one of the youngest professors ever dismissed from Bryn Mawr. Helmsley said they found him a threat to convention; an old colleague quietly confided that it was psychological instability.

I had met him on the F train two years earlier. He was reading Ulick Varange's book *Imperium*. It was a very hard book to find and few knew about it. Whether it was worth getting or knowing about was another question. He claimed that it was a mild poly-philosophical work but it was wonderful prose satire. When I asked him how he could dismiss a poly-philosophical work as satirical prose, he explained that he viewed our present era as nothing more than a retrenched "Age of Reason." He showed a preference toward the animist perspective, which preserved the life-force, to man's harnessing perspective, which was simply a castrating method analysis.

And we spent the night riding around on the F train with him usually talking and me usually listening. I had a lot more patience back then and was easily dazzled by bullshit.

Beyond maintaining his life functions, Helmsley spent almost all his time on two activities: writing and reading. He explained to me that he used to write more than he read but lately the scale had been tipping the other way. He had had two thick and confusing books of poetry published in an extremely limited and costly edition by the now-defunct Necro Publications.

Helmsley claimed that the two works quelled all further desires to be published. But occasionally I'd find form rejections in the garbage can, and I strongly suspected him of being a closet submitter. He actually had a decent reputation as a reviewer and had a growing reputation as a translator. Inexplicably he regarded this as hack work, published under a pseudonym, and never boasted about a publication.

He still wrote and wasn't shy about the creative process. When he was working on a project, you knew it. He would completely immerse himself in the subject. Although everything was poetic in form, he was paying more and more attention to different cultures through history. He would frequent the museums, attend seminars, study languages, and although he never did, he always longed to visit the subject country. Usually he tried the next best thing, which was re-creating the psycho/eco/politico/-environment and wrestling with the questions that might occupy one of his poetic foils.

He took this study to all ends. One time, while he was studying revolutionary France, he spent a week attempting to re-create the heartburn and gastritis of the time. Could a mushy crepe significantly contribute enough fury to provoke a revolution? I did my own cooking that week.

Due to the ten-percent money-market return that existed in 1983, in which he had invested his parental inheritance minus only the pittance that he lived on, he was actually able to save a little each month and had no need for a job.

"Just from the garbage America throws out," he once said, "one could live like a well-to-doer in a third-world country."

His thrift often breached into pettiness. His rent controlled apartment was stocked with charitably resold bargains, irregular discounts, and damaged goods. He pedalled an old cast-iron bike around the town, and his pockets were usually lined with hurriedly snatched packets of sugar and other assorted sealed condiments which he would habitually take when the opportunity arose.

Although he was a passionate lover of all arts, literature was what he tried to produce. To hear him casually rattle off a favorite passage or stanza in which each intonation had been rehearsed to a grace—I would imagine it was like listening to Caruso sing his favorite opera. He easily could sound pompous but he was actually very modest. In fact, he preferred relating to the arts alone. On those occasions when I bore witness, he seemed to go beyond propriety with his eyes rolling and his body swaying like a Shaker in a spiritual fit. I'd get nervous, and try to snap him out of it.

I would usually see a lot of Helmsley for a couple of weeks and then a stretch of time would pass without so much as a phone call. I hadn't spoken to him for at least two months, but whenever we resumed our friendship it carried an instant familiarity, as if only a day had gone by. He always seemed glad to see me and always had a place on his couch if I needed a bunk. When we first met, I was writing my premature memoir. He was impressed by the idea, and the amount of time and attention I was giving to it. Because of that I think that he convinced himself I would someday be a bona fide writer.

The subway screeched into the Carroll Street station. It was cold and late and my arms were full with my belongings as I trudged to Helmsley's house. When I knocked on his door, he mindlessly threw it open wide. Despite his under-heated apartment, he was completely nude and bathing in sweat. In his right hand was an old Modern Library copy of *Light in August*. When I first met Helmsley, he explained how he had put together his own anthology of selections and which, for the sheer pleasure of reading, he would reread, again and again.

"You mean you just reread excerpts? Is it fair to take a work out of context like that?"

"When you want to hear a song, do you feel compelled to always listen to an entire album?" The particular tune that I had walked in on was the last two pages of Chapter Eighteen—the execution and castration of Joe Christmas. It was high on Helmsley's hit list.

"What's up?" he asked as soon as I dumped all my worldly goods onto his hard couch.

"Sarah gave me the old farewell."

"What happened?"

"I fucked up."

"You got into a fight?"

I went into his kitchen, filled a glass with water, emptied it in a gulp, and replied, "No, I transgressed."

He stopped asking questions and just gave me a wide-eyed expression.

"I drew water from the well of another."

"I hope she was worth it."

"That, I'll never know." He gave me another of his curious expressions.

"Are you telling me that you lost everything for her and you didn't even score?"

I lay on my smelly worldly possessions. "It was a turgid punishment; a flaccid crime."

Helmsley marched back into the living room fully dressed in his second-hand clothes. "I was about to go for a walk. You're invited if you like."

I needed to stew for a while, so he left. I turned off the lamp and thought about Sarah. I had always wanted to believe that love was a hypnotic and sustained state of lust, respect, etc., but that never happened with Sarah or anybody else. We did have a good relationship. Sarah was a nice, attractive, intelligent girl. We functioned well together. To be young and alone in New York City meant you either had to have a lot of parental assistance or have a lot of luck, and I had neither. Entry-level salaries for most good jobs could not pay for basic living expenses. Unless you wanted a quirky roommate, the economy encouraged you to find a lover. Sarah and I complemented each other well. We were emotionally matched and although things never got too sweet, they never got too sour.

At first, as always, the sex was sublime, but after a couple of months that petered out, and if we were lucky, which was about once every two weeks, one of us would discover or rediscover some novel aspect that would serve as arousing. We enjoyed each other's sense of humor and knew each other's moods, and how to provide mutual comfort. But also I think we both understood that appreciation grew with distance and every so often a controlled neglect was healthy.

But I had damaged the works and proved myself the adulterer and probably gave the impression that I didn't give a damn about her. All I could do was sit there and brood.

Soon Helmsley returned and attempted to start me talking. "So what did you mean when you said you lost your job?"

"I got canned." I was preoccupied and didn't feel much like elaborating.

"Why?"

"I forget, I was implicit or something like that. I don't want to think about it now."

"Well, excuse my persistence, but how will you live?"

"Are you kidding? With a year of ushering under my belt I can go anywhere."

"I know an opening as a packer at the Goya plant." It was a warehouse near his house.

"Look, I'm still basking in disgust and self-pity. Can we rebuild my life tomorrow?"

He thoughtfully retired to his room, but before turning out his light, he placed a half-full bottle of Scotch on the night table along with an old shoe-box filled with K-Tel hits of the seventies that he had purchased through a TV commercial. "If you're going to listen to mood music, do it on the headphone, and if you want to cry do it in the pillow." And then he left.

I thought for a while about the real tragedy of the breakup. Of course, it was deeply rooted in vanity; I had slowly regained a normalcy that I had lost years ago when I first left my parental home. Under Sarah's tutelage, I had been redeveloping healthy habits like brushing my teeth and hair. I was also sleeping and eating well. I had lost the bulge of pounds that I acquired when I first came to the city. I was going to NYU Dental School for cut-rate, semi-annual checkups and, most of all, I was finally conquering that Himalayan peak of unlaundered clothing. Once a week I would push all my things—which were presently sprawled along Helmsley's couch—into a seventy-five-cent machine and read a magazine. Everything was slowly coming together; a decency was winning; people were slowly coming to treat me with more respect; I was in less general pain and was finding greater comforts. I even thought more lucidly. As the mercenary and the maniac were slowly being exorcised from me, life was becoming both more peaceful and productive. For not even a nipple's pinch, I'd lost it all. Strapping the headphones over my scalp and taking a painfully long guzzle of that mouthwash Scotch, I listened to an unknown band singing depressing tunes of the seventies.

The next morning, I got up slowly and found a note from Helmsley informing me that he had gone to some arcane exhibit. I showered and began to shave, but after doing significant damage to my features I conceded I was still too wobbly. With Helmsley's toothbrush I scrubbed my teeth. Closing my eyes I must have dozed as my hand mechanically kept brushing. When I came to a moment later and tiredly inspected myself in the mirror, my face was snagged with nicks and my traumatized gums were lined with blood. I cleaned up, dressed slowly, and boarded the F train, returning to Manhattan.

While on the train, I thought about my imminent grand appeal. First, I would beg for my job back, and next I'd explain to Sarah that one misadventure didn't warrant a breakup. One sexual excursion was the permitted allowance in any modern relationship, and I hadn't even gotten that.

Once back in the East Village, I called Sarah but only got the dispassionate recording. I figured that she was probably there and a whiny plea would only alert her that I was back on the prowl. I still had her key, so I decided to go straight to her house. It was late in the afternoon and now that school was over, there was no reason that she shouldn't be at home. When I finally reached her apartment, I knocked politely. When there was no answer, I tried inserting my key in the lock.

In the few business hours that I had slept through that morning, she had called a locksmith and had her lock cylinder changed. It was only then that I realized the unshakeability of her resolution. I got pissed and started to kick the door, but after a while I calmed myself and decided to leave a note: "All is not as bad as it seems. I swear that in the course of our relationship, I never made love to anyone but you. If you don't believe me you can ask the popcorn girl. I love you dearly and it pains me that you won't even talk to me. I am staying at Helmsley's. Please give me a call when you can. I love you."

When I left her building, I was so confident that everything was repaired that I marched full steam over to the cinema to reclaim my lost job. When I got there, I asked the box office girl if I could see Pepe. She spoke to him on the intercom and then said go right in. As I passed through the theater, I saw some new kid holding a flashlight and laughing at the film. He had obviously just been hired to fill my spot. When he noticed me heading for the office, he intervened.

"What the hell do you want?"

"Pepe," I replied.

"Oh, you're Pepe." He didn't even have the brains to figure out that I was probably too young to own a theater.

"I'm sorry boss, go ahead." This kid wasn't going to last the week. Pepe was at his desk reading something when I opened his door. Without looking up he asked, "What is it?"

"Pepe, if I could have my job back..."

"No."

"Just hear me out. I can work twice as hard and you can even lower my pay. How's that?"

"No."

"But look, it would be a better example, because if you just fire me I might go and get another job with better pay. But this way you can degrade me and then people will never think twice about even asking for a raise."

"No."

"I'll tell you what. I'll work here for two weeks free and then you can decide."

Pepe thought about it a moment and then in the same bland tone repeated, "No."

He never told me to leave; for that matter he didn't even have the decency to look up from whatever he was reading. He just kept repeating that word. As I despondently retreated down the stairs, the usher who had effortlessly replaced me dashed up.

"Are you having a good day, boss?"

"No, you're fired."

"What?"

"You're fired, now get the hell out of here!" I yelled. By being so available he had conspired in getting me fired.

"But...but..." Inarticulation turned to rage. I watched his face turn red and redder. He was taking it even worse than I had.

"I'm fired, huh? I'm fired, huh?" he screamed in duplicate. I promptly realized my cruelty. But he was quicker in reprisal than I was in rectification. Instantaneously he grabbed his jacket and dashed into the lobby.

"Wait a second," I said, and pursued. I was about to hire him back, but before I could I heard the sudden crash. Rushing out to the lobby, I saw that he had toppled the new cigarette machine to the floor, and before dashing off he yelled, "Go fuck yourself!"

"What the hell is going on!" Pepe appeared a moment later amidst a crowd that had formed around the smashed machine. He asked the candy girl what had happened.

"Da new usher, he say...he say bam! to dat machine and den he say go fuck you and den he run off."

Pepe was confused. The new guy was working out well. All were baffled. I felt bad. With nothing else to do, I slowly walked down the Bowery and over the Brooklyn Bridge to Helmsley's house.

Fumbling for the key outside his door, I could hear Helmsley within, holding some frantic kind of recitation. I knocked. Letting me in, he interrupted me before I could tell him about the theater mishap.

"I have bad news for you."

"What?"

"Well about a half an hour ago, Sarah called." He paused with a bleak expression. "She told me she got your note and that she didn't care to see you again."

"What?"

"She said that this seemed like a good place to end the relationship considering she was going to graduate school and all."

"She told you this?"

"Well, I told her to speak to you; I said that I really didn't want to get involved in all this."

"And what did she say?"

"Just that if I didn't take the message, you'd never find out."

"Didn't you plead my case at all?"

"'Course I did, I told her that you truthfully told me that you never screwed that little candy tramp and that underneath it all you were one of the finest people I had ever known."

"What do you mean underneath it all?"

"You know, underneath all the crap that life does to us."

"And what did she say?"

Helmsley sighed. "It didn't go well. Why don't you come with me tonight? Find a new girlfriend."

"What did she say when you told her I was one of the finest people you know?"

"She said that I could have you."

"She said that?"

"Well, that and more."

"What more?"

Well, if you insist, she said that after a month of living with you, I'd get to know..."—he looked up a moment and recounted each adjective on his fingertips—"...the snot-nosed...egotistical little cocksucker...that she had to put up with all these months. She also made it clear that she didn't want to see you again. I don't remember that part exactly. She might've just been in a disagreeable mood but I think she despises you."

I dropped to the couch. I was a snot-nosed, egotistical little cocksucker? "Did she actually say all those things verbatim or was that just the gist of it?"

"Look, I'm going to a very promising party tonight. Why don't you come along?"

"No thanks."

"Look, there will be other people there like Sarah, other girls."

"I'm in no mood for a party." I felt hollow. We had lived together all these months. I had no idea she had been bottling up all that hostility.

"You've got to come with me," Helmsley insisted. "I have no intention of coming home tonight and finding you dead in the tub. That once happened to me, you know. I found someone dead in my tub." He went on to inform me that I'd be able to exchange my sob story for a date with any girl there.

"Try to get a tear in your eye by the time you come to the part about how your girlfriend dumped you and how you're a frustrated, unemployed orphan. It'll be a clincher."

All of last night's mouthwash Scotch was gone. If they had nothing else at academic parties, they had booze. They needed it to loosen up. I was about to complete the shaving job that I brutally initiated that morning, but Helmsley stopped me. "Don't even comb your hair."

"Why not?"

"You haven't got a chance for the slick look. You're going after the shaggy dog appeal. If you're trying to show that you're a mess you've got to look and act like it. So let's go." We both grabbed our jackets and were gone.

We took the F train to Fourteenth Street and walked through the long uriney tunnel that passed from Sixth to Seventh Avenue. There, we took the IRT up to Columbia-land, 116th and Broadway. It was the winter intercession for most schools. This particular party was a graduate affair filled with doctoral candidates, master's students, all affiliated with Columbia's anthropology department—enthusiasts of mal-developed skull fragments found around Kenyan lakes.

At first I tried. I found girls who reminded me the most of Sarah personality-wise and tried to joke around comfortably with them. I panicked about the shaggy dog appeal, matted down my hair and small-talked with one young protégée of Margaret Meade who, when she asked me about myself, I provided a thickly veiled description of the truth. "I was just transferred"—instead of fired—"from my job at a corporate law firm"—instead of stinking movie theater—and had "recently moved into my own apartment"—instead of being dumped by my girlfriend...and so on. She quickly dusted around the old bones of truth and realized that my tale of mediocrity was actually of woe. Instead of a safe bet I was a loser.

I drank some alcohol and looked for prospective girls while considering a new approach. Tolstoy—Helmsley had informed me—before marrying his wife, Sophia, had let her read his hold-nothing-back journals to show her that he was just another slime bag. It was a deliberate effort to destroy any romantic notions his eighteen-year-old bride might have of him. This was my next strategy, my new approach. I sat down alongside my next victim, who was standing innocently alone by a partly opened window, unprotected. I quickly introduced myself and launched into the new approach, "Isn't this something?"

"What?"

"My girlfriend dumps me, I lose my job and apartment, and it's the third anniversary of my being an orphan."

"Poor you," she replied sympathetically. It was working.

"I tried to sleep with another girl, but that's another story. See here," I pointed to my raw gums that I overbrushed earlier, "and here." I pointed to the barely visible cracks in my facial flesh. "I felt so bad last night about her leaving me that I got drunk this morning and then I woke up and did this to myself."

"Oh," she replied.

"My father died in a plane crash, but don't feel sorry for me," I remarked.

Some guy wearing a turban heard me. He joined us uninvited, holding two drinks.

"A plane crash?" he said, "Oh, my!" He handed his girlfriend one drink, and she pointed to my gums and jowls and informed him about my recent misfortunes. I excused myself as they continued their conversation about me. I drank some more, but I didn't really try socializing. I think stories started circulating about me. I think someone pointed at me. Eventually a bevy of cute girls entered together. They couldn't have heard about me yet. They were dressed to the hilt, hair cut and colored like tropical birds, with the smells of perfumes named after TV stars. I shagged up my hair again and introduced myself to the most extreme of them. She was a delightfully perfumed pet who said she was in her last year at FIT, and then she asked me what I did. Confident that the new approach was working, I replied truthfully, "Unemployed, unconnected and unmotivated." She was uninterested and vanished. With that strike, I was out. I promised Helmsley I wouldn't pull a Jim Morrison in his bathtub and left.

THREE

The next day, I wrote a deliberately nebulous resume, a resume Helmsley later referred to as my greatest piece of fiction. It might have qualified me for everything from a shoeshine boy to an astronaut and off to the Goya Plant I went. They found me overqualified. Intelligence had become a liability; education, a hindrance.

I borrowed Helmsley's suit, bought the *New York Times* and took the little resume on a walk. We went to endless job agencies. But it was the same thing every time. After a flash interview by a variety of look-alike agents, they'd say more or less the same thing, "You're just the right man for something that should emerge any day now." None of them ever called me back.

By the end of the second week, I stopped getting up before noon, and by the middle of the third week I stopped shaving altogether. I'd lie around in bed watching daytime TV, which is the first sign of nervous breakdown in an enlightened culture. First, I watched the noon news and talk shows, then the game shows, onto the late-afternoon talk shows, and finally I was glued to the soaps. After that TV-mangled period, I stopped watching and just slept a lot. Helmsley realized I needed solitude and went out frequently.

As the components of your life are stripped away, after all the ambitions and hopes vaporize, you reach a self-reflective starkness—the repetitious plucking of a single overwound string. I was too poor to even have an etherizing vice like drugs or alcohol. Slowly I became a Peeping Tom of finer days, a vicarious liver through my own past. Years ago, forecasting the quality of my life to come was a cinch. By five years' time—which would have been five years ago—I would've graduated with a degree in architecture, and with a guaranteed job in my father's growing real estate development firm. In sum, I'd be kept in clover. Envisioning my future was like watching a lucky contestant on a game show, whose winnings increased with each spin of the wheel.

That's not the way things worked out; my life changed viciously. But it happened in a kind of aloof suddenness that someone might possess when pushing an elevator button or hitting a light switch. Five years had passed since the switch was thrown, and I was lying on an old couch in Brooklyn, considering the variety of ways in which my life was miserable. My mother had died when I was young. When my father was killed, my sister went off to live with relatives, and I was alone.

By the fourth week of my stay at Helmsley's, I was leaning as much over the edge as possible without tumbling over. I hadn't eaten in two days and I hadn't slept in three. I wasn't really in pain, in fact I was undergoing this bizarre type of euphoria, the kind of numb yet heightened elation an anorectic might feel in denying oneself that final crumb. Everything was dreamily wonderful, a preview of what was to come. I only got out of bed to go to the bathroom, and though I was wide awake I had neither thoughts nor moods.

I felt like a television camera just tracking and panning and registering responses. I knew my legs were very cold but was not bothered in the slightest. Helmsley finally came in the room and asked, "How are you?"

I waited along with him to hear how I would respond, and I was glad when I finally heard myself say, "Fine."

He put his hand on my forehead and it felt strangely soothing. He mumbled, "You're sick. When was the last time you ate?"

"Yesterday, I think." Time was flat. Everything seemed to have occurred a yesterday ago. He led me into the kitchen and prepared a meal for me that made me realize how hungry I was. Recalling the recuperative weeks that followed, remembering Helmsley's concern and affection, my Adam's apple suspends like a pendulum. He fussed over me like a mother. He woke me in the mornings and would prepare breakfast for both of us. Then he made sure I had showered and brushed my teeth; he nagged me into laundering my clothes. We would go on brief walks, full of optimism and esteem-building conversation. Up until then, I had always admired Helmsley's lofty knowledge, but I categorized him as a lover of mankind while ambivalent about man in any specific sense. He was unsympathetic to ghettos, passing them all by with the usual blindness that most New York natives seem to have.

During the chilly January days, the coldest days of winter, after the weeks of being indoors, I was stir crazy and spent as much time outdoors as my circulatory system allowed. In the mornings I would take the train back to the East Village and wander around. All those air-conditioned stores that I would cool off in during the previous summer's swelter were the same stores that I warmed up in during those frosty days of winter.

"Strange," Helmsley commented out of the blue one chilly morning. "Your generation is the first in years that hasn't produced a convincing sub-culture."

"How about punks, what do you call them?"

"Unconvincing. Now, you take hippies. They had a talk, a literature, central figures, splinter groups—a vision. They were political and they were even anti-fashion. Punks are kind of a negation of growth, at best a fad."

"That's not true. Punks have a music, and a style." But he had a point. I did feel that this was an inopportune time to be young.

"The only ones who have any kind of legacy are those who have. There's no distinguishable counter-culture..."

"What's in a counter-culture? It isn't that important," I responded, sick of hearing him bad mouth "my age."

"The counter-culture eventually becomes the culture. Max Eastman, a commie as a youth, was a power-broker when he got older. Angry young men eventually get the reins, still have enough steam in them..."

"Change the subject."

"See, you're so apathetic, you're an old man. You should have more of a youthful identity."

"Youthful identity?"

"Sure, did you ever see the film *Woodstock*? You should go to some Woodstock. Where do the young folks gather? You should go there."

"Where do young folks gather?" It sounded like a Peter, Paul and Mary tune. With all the free time on my hands, I decided to hunt down some young. I got off the R train at Broadway and Eighth and slowly walked down the east side of Broadway. The street was a bustling youth industry. Chic teen stores, stocked with the latest fashions-for-juniors crowded the block. I flowed in and out of each one, pulled like a cork on the consuming post-adolescent sea. Tower Records, appropriately located at the end of this succession, on Fourth Street, was the apex of teen exploitation, the drain at this ditch.

With MTV-tuned televisions posted every ten feet or so, hung up high but aimed downward precisely at eye level, allied with Dolby-blasted music, this was too much for a youngster to resist. By and large, I found the whole rock 'n' roll racket sordid. Motivated by a shameless ocean of dollars, basic adolescent compulsions—principally sex and violence—were serviced. Catchy tunes and sappy lyrics were wound together, moronic DJ's repetitiously played them out, and by the time they were on Casey Kasem's "American Top Forty," most kids felt like pariahs if they didn't own the selected album.

Flipping through twenty years of rock albums—the hippie albums of the sixties, the disco motif of the seventies, and on to the punk appeal of the eighties—you could see the development of fashions. The contemporary hype was colorful androgyny, which allowed a kind of guilt-free flirtation with homosexuality. One could feel strange attractions to these semi-boy, semi-girl entertainers that looked like sexy Dr. Seuss creatures.

It was after five, and the rush hour was in effect. While wedged between angles of sweaty anatomy in the Brooklyn-bound R train, I was subjected to bland disconnected lines of conversation.

"The man's not for you Dana, he's a sex pig." Another lady as tall as she was wide, squeezed next to me jerkily and pulled off her yak-like coat revealing a sleeveless, tasteless print dress. Like a fish in a filthy aquarium, I kept gasping upward for air. When the train screeched into Rector Street, she fell on me just as I was inhaling open-mouthed. Her bearded armpit sunk into my mouth; it tasted like a Big Mac.

She unloaded with a herd of people at Whitehall Street, the next stop. Carefully I maneuvered myself into a more guarded position by the door. A girl with an accent and a bunch of luggage was talking to a spindly, oily fellow who looked like a future presidential assassin. "Listen to me, all you have to do is go to Twelfth Street and ask for Miguel. Tell him Tanya sent you. He's promised me it's yours."

"But I have no idea how to manage a movie theater."

"There's nothing to it. It pays well and it's the easiest thing in the world."

"But I don't even have a work visa."

"Listen, I told you this before—just make up a social security number. They never check; if you're really worried pay someone a couple of dollars and use theirs. Everybody does it."

"What's the pay?"

"Five bucks an hour."

"Well, let me think about it a couple of days."

"Say," the girl said, peering at the digits of her watch. "My plane leaves in fifteen minutes. Where is this train to the plane?"

"It's supposed to be at Jay Street," the greasy youth replied as our train pulled into Court.

"Get off here and walk to Jay," I warned her. The doors opened and both of them looked at me strangely.

"This train doesn't stop at Jay Street," I yelled as I hopped out between the doors sliding shut. As the subway slowly tugged out of the station, I watched the girl's face turn to panic, and she quickly questioned people around her. There was no way in hell that she was going to escape from the city today.

As I walked out of the station and down Court Street homeward, I felt sorry for her because she had unknowingly just given me a job. If that oily kid could do it, so could I. He was not sure he could handle it and was going to think it over for a couple of days. Think away, oily boy, I'm going to grab that job tomorrow. As I walked, I wondered what kind of theater it could be; it had to be either a second-run or a repertory theater. Those were the only ones that would pay five an hour and hire someone with no prior experience. If that schmuck could do the job, I certainly would be able to handle it.

The next day, I spent as much time as I ever had in preparing a good appearance. I wasn't sure as to where on Twelfth Street this miraculous theater would be, so I took the IRT to Fourteenth and Seventh, got off at the Twelfth Street exit, and started walking.

The first theater I saw was the Greenwich. While working at the Saint Mark's, I heard that these conglomerate theater companies were very "by the book." They certainly didn't hire people off the street and make them instant managers; you had to work your way up tiresome and tedious ranks. I passed by that theater, heading east. The subway export said, "Just off Twelfth Street," which might've meant Thirteenth. Since the Quad, "four theaters under one roof," was on Thirteenth, I checked it out. Going up to a glass screen with a hole in the middle, I asked if there were any jobs available. Someone yelled no, and on to the next theater. Back on Twelfth, between Fifth Avenue and University Place, was a small repertory dive called the Cinema Village. I figured that this had to be the one. I went up to the outdoor box office. A cool brunette was sitting on a stool. I gave her a foreknowing grin. I knew that one day we'd be great friends, we'd maybe even sleep together. It would be funny, one day, to look back on this first time when we saw each other. When she finally looked up from the curriculum she was reading, she snapped her gum.

"Hey there," I finally shoved my face up to the dome-shaped hole where cash passed hands.

"If you want a ticket, it's four bucks."

"You know, dear, I'll give you a pointer. You should be nicer to strangers. One day they might be your employers."

"If you're waiting for someone do it over there." She pointed away from the door.

"I'm here to see your boss."

"One second." She picked up a phone and mumbled something into it. In a moment a short stocky guy in his thirties with curly hair and wire-framed glasses appeared.

He opened a big glass door allowing me into the lobby. "I'm Nick Miedland, the manager. Can I help you?"

"Yeah, do you know Tanya?" I said in a low voice.

"Yes," he looked nervously at the box office girl, "what about her?"

"She sent me."

"Tanya?" He said looking behind me.

"Right," I murmured as I moved farther down the lobby away from the bitchy ticket girl.

"Tanya said you had a managerial opening for me."

"She said that? Well, I'm sorry but there are no openings." I gave him an insider's smile.

"Come on, Nick." I took the liberty of using his first name. "Tanya said just yesterday that there was an opening."

"One second please," he said and then looked behind me. He addressed the girl in the ticket booth, "What's all this about a manager's opening?"

"What?" she replied.

"This gentleman claims that you've been telling him about some kind of manager's opening?"

"No, not her," I corrected, "Tanya told me about it."

"This is the only Tanya I know."

"I must have the wrong place," I muttered.

Without a further word, he turned and went back to his office. Two Tanyas in two days, what a fluke. I smiled apologetically at the present Tanya as I left, but she only gave me a nasty expression. At least she had a job. As I walked away, I felt increasingly foolish. Half way up the block, I turned and yelled back, "Fuck you, Tanya!!"

I didn't know of any other theaters on Twelfth Street and wondered if I'd gotten a bum steer. So I wandered down Twelfth and stopped into the Strand Bookstore. There, I took the elevator up to the seventh floor to drop in on Kevin. Helmsley had introduced me to him a couple years earlier, when he was working part-time in the basement and had just entered some Columbia master's program. Over the years, Kevin had slaved his way up to the rare book room. Whenever I wanted to buy a book, I brought it up to Kevin and he would purchase it for me with his employee discount. We talked a bit about books and finds. Eventually he had to get back to cataloguing books, so I went downstairs and browsed a while. Fortunately nothing caught my interest. I wouldn't have been able to afford anything anyway. I wandered with increasing worry along Twelfth, eastward. At least, if all else failed, I had enough to get a slice of cheese babka at Christine's Coffee Shop on First Avenue.

At Third Avenue, on both Twelfth and Eleventh Streets, NYU dorms were erected around 1986; students rinse the area. But back in the early eighties parking lots filled the sites. The emptiness was a marketplace for prostitutes. They would hook their tushies on car fenders waiting for a trick. I remembered their tight bright clothes were making promises that their wasted bodies couldn't keep, and for a while I watched the middle-aged, fat-assed men decelerate their long American cars with Jersey plates and consider the day's slim pickings.

The morning had started with hope for a good job, but that belief was slowly sinking with the sun. Each of the blocks went by without a theater. In despair, it seemed somehow appropriate that these lost souls were stationed here. Each of them must've had a day like this when their hopes started strong and erect, but slowly, one by one, all possibilities dwindled until they wound up on a street like this one, watching other girls hanging their sides on fenders like meat on a hook, waiting for a buyer. Seeing this they must've figured, "I've got nothing else going," and then joined the others.

Looking northward up Third Avenue, I noticed a guy walking with a pretty blond boy in a sailor's outfit. Together the pair walked, arm in arm, heading toward the sleazy porn theater half a block up. The entrance of the place was circular and covered with dirty brown shag carpet, a giant orifice. Above it proudly flapped a flag: "The Zeus Theater."

Quick as a fart came the revelation. This was a theater near Twelfth Street! Even though AIDS was widely known, this was about a year or so before the Post ran headlines like "Grandma Dies of AIDS." The hysteria was still a ways off. Between the NYU dorms and the pandemic pandemonium, the Zeus Theater had little chance of survival. It was closed down in the late eighties. Instead of taking the view that I'd be exposing myself in a pathogenic porn theater, it looked like just another offbeat job.

So I pondered for a moment with a renewed hope. Could this be the place? And if I did go in and was offered a job, would I take it?

My affections were never inclined beyond females. But this was a job and I was broke. I had dropped out of college just before my graduation. I had no marketable skills, no connections, and no real ambition. After a succession of degrading minimum-wage jobs, I finally might luck into something with a salary, in which I'd most likely be unsupervised.

Checking both ways, just to be sure that no past pillars of my old

Midwestern community were lumbering by, I followed the middle-aged man and his Ganymede inside. They paid and together they romantically squeezed through a single angle of the turnstile. I looked through the dirty bulletproof Plexiglas and saw an elderly olive-skinned lady sitting on a stool.

"Excuse me," I yelled through four small vertical slits.

"Please turn it," she interrupted, pointing to the turnstile. "They only turn it once."

I turned it and yelled back in, "Is Miguel in?"

"A segundo." She replied in an accent, and then yelled into a cheap intercom. "You wait here."

I stepped to one side, turned away from the door and waited. After the turnstile spun a couple of times, I turned to the entrance and watched those coming through. They were mainly businessmen types, family men who didn't fit my naive idea of what gays looked like. A door finally opened and a very young man with only dark peach fuzz for a moustache introduced himself as Miguel and asked if he could be of any assistance.

"Yes," I replied, shaking his hand, and in a conspiratorially low voice I explained, "Tanya sent me."

"Oh, I've been waiting for you. Come this way." He led me around the turnstile and down a narrow hallway in the theater. "So how's Tanya faring?"

"Fine, fine." The whole place was darkly lit. Occasionally I would brush shoulders with some passing patron. Finally stopping at the end of the corridor, he opened the door and flipped on a light. His room was a modified closet, the fluorescent bars of light revealed a macrame Yin Yang calendar, a small refrigerator, and a tiny television set.

"One second," he said, flipping his desk lamp on and turning off the fluorescent flood. He offered me a group of film canisters as a seat. When I sat, he leaned back in his swivel chair and began, "So talk to me."

I told him my name and gave him Helmsley's address and then explained that I had theater experience at the Saint Mark's. About to elaborate on my theater know-how, he interrupted.

"I don't want a resume."

"Pardon?"

"I want to know what you're thinking."

"About what?" I asked.

"Just about." And he leaned back further in his swivel chair and set his thin arms on the rest of the chair and threw his head back.

"Well," I said, leaning forward on the dented canister, "I'll level with you. I'm in dire straits for a job, and I'm probably not qualified, but I am willing to put a lot of energy into learning, and I guess that's really what I'm thinking about."

"Well." He grinned. "Let me first ease your tension. You've got the job. Now, I'd like you to feel unencumbered. Go ahead and shake out your arms and legs."

He started shaking his arms and legs demonstrating how it was done. I followed him. "Now, tell me how you feel and what you're aware of."

This was all very weird. "I feel very happy."

"Is that precisely how you feel, pleased as opposed to satisfied?"

I thought about it a moment and replied, "Well, I am exceptionally pleased, but as I adjust to the news of being hired—security, authority, responsibility—as this sets in, I taper off into satisfaction."

"Good, very good. Okay, now I want you to close your eyes and think about this: I was only lying to you. I'm sorry, but you simply don't have the qualifications. I simply can't give you the job." He then paused. I thought about this a moment: punch this guy in the fucking face and get out of here. But then I realized that to him this was one big controlled setting.

"I am unhappy." This guy wanted me to do some kind of Isadora Duncan dance, symbolizing and acting out feelings. "I am shrouded in constant shade, waiting for liberation. I am a barnacle forever stuck to the bow of a ship."

"Good, good." He nodded approvingly. "Now you've got the job again and you know that you have it. But you've experienced the knowledge of not having it."

I paused and didn't know what to do next. "So?"

"So what does this knowledge offer you? How do you see yourself here?"

"I don't understand."

"I want to see not anticipation, but action. I want to see you working here tomorrow, right now."

"You mean you want me to envision myself working here?" I looked over at him and he just watched me. "All right, I can do that." I closed my eyes and tried to see myself walking through my theater. "Yep, there I am."

"What are you doing?"

"I'm handling the many chores and duties that occur in the course of a given day." Then opening my eyes, I asked him, "What kind of chores and duties occur in the course of a given day?"

"We'll go into that later, right now I want you to explore your anxieties."

"Huh?"

"Look, you don't realize this, but you are on those dimensions simultaneously. Recollection is just calling forth those moments. Think about it. With any given situation there's usually a predisposed action."

"Yeah, so?"

"So when I ask you these questions you don't have to think. Simply look and tell me what you see."

"What was the question again?"

"We were talking about your sensations on this matter."

I took a deep breath and closed my eyes and went under: "I feel an impediment, I'm not as well trained on this as you.... I feel a certain anxiety over what might happen." I was running dangerously low on bullshit.

"Have you ever participated in EST?" he asked.

"No."

"Do you chant?"

"No."

"Crystals?"

"No."

"All right, we'll go into more of that later. You're lucky we met, I see a lot of headway I could help you with."

"I'm looking forward to that." Closing my eyes I suddenly started groaning. "Oh, I'm registering something within."

"Good, good, what is it?"

"It's stifling...I see...money...." I was answering like someone hearing voices at a seance. "It's the stifling question of wage."

"Yes." He leaned forward energetically. "Good, go with it."

"I'm speculating about the whole power structure."

"Okay, that's Pentagon; you're referring to Pentagon," he explained. Who the hell had mentioned the Pentagon? But I got the picture. This was a West Coast hippie with short hair whose destiny as a Haight Ashbury health food cashier had somehow been derailed and instead he had wound up in this bizarre and forsaken spot. Wherever he is nowadays, a transchanneler and a crystal would certainly be nearby. I was getting sick of his shit: "To hell with the Pentagon!"

"Good, excellent, get rid of all that hostility, but then let's get back to the issue. Specifically, I'd like to hear what you thought when you saw me for the first time."

This was going to be easy. He wanted to be flattered. "Well, I felt...an energy, you know, like a compass needle pointing north." I then paused a moment and looked enlightened and blurted, "Of course, it all makes sense now."

"What does?"

"Well, for the past few days, all these auspicious and portentous things kept happening."

"Really?" he replied eagerly. "Like what?"

"Well, I felt this kind of Buddhistic suspension, as if nothing and everything mattered."

"Really?"

"I broke up with my old lover."

"What a sacrifice."

"And moved out of my old house."

"Holy Tao!"

"And I was drawn here randomly by an overheard conversation on a subway."

"What karma!" he hollered, leaping out of his chair and giving me a hug. I softly pushed him back into his chair.

"Well," I resumed calmness. "When would you like me to begin?"

Taking a deep sigh, he wiped the sweat off his brow. "How would you feel about starting your training tonight, right up until closing?"

I didn't want to spend the night in this sleazy theater. "Well, I'm feeling a fear, a panic, my heart is palpitating, panting deeply, quickly. But I'm willing..." I faltered as I put my hand over my heart. "I'm willing to give it...a stab."

"Maybe tonight is a bad idea. In fact, you better get some rest. You know, what you need is some miso and rest."

He walked me to the door and concluded, "Give me a call tomorrow and we'll arrange a time."

"Thank you," I said, breathing more easily. When he closed the door, the significance hit me. The replaced esteem, especially considering the long decline into hopelessness that had been averted by this eleventh-hour reprieve, the full impact hit me as I dashed excitedly through the dim, nefarious halls head on into some small guy, knocking him flat to the ground.

"I'm so sorry," I said as I reached down, unintentionally grabbing him around the chest to help him back to homo erectus.

"Hey!" I heard a high-pitched squawk. "Get off, sleazebag!"

I realized that through the shirt I was juggling a set of boobs. Quickly I let go and she fell back to the ground.

"You're a girl!"

"I'm a woman, manboy!"

"What are you doing here?"

"I'm the projectionist," she replied. "What's your problem?"

"Oh, sorry," I replied, flustered. Not knowing what else to say, I nervously said, "How do you do? I'm straight." And then I bolted out.

FOUR

I retreated back across Twelfth and down Broadway intending to return to Helmsley's with the heartening news. But as I passed by the NYU dormitories, specifically the one that housed Eunice, I thought about that olive man in the white suit. Instant anger and hurt eclipsed the jubilation of the new job. I realized that this was something that had to be resolved. I wondered if they'd be together now.

It was still the lighter side of twilight, so I decided to try to find her. A guard insisted on announcing me, so she was on guard when I got to her door. When the elevator stopped on her floor and the doors slid open, she was standing there, leaning against her door holding a can of Tab, which she was sucking through a straw. We entered the room.

How could she do that to me? I stood still and stared at that milky, silky soft skin, her shadowless face. At first, I tried to remember and then I tried to forget his filthy hands fumbling over her and then I tried not to imagine what might've followed.

"Aren't you going to say anything?" she asked after a patient interval.

"You probably heard I was fired."

"I heard, but I couldn't believe it...." She rambled on about what a shit Pepe was, and gave me some cinema updates. It sounded all so innocent; she didn't realize that I saw her being felt up at the Ritz.

"I missed you dearly," she soon concluded.

"How much?" I mumbled. I took a single step toward her and she took a couple of steps backwards until she was up against the small pullout sofa.

"What do you mean?"

"I mean I know you didn't go out West to visit the folks."

"What do you mean?"

"I saw you at the Ritz the other night with that old guy, letting him kiss you and feel you up."

"I don't see how what I do is any business of yours."

"It is when I spend two months dating you in the cold until I lose sensation in my fingers, and my girlfriend and job."

"Wait a second. You can't dump all that on me."

"You knew what I wanted."

"And you knew what I wanted."

"Yeah, to make yourself feel pretty at someone else's agony. Fuck you." I slammed the door behind me and left.

When I arrived back at Helmsley's, I told him that I had the job.

"Good, this can be a double celebration. What are you doing tonight?"

"Nothing, why?"

"Because there's someone very special I want you to meet tonight."

"I'd be honored, but to be honest I'm tired, starving, filthy, and broke. Tonight might not be the night of nights." It was only around six. He suggested that I nap an hour or two, take a shower, and then maybe we would go out, his treat. "It's important that you meet her tonight."

Three hours later we were at a local restaurant where Helmsley ordered the most expensive dish in the pasta category.

"A fine meal can alter one's entire perspective," Helmsley quipped as I gobbled deeper and deeper into the high-sided plate. I felt like Godzilla as I tore through the many pasta roofs and cheese floors. To do any real damage to that tomato and garlic structure was a gluttonous task. All Helmsley did the entire time was pour from a select bottle of vino and snicker. Eventually, though, he attempted to start a sentence, an opening to something he didn't seem to know how to close.

Finally, when I was full, I asked him what was going on.

"Well," he replied, "it's a little hard for me to say."

"Is it concerning that special friend that you mentioned earlier?"

"Yes, in fact." He smiled a bit. "I'm trying to give you an idea of what to expect."

I could easily imagine her, a fair-skinned cutie who had probably graduated from an Ivy League and developed a shapely resume. "I've been in love, Helmsley. I know, you want to tell me that she's different from any other girl you've ever met..."

"Yes, but there's more..."

"There's always more. You're nervous, that's all, just calm yourself."

Helmsley, as far as love went, was just entering puberty. In this area I felt a bit like an older brother and was about to mention how beguiling love is and the disappointment that inevitably follows, but I caught myself. I wiped the oil and sauces off my face, he paid the bill, and we left.

We went to the nearby bar where the fateful rendezvous was set to occur. A sign outside said it was an American Legion Post. Once inside, I noticed a cool tension that I learned was due to the two types of patrons: the recently arrived yuppies, who'd found that quaint Cobble Hill was only minutes away from their beloved Wall Street, and the third generation Italians who resented the young professionals, probably for jacking up the neighborhood's cost of living. Helmsley quickly brought two bottles and mugs over to a booth by the door. Once seated, I could feel poor Helmsley's anxiety multiply.

"Calm down."

"It's just that, well, you know, I don't have many women friends and I feel very different about this one..." He then launched into a poetic preamble about man's profound and incurable loneliness and how the soul itself is a piston-shaped apparatus that creates a series of vast obliterating implosions which are the true motivations of all man's actions. Nothing was simple. After the earlier session with Miguel, I couldn't stomach any more.

I grabbed the beer mug, shoved it to his lips, and turned it bottoms up. He started guzzling as he struggled for the handle. When he finished it, he put the mug down and apologized.

The door suddenly whipped open with such a bang that Helmsley's empty bottle fell over. A gang of young locals stormed in. The last of them broke from the rest and shoved into our booth. Pushing up against Helmsley was an older lady. She took Helmsley's hair in her hands and gave him a hard unexpurgated kiss on the mouth. I couldn't believe it.

Angela was a small, butchy mama who couldn't have been any younger than forty-five. Her dark wrinkled skin sagged loosely away from all bones, and as she banded her arms around Helmsley, I battled a grin.

"So whatchu boys talkin' 'bout?" All I could do was hold back that grin and look at him—so this was his salvation from ruin, the melter of his stalagmite.

"We were just waiting for you, dear," Helmsley replied tenderly.

"Ain't talkin' dutty, eh?" The she-wolf grinned.

"No, hon, I was just mentioning you, in fact."

"You tease," she replied while yanking Helmsley downward so that his head was resting across her lap the same way Sarah's head had laid across that chunky punk's lap in the teen-bar a couple of weeks before. As he struggled to rise, she splat her lips on his and the two of them tumbled underneath the table.

In time a hand reached up from under the table, and feeling around the table top it snatched my half-finished bottle of beer and disappeared with it back under the table. In a gulp's time, an empty bottle was replaced on the table top. I looked around the bar uncomfortably. The table started rumbling and up popped her head. Extending her hand over the table, she hollered, "Helmslock told me a lot aboucha."

"Dat's swell," I replied. When we shook hands, she squeezed my knuckles into a painful bundle. She laughed when I retrieved my injured hand and asked, "What's a matter, not man enough?"

Helmsley slowly reappeared from under the table. His hair was tousled and he blushed as he straightened it with his fingers. Silently he rebuttoned his shirt.

"So yer friend 'ere ain't man enough for a little handshake."

"No," I retorted. "I gots ta idmit it, Helmslock, the little lady's gots da man's grip."

Helmsley replied with a swift kick from under the table. Out of respect for my friend, I took the back seat and watched as Angela ruled the evening with filthy remarks and vulgar jokes. He was almost as attractive as she was ugly. When Helmsley's glasses were off, if his old pants and hair-style were updated, he could resemble a manly Mel Gibson. He was muscular and had dark, deep-set eyes. His appearance was as remarkable and singular as his character. Unfortunately one fork in this road to gorgeous was that while his intellect was unremitting, he usually froze when dealing with people whom he hadn't known for a while. Subsequently he had no luck with small talk and usually came off as a nerd.

While stuck there soaring to new heights of boredom, I speculated on possible motives for Helmsley's interest in her. Lately he had been involved in the study of early man. Perhaps he was immersing himself in a Neanderthal woman. Or perhaps this was the first girl he had ever met who just reached down into his pants and plucked out what she wanted; fuck the small talk. I could see how this normally crass feature would appear charming to a guy who had always been too shy to present himself.

But still, she seemed hideous at the time. Could love bridge the intellectual and cultural abyss between them? Could love amputate the fifteen or so years that tossed her ahead of him? Could love repair so much? If so, then for the first time in my life, sitting there, I realized how love was truly great.

It had always been easy for me to fall head over heels for some bouncing blonde from Texarkana, Texas, to sip her like a dry martini and smash the crystal in the fireplace of fate. But it was only Budweiser that my dear pal Helmsley was guzzling, as he nestled his head into the folds of her belly and looked into her cavernous nostrils.

For different reasons, we had all downed what would have measured out to at least a half-keg of beer. Angela, who had drunk twice as much as Helmsley, was no drunker. Suddenly Angela jumped to her feet and, yanking

Helmsley up, decided it was time to go. Before departing, though, she cut a profound fart. I was too drunk to mind, though; I knew I wouldn't make it even as far as the door. I sat there and ordered another beer.

Alcohol corrodes one's dexterity and sense of proportion, but it also heightens one's emotions. Smelling that fart, I thought of Helmsley in love. Had I spent my whole life confusing love with a series of erections? Love to Helmsley must have been an utter necessity, whereas for me it was always just a luxurious distraction. I wished that I had the need to lust after some goiter-necked, tooth-decayed, leg-blistered old bag. If I could love like that it would be a pyramid of emotions, an Arc de Triomphe of affection.

When the time arrived for the bar to close, I had to be helped out. No sooner did I plop myself down on a neighboring stoop than my stomach reared up. Staring down at the pool of vomit that had fountained out of me, I made out the expensive Italian meal I had eaten earlier that evening. The regurgitated pasta and cheese were little islands in a vast sea of beer. I recall feeling through that drunken stupor a deep loss; it had been a magnificent meal.

If I could love it enough, I would be able to eat it up all over again. It probably would taste just as good, once I got over the disgusting appearance. I knelt in the slop and gazed into it with as much devotion as I could muster. Dogs eat their regurgitation, I prompted myself. Slowly stretching my fingers out, I stroked along the meaty lumps and cheesy threads, and then brought my fingertips to my lips. I tried, but for some reason I just couldn't get beyond the bilious stench.

"Hey," someone yelled, following it with a prodding kick to my ribs. A large guy with mountainous shoulders loomed above me.

"What da fuck you doin'?"

A gang of teenagers behind him were looking down at me grimly. They knew when a good beating would be therapeutic. As I scrambled to unsteady feet, I realized there was no chance of running away.

"Well, I was just eating, you know, a meatball hero, and I look at my hand here, and my high school graduation ring is gone, so I...uh, upchuck here, and I was just looking for it, you know, it had a diamond stone."

"Diamond?" the most brilliant of them queried. "What public school has a diamond for a graduation stone?"

"Who said public?" I countered. "It was parochial."

"Which one?" asked the guy with the twin tower shoulders.

"Maternal Lamentations. Over in Sheepshead Bay."

"We just beat them in basketball," one of the morons said, to my relief.

"Fuck it," I said, looking wistfully at the vomit. I slowly walked away. After I had staggered away half a block, I looked back and saw the bastards kicking through my poor puddle of barf. As I turned away, I heard one of them yell to another, "Gypsies steal gems that way."

Late afternoon the next day, I awoke with a punishing hangover. I arose slowly and remembered the previous night with disbelief. I peeked into the slightly opened door of Helmsley's bedroom to see if he was sleeping alone. The room was empty and nothing had been altered since yesterday. He had been out all night. I went back to my couch and retreated back into sleep. When I awoke again, it was dark out and I was starving. I recalled the barf episode of the night before, and quickly brushed my teeth. It was only six P.M. I took a shower and a couple of Tylenol and called Miguel to ask him when I could come in to start training. He instructed me to come in as soon as the energy was right. I dressed and got the F, then changed for the L to Third Avenue where I walked south to the theater. Upon my arrival, Miguel asked me, "Are you sure you're in the right energy so soon?"

"I stopped in a nearby Radio Shack and checked on the meter. I'm ready."

"All right," he said, and we began with a tour of the theater.

"This is your theater," he explained as we walked to the stage. "You must look at it as if it's a part of your own body." Sex was lurking all around us. It was crouched low in the darkened seats and projected high on the stage.

"This way." He led me to a staircase behind the stage and to a downstairs room. The place looked and sounded like a medieval dungeon, with dark stone walls, puddles of water, virtually no lighting, and the moans. There was constant moaning all around. A hand out of the darkness groped my thigh.

"Fuck off!" I yelled.

"Shhhh," Miguel whispered back. "Occasionally someone might reach out; all you do is simply take their hand and push it away. Not rudely or quickly, everyone here is as human as you are."

We went back up a staircase to the front of the theater. "Now look here." He pointed to a burnt-out bulb. "Ow, see that? Ow ow, you should smart when you see that. A bulb is burnt-out and now the theater is in pain. Say ow."

"Ow. Why?"

"You should be in pain until you replace the bulb. You're both the nerve system and the lymph node system of the theater."

"You mean the white blood cells," I corrected his little metaphor.

"Why not the lymph node?"

"Well, isn't the lymph node just sweat and pimple pus?"

"So?"

"Well, the white blood cells destroy foreign objects that enter the body. Didn't you see the movie *Fantastic Voyage*?"

"I thought the spleen does that."

"No, the spleen stores blood, and I think the liver cleans it."

"All right, enough. You're the spleen, the liver, the white blood cells, the lymph nodes. You're all of that and anything else you can think of."

He gave other pointers as we walked back through the dark theater. Looking up at the beam of projected light, I saw something strange. As I walked down the aisle, I noticed the ray from the projection booth was parallel to the seats. Out of an architectural interest, I squatted to inspect the incline of the floor.

"You wouldn't have a level, would you?"

"Very good," he replied, and yanking me up to my feet, he quickly put his finger over my lips and murmured, "I'll explain later."

"Explain what?" I asked as soon as he closed the office door behind us.

"Did you notice the angle of the screen?"

"No, what's wrong with it?"

"It's slanted backward at the top. And all the seats are anchored at such an angle that everyone sitting has to apply a soft but constant thrust to sit back in the seat.

"Doesn't anyone complain?"

"No"—he grinned—"they just leave. No one can bear it for more than a couple of hours."

"You can probably get a team of carpenters to fix it," I replied. "Who fucked up?"

"Fix it? That's like fixing the Mona Lisa! It's brilliant."

"Brilliant?"

"Look, porn theaters aren't like other theaters. People come to a porn theater and they stay forever. This way they either leave or they suffer." It was an interesting theory, but who could guess how many patrons never returned because they didn't care for the back strain?

"Who thought of it?"

"Only one man could come up with something so ingenious, Otto Waldet. Did you ever see the last scene of *Lady from Shanghai* ? Otto built that set for Welles. He was a set designer up until the early fifties, when he was blacklisted. By the early sixties, he started one of the first chains of gay-porn theaters. He just died last year."

"Is that why the projection booth is at that strange angle?"

"Oh no, that's something entirely different. This theater was initially a nursery school. The projection booth was built between the second and the third floor."

I was introduced to my staff: a middle-aged box office lady named Rosa and a Cambodian porter named Thi. Miguel finally led me back into his office and had me fill out a W-4 form and then we agreed on a mutually accommodating schedule.

"Why don't you work with me the rest of this evening so we can get to know each other?"

The evening was almost over anyway, so I decided to stay for the remainder. Opening up a compact refrigerator hidden under the desk, Miguel took out a couple beers and a bag of banana chips. Then he pulled out a small television and we decided on a football game. It was a remarkably American evening for a neo-hippie in a gay porn theater.

As we watched the Forty-Niners beating the Jets, I remembered how in the past working had meant something far more physical, under the constant supervision of usually someone conspicuously dumber. I sputtered through a mouthful of chips, "I can't believe I'm getting paid to do this."

"This is really a pretty smooth operation and if nothing's broken..."

"Sounds comfy."

"It's boring, that's the real job." And we didn't talk much more until the end of the game. By the time the Jets had won, we were both pretty tired from the beer and the little room had gotten pretty humid, so we stepped out front and watched guys stray in and cars cruise by for corner whores. Miguel took out a cigarette.

"Aren't those bad for your health?"

"They're organic," he replied, and lit up.

Suddenly when a long American car turned up Third toward us, Miguel snuffed his cigarette and spoke under his breath, "Quick, get into the theater."

"What's the matter?"

"Ox is here. He's the district manager. I didn't tell him I hired you yet, and he lives to yell. I'm sure he won't pass up this opportunity. Just make like a patron until he passes."

Out of a purple Cadillac that pulled up in front plopped a pudgy middle-aged man with a curly beard. He was wearing such a distinctly tasteless suit that it seemed to make a kind of agonizing fashion statement. His upper torso rocked solidly as if he were entering a boxing ring.

"You sure I shouldn't meet him now?"

"Just disappear until he does."

Hastening into the bathroom, I started to urinate but kept hearing the sounds of fumbling in the adjacent stall. I concentrated on a hand-lettered sign that Miguel must have written. It read, "Save water, New York is going through a drought." Underneath it was all the predictable graffiti, "Fight Aids not Gays. Save Soviet Jews...Win Prizes. Ernie loves Tony loves Casper loves Ira loves Bozo..." The sounds in the stall got louder and louder. So I retreated into the theater, took a seat, and discreetly checked around me. Most of the guys were hunting around for someone. Three aisles in front of me, I caught the outline of a couple occupying the same seat in a contorted position. I watched the film awhile. Apparently a jogger named Mario had bumped into a handball player named Sheldon. It turned out that they had been noticing and admiring each other for some time. Their characters were left undeveloped, but they were both eager to advance on to the subsequent scenes. Neither of them had any other appointments, obligations, or occupation. Sheldon, it seemed, played handball and slept, and Mario jogged and slept. As the unlikely plot progressed, Mario invited Sheldon up to his house, which was conveniently near. There, they each made comments like, "Sa-a-ay, I'll bet you're pretty big with the ladies," and, "You look good enough to eat," and so on. Finally they stretched out on a sofa and started making out. Sheldon's hand started moving down to Mario's flimsy shorts.

Simultaneously I felt a liquid hand slide into my lap and I hopped up. It was Miguel, laughing.

"He's gone." I rose and followed him back into his office.

"Why does he come? Why couldn't I meet him?"

"Well, I wanted to tell him I hired you before you met him because sometimes he acts like an animal. He usually comes by about twice a week just to make sure everything's okay. He makes the rounds."

"What rounds?"

"The rounds of the chain. Otto's family owns it and he does most of the administrative work for them."

"He looks like an asshole."

"He looks dumb; in fact everything about him is dumb. Only he ain't dumb."

"How do you know?"

"His actions are very calculated, almost predestined."

Soon it was closing time. Miguel collected all the money together, wrapped a filled-out bank deposit slip around it together with a rubber band, shoved the bundle into the green deposit bag, zipped it up, and locked it.

Together, we walked to the nearby bank, and he put the money into a night drop. Then we went back to the theater. Rosa, the listless box office lady, went home, and we went into the office. After Miguel filled out a variety of forms, which created the illusion that an authority was checking us, the projectionist buzzed down to warn that the film had come to an end. Miguel turned up all the lights in the theater and turned out all the outdoor lights. Together we inspected both the theater and the dungeon downstairs to clear out all malingerers. The place was empty. While checking the toilet, I asked Miguel if plunging the toilet was among our many duties.

"The last time the toilet got plugged up was sometime last October—anyway, I had to unplug it."

"I used to do that all the time at the Saint Mark's. Awful business, unplugging a toilet."

"Oh," he responded. A memory was apparently set in motion. "Last October when I started plunging, first blood started coming up, and then black feathers."

"Christ."

"Finally a small bird came up."

"I once unplugged a piece of red meat at the Saint Mark's, I think it was Kielbasy."

"Well, I didn't finish my story. The toilet still wouldn't flush so I kept plunging and plunging and finally a filthy black pelt came out."

"A what?"

"The pelt of a small animal. It looked like a gerbil. And I flushed again, but the toilet still flooded."

"Still? I'd be on the phone to Roto-Rooter by then."

"Well, I wish I did that," Miguel replied, "'cause I finally sucked out what looked like a fingerless hand."

"Christ!"

"It was just about this size"—he distanced two fingers a couple of inches apart—"like a child's hand. But it wasn't as awful as it sounds."

"You found a baby's hand and you weren't worried?"

"Well, I had a pretty good idea whose hand it was."

"Whose?"

"This nut that used to come by a lot. He got pissed once because I found him trying to stuff a...well he got mad at me, and later I heard that he worked with cadavers."

"You should've called the police."

"Let me warn you right now. Never, but never, call the police. They've been trying to close us down since the beginning. I just tossed the hand off the back of the roof. No one'll ever find it."

"But what do I do if something happens to me?"

"I'll tell you exactly what Ox told me when I first started working here. If you can take them, beat them; if you can't, run. There's a bayonet and a baseball bat in the office. If you kill anyone, drag them into the office and Ox will get rid of the body for you."

"That's reassuring."

"I think he was kidding, but listen, nothing serious ever happens. We're open every day of the year here for twelve hours a day and since we're in a low-income non-residential district, we're subject to a lot of crazies. You can't let them get to you."

The evening was over, everybody had left, and the lights were out. But Miguel said he still had some tedious business requiring his attention.

"I'm wide awake. I might as well take it all in." So he told me how much money the theater had made that day.

"Now the way we check this is..."And he showed me a little glass-enclosed dial above the desk, cemented into the wall. "Each time the turnstile spins, this number increases by one. We subtract the amount that the dial displayed at the beginning of the day from this figure, and the amount we're left with is how many patrons came in today. We multiply that by four, which is the price of admission, and that's how much money we should have. Understand?"

"In theory," I replied, and began to ask a question, but interrupted myself with a yawn.

He smiled and said that we could do it again the next day when my energy level was maximum. He walked me to the door. Thi, the porter, had already started cleaning the theater. Miguel wished me good night. I started walking to the subway, but I decided that I didn't want to be stranded in Brooklyn wide awake.

FIVE

As I passed Eleventh Street on Third I saw the big bright sign of the Ritz. Jersey kids were still stumbling in, so I walked over to the door. There was usually a five-dollar admission but an accord had been arranged between Pepe and the manager of the Ritz: their respective employees were allowed free into each other's places. I approached hesitantly. The doorman, who was chatting with a group of Jerseyites, apparently remembered me from my many previous entrances. Unaware of my dismissal from the Saint Mark's, he just waved me in.

Once inside, I had just enough to buy a beer. I was wide awake, so I decided to try dancing off some energy. I approached a skinny girl leaning against the bar and we danced for a while. She kept trying to dance slower and closer, and I kept pushing her away and the tempo up. Finally when it took more energy to repel her than to dance, I thanked her and left the floor. I saw an attractive, healthy girl put down an almost full bottle of beer and leave. I would kiss her if she let me, and with that criteria I wiped off some lipstick at the nozzle and poured it into my mouth without touching the rim.

I finally felt tired enough to fall asleep on Helmsley's sofa, which seemed to be getting harder and harder every time I was on it. Heading toward the door of the club, I was suddenly stopped by two soft hands shoved before my eyes.

"Guess who?" murmured a disguised voice.

"Sarah?" was the only name that came to mind. Pulling off the blinds and turning around, I found myself face to face with Eunice.

"How are you doing?" she asked as if no preexisting clash had ever occurred.

"Are you here with him?" I asked, looking around.

"No," she replied.

"Why did you lie to me," I leapt right into the fray, "saying that you were going to visit your parents?"

"Well, I was going to. But do we really have to go through this?"

"But you lied to me! That's what I most resented." No anger still existed but for some reason I felt compelled to continue the fight, to hold to some righteous platform.

"You swine!" She gave me a token swat. "You have a girlfriend, and you have the audacity to yell at me for having a fling."

"Ah ha! But I told you about it!"

"Is that how it works? If confession makes everything all right, then why don't you tell her about us?"

"She already found out," I confessed with a hung head. "I told you. She left me."

There was a stretch of silence, so I gave a slight farewell smile and resumed walking.

"Wait a second." Eunice caught up. "She left you?"

"Yeah."

"Do you want to dance?" she finally asked pliantly.

"No thanks, I'm tired." And resumed walking.

"Wait a fucking second," she said this time, angrily. "Can't we try to be friends, I mean does one fight end the friendship?!"

"Yes!" I yelled. "You teased!"

"Tease? I told you right up front exactly what I was up to when you asked me," she answered.

"You left me hoping, you left the possibility dangling."

"You're crazy!"

"Fuck you!" I shouted unconcerned that we were the center of attention in the place. She, on the other hand, had become visibly embarrassed. I continued, "I made minimum wage and spent every cent on you! I spent all my available time with you!"

"Look, I was interested in you as a boyfriend, I admit it."

"Ha ha!" I exclaimed idiotically.

"But I'm not going to be the other woman. Now that you're unattached, there's a new context."

"Well fuck you!" I yelled. "Go fuck that old fart I saw you with."

"Well fuck you too!" she yelled back and vanished back into the masses. If not getting involved with her was something that I would ever come to regret I couldn't feel it then. All I wanted was sleep. On the ride home I couldn't help but think how just one month earlier I would've died to have what I had just rejected.

Sleep was prematurely cut open for me by a sharp angle of sunlight that pierced my closed lids like a can opener. I turned over, but outside the battle of car horns finished off the beleaguered sleep. I lay there awhile with my eyes still closed and thought about old times, and then it started happening. I could feel the rapid palpitations and the sweat. The snail had visited last night; a thick film of oil seemed to be evenly licked over my body. I tossed the blanket to the floor, and with a towel I wiped my face dry. Helmsley's door was open and his room was bare. Stepping under the shower, I felt the cold water slowly turn hot and then cold again as I tried to scour away my epidermis.

I dressed and wolfed down the ninety-cent breakfast special at the corner diner. It was a wonderful morning. Everything seemed real and luminous. I breathed deeply. A cold wind that days earlier had swept across arctic ice pans settled above Brooklyn and chilled everyone away, indoors. The sun was bright, but ineffectual. The few folks out looked more rugged than the usual anemic breed of New Yorkers. I had nothing to do, so I walked. After breakfast, I walked down Clinton Street, through Brooklyn Heights and across Cadman Plaza to the Bridge. The Brooklyn Bridge was reconstructed in the mid-eighties so that it became one graceful incline, more accessible to cyclists. But in crossing it by foot, I constantly feared I was going to be hit by a speeding bike, and preferred the way it was before, divided into roughly five parts by short series of stairs. By the time I finally reached the Manhattan side, I had both a chill and an appetite.

Walking south on Broadway, I realized that I had enough change for a coffee in a Blimpie's. When I opened the door, I was shoved to the floor. When I looked up, someone was holding a fat handgun and wildly waving it around.

"Stay on that fucking floor!" I stayed. The gunman, a spindly Hispanic, was pointing to the till with the pistol. "In de bag," he shouted. "Put it in de fucking bag."

Suddenly the door swung open and in walked a preadolescent girl in a parochial school dress, probably for a pack of Yodels. He grabbed her and she screamed and continued screaming.

"There are cops all around here. Get out while you still can," a career lady behind me said. I didn't notice her until that moment.

"You're next bitch," he screamed at her. Grabbing the screaming little girl in his arm, he frantically tore at her dress. "Shut the fuck up!"

I guess he interpreted her screaming as insolence instead of fear. Spontaneously an old man leapt at the fucker's gun hand. After hearing the discharged blast, the cashier jumped at the gunman, but he kept slipping backwards. The school girl broke free and dashed out the door. The old man dropped to the ground. I jumped up thinking the situation was defused. The gunman released two more shots. I jumped away, falling through the coldcut display case, and the gunman was out the door with his bag of money.

A tray of coleslaw had spilled over me, and as I tried to rise I felt a numbness in my right arm and saw blood mixing in with watery mayonnaise. The cashier leaned over his old friend. The old man was calmly on the ground, blood was drilling up out of his belly. The cashier was holding a rag on the puncture. The lady hung up the phone after notifying the 911 people. She looked at my arm; through my jacket and shirt there was a deep cut.

"I'm okay." I trembled with false modesty. "How's the old guy?"

"Did you know him?" she asked solemnly. I shook my head no.

The lady wrapped a tourniquet just below my shoulder. Soon people from the street started pouring in and asking me dumb questions: "Did it hurt? Are you all right? What happened?" In what seemed like forever, I could finally hear the wailing sirens, and then an endless flow of police started streaming in as if they were compensating for the prior lack of security. The cashier was sobbing over the dead body until one group of paramedics put it on what looked like a large tray and then covered it with the white sheet. Finally one medic, a big guy with a name tag reading "Luciano," took a scissors and cut the jacket and shirt right off my arm. He started looking for a bullet hole.

"It was a piece of glass," the career lady explained.

Upon hearing that I had no relations living in the city, she offered to escort me to the hospital. We spoke during the ambulance ride to Saint Vincent's Hospital.

"What were you doing in there anyhow?" I asked her. She was attractive, articulate, well-dressed, and simply didn't look like a Blimpie's type.

"I work in the area."

"As what?"

"A stock broker," she said and then asked what I was doing there. I explained that I had just walked over the bridge.

"Didn't you have a token?"

"The IRT isn't as poetic as the Brooklyn Bridge."

"Oh," she replied with an inspired smile, "you mean not many dawns chill it from its rippling rest..."

"Very good." I was surprised. She asked me if I knew the reference.

"What kind of bogus, never-completed-a-page, cappuccino-slurping writer would I be if I didn't know the opening of 'The Bridge'?" The odds that two people knew the same poem seemed rare in these illiterate days.

"Is that what you are?"

"Well," I replied, "maybe I completed just one page."

As the siren wailed and the ambulance precariously cut off other cars, she started loosening up and telling me about herself. Her name was Glenn, modernized from Glenda. She was a thirty-two-year-old divorcée with a fair income and her ex-hubby's Brooklyn Heights townhouse.

At the hospital, they checked out my arm. There weren't any bones broken, no arteries severed, nor vital organs damaged. I had spilt a bit of blood, but all in all I had plea bargained well with fate. After the bandaging, a cop kept reviewing the incident over and over. Maybe, if I revised the facts, circumstances might retroactively right themselves. The career lady correlated all the details so the cop finally left me alone. Initially the hospital wanted to keep me overnight for observation. But after I explained to the nurse with the metal clipboard that I had no insurance plan, no Blue Cross and Blue Shield and no money, my situation seemed less serious. Before Glenn left, I asked her if she would ever care to dine or something. She said that she didn't think so.

"Well, can't I at least speak to you again?" I appealed. "You aided me in a time of need and I feel obliged."

"Don't feel obliged."

For that fearful moment in the Blimpie's, she made me feel very protected. I asked her, "Do you have a child?"

"No, why?"

"Think of me as one," I replied.

"Look, we can talk on the phone, but I'm involved and I wouldn't want to give you the wrong idea." As she said this, she took out her appointment planner and scribbled down a telephone number with an extension. She then tore out the page, handed it to me, and was gone.

I had a buck-fifty and needed to be at work in a half an hour so I started walking east. After spending hours in the gloom of that hospital, it was good to be out and away. When I finally got to the theater, the box office lady asked if I would mind the box office a moment so that she could relieve herself. I sat on her stool and waited. After about five minutes, during which time three young bucks sporting ten gallon hats moseyed on in, I found myself deeply attracted to the cash in the till. I finally counted it. It amounted to more than I had seen in years. I finished counting before the lady returned to the box. The balance came to two hundred and fifty-six dollars. Two patrons later, Rosa resumed her place. Going into the office, I coughed through a thick cloud of marijuana smoke. There were burnt-out roaches in the ashtray. Miguel was giggling on the phone to someone. I caught the phrase "mobilization on Washington" and stopped listening. WBAI was playing ancient Siberian folk music and interlacing it with an explanation about these lost people and their futile attempt to protect their vanishing heritage. In mid-sentence Miguel looked up and noticed that the right sleeve of my jacket and shirt had been amputated. Upon seeing the iodine-stained gauze that was packed around my shoulder, he quickly concluded his conversation. "What happened?"

"I walked in on a robbery and fell through a display case."

"No shit?"

"No shit. Someone got killed."

"How?"

"He tried to grab the gun."

"He was asking for it then. Were the robbers black?"

"No, it was a Puerto Rican guy."

"I know a homeopath, like a doctor. He can look at your shoulder."

"No, I've spent enough time with doctors."

"Well, just relax. Want a medicinal joint?"

"No thanks."

"I've got a case of the munchies myself. Want anything at the store?"

I didn't. He threw on his jacket and went to the newly opened Korean fruit stand on the corner. I turned on the small TV that was on his desk. Richard Dawson was kissing a mother, and then he kissed a daughter, and then I turned off the TV. Trying to appear responsible, I started clearing off the desk top. I threw away an empty Dannon's yogurt cup and then wiped up all the granola crumbs.

Checking the register dial that showed how many people had come in since the last cash drop, I counted twenty-six and multiplied it by four. The sum came to a hundred and sixteen dollars. But I had just counted over two hundred dollars in the box office. I checked all the math again, something was wrong. Obviously I had screwed up somewhere, so I decided to just keep quiet and let him explain everything to me. I turned the TV back on and watched Richard Dawson kissing some more relatives until Miguel arrived. He put a quart of Tropicana Orange Juice on the desk and, after watching a bit more of "Family Feud," started instructing me about the job.

"We didn't do too well today," he said. Out of his pocket he produced a rubber banded roll of bills. He then checked the gauge that I had checked and did the same computations I had, coming to the same conclusion.

"Yep, a hundred and sixteen bucks," he said, and then added, "This is pretty average for a Tuesday matinee."

He then counted the stack of bills: it amounted to the same figure.

"Let me ask you something," I asked. "When you take a drop, you take everything but fifty bucks right?"

"Right, why?" he asked calmly.

"Just getting the facts straight."

"Well, I just collected all the matinee, so there is now fifty bucks in the till."

I watched him put the money in an envelope, fill out the front with the present gauge number, and calculate the sum total of the matinee. He then put the envelope into the deposit bag for the nightly deposit.

Something fishy was going on.

The night spun on as quickly as the digits on the gauge. Miguel gave me a few pointers on the porno business. He talked quickly about the illicit side of the trade, specifically the shakedowns and the pirating of porn films. But he elaborated on the nuances of location. Aside from zoning rules that dictated the locations of gay porn theaters, it was each police captain's private policy in his individual precinct that usually dictated whether sex was permitted in the theater or not.

"For example, Ox had to sell the theater in Queens because a homophobic commander was transferred there, and he had the vice squad staking the theater out regularly," Miguel explained.

He also mentioned that business had slackened for a couple of weeks the previous fall because the condom dispenser in the lobby was busted and the boys were afraid of contracting AIDS.

"Anybody can do what they want in here but everybody is given a safe sex pamphlet, I make sure of it," he said proudly, "and nobody wants to die."

We spent most of the evening drinking beer and talking. We rambled on about our pasts, and to compensate for our lack of experience due to youth, both of us were unintentionally drawn into colorful hyperbole. He told me about his semester at college in Boulder, Colorado. He lived out of a motorless van and had long wavy hair. His favorite recollection, which also seemed to be his vision of the perfect future, was the time he went to the Rainbow Gathering. This was a festival for orthodox hippies who met once a year somewhere in the undisturbed wilderness. For the duration they met, it was like being a hobbit in a carefree world, provided it didn't rain. I didn't care to dredge up my drab and depressing past, so I made up a lively yet realistic background.

"I was raised in New York, but I can't bear dealing with parents anymore."

"Where did you meet Tanya?" he asked and for a moment my mind was a blank. Then I remembered the girl on the train.

"On a train," I answered, almost truthfully.

We talked about other things and just when conversation was getting completely absurd, the intercom buzzed. The box office lady said that there were two people in the outer lobby waiting to see Miguel. I followed him out and met his guests. They were two punks. One was taller, appeared older than the other, and both of them had wide grins. With their mohawks and leather gear they looked like characters out of *The Road Warrior,* Wez and his motorcycle-mate. One of them was holding a pail and the other one, the taller one, had leaflets.

At first Miguel appeared flustered. He greeted them with the words, "I thought you were coming tomorrow."

"We were out gluing up flyers for our gig and since we were passing we wondered if we could check out the sound system," explained the smaller one.

"It'll only take a moment," concluded the other. I moved in closer to inspect the mohawks. They were spectrum-colored with glistening speckles. I could see that they were erected with the help of Elmer's glue.

"Okay," Miguel consented nervously. So they left their glue buckets and flyers in the box office and followed Miguel into the theater.

As Miguel and the taller one quietly led the way through the dark theater, I walked alongside the diminutive sidekick. He had what resembled the coastline of Asia minor shaved carefully into his bristled scalp; I could make out the Aegean fingering into the Bosphorus. In conversation with the punk,

Miguel unlocked the projection booth. The projector was on, but there was no operator present. The two punks quickly went through a checklist and at one point I overheard the head punk whisper to Miguel, "I didn't get you in any trouble, did I?"

"No, no," Miguel replied calmly, "everything's still in orbit. Only, as a rule, try calling ahead."

Miguel then introduced us. "This is the new manager, but he's real cool."

We all shook hands and Miguel explained that these were two young vanguard filmmakers. Apparently Miguel had many acquaintances from both the NYU Film School and The School of Visual Arts. Since the Zeus Theater had a superb 16mm projector, Miguel rented the theater for private functions at a nominal cost.

Since Hans—the taller one—and Grett—the smaller one—were collaborative members of an important local band called Slap, and since they were able to get Miguel on the guest list of several local after-hour spots and clubs, he was going to let them view their film for free. It was going to be screened the next day, when I wasn't working.

Miguel talked with Hans awhile, and Grett watched the dirty film. In a moment the two had concluded their business. Hans and Grett exited, but before we could retreat back down the steps, a small door whipped open and out jumped a cute young lady wielding a crow bar. It was the same girl that I had bumped into a couple of days ago when I first got the job.

"What the fuck's going on here?" she demanded, lowering the bar.

"I'm sorry," Miguel replied, "I should have buzzed first."

"If it's not asking too fucking much!" she yelled back. "I thought you were a rapist. And besides, it's in the union contract with all theater owners, 'the projectionist must be duly notified before entry is gained into the booth...'"

Miguel apologized profusely, but as he did, she turned her small back to him and suddenly glared at me. Trying to ease the tension, I introduced myself.

"You're the straight one," she said.

"What?" Miguel cried with astonishment. Turning to me, he asked, "You're straight?"

"Of course not."

"He specifically told me he was straight," the projectionist replied. "I bumped into him downstairs. He grabbed my tits and all he could say was that he was straight. Then he runs off."

"What?!" hollered Miguel.

"Wait a second," I replied. "I bumped into you, I tried to prevent you from falling and said I was late, not straight! That's why I was running. Why the hell would I say I was straight?"

"To show why you were molesting me is why," she explained.

"She's crazy," I pointed out.

"Then you are gay?" Miguel asked. They both peered at me like a spy on foreign soil. After years of institutionalized bias, I was sympathetic to certain cases of reverse discrimination. But despite my sympathies, I still needed the job.

"I'm nothing," I finally replied.

"He might be nothing, but he's a straight nothing," she replied.

"What do you...you know...do?" Miguel asked after a period of silence.

"Quite frankly, I don't penetrate anymore."

"You don't what?"

"I stopped penetrating."

"Well, what the hell do you do?" she asked.

"I...I guess I just fondle."

"But what do you fondle, guys or girls?" he asked.

"Guys, I guess."

"You guess?" the projectionist said. "What do you fondle, ears?"

"Guys," I declared, "with guys."

"So then you are gay?" Miguel added.

"Well, I've fondled girls, too. What the hell is the big deal?" I finally got tired of being cross-examined. "Is it a crime to be straight?"

"We're still something of a persecuted group," Miguel stated, "and quite honestly, I just feel that for this particular job I believe a gay person is more fit."

"How about you?" I asked the cute projectionist. "Aren't you straight?"

"No longer," she replied plainly, and then added in a kind of disturbed and distant way, "I don't involve myself with...anyone anymore." Small wonder.

We went back downstairs to the office where we continued with the routines of the night, but periodically the issue reared its ugly head.

"Look," Miguel said sanctimoniously, "it's not that I'm anti-straight or anything. I really have no hang-ups there. But this is a gay porno theater, and a certain understanding is needed, an understanding that comes with being. And besides, if you were straight, working here might be..."

"Dangerous to my health?"

"Disorienting, that's all."

"You make homosexuality sound like leprosy."

"It's like trying to explain color to a blind man."

"That's no answer," I replied and then declared falsely, "I'm gay, I should be able to understand your argument!"

"Because it's a violation!" he insisted. "When I was in high school, I didn't mind the kids who disliked me for being a faggot. But I hated the bastards who claimed to be friends. The ones who were interested in how it was done. Who looked at you like a lab rat they were studying. Condemning it on one hand and getting off on it with the other. It was pure deceit!"

"I'm not straight!" I insisted.

"I suppose not," he finally concluded and added, "Tanya doesn't deal with straight guys."

Soon it was closing time, and quietly we did the nightly tabulations together. Miguel subtracted the amount of people that came during the night from the amount of people that came during the matinee, then he multiplied the sum by four. While in the midst of further calculations, I got up to take a piss. "I'll pick up the money on the way back," I offered.

"That's all right," he said, "I'm responsible for it."

"It's no problem."

"No!" he was suddenly angry. "Only I'm allowed to deal with the money!"

Perhaps he was still angry over the night's argument. I pissed quickly to the copulating moans in the abutting stall and wondered why Miguel was so touchy. Miguel returned to the office and put all the night's money into the drop bag and locked it. After looking at the tally sheet, I was surprised to see that the theater had only earned four hundred bucks. That meant that only a hundred people had come—but the theater was full all night.

While locking up the place, Miguel said that he felt there was still a tension between us due to the discussion, so he invited me for a beer. Instead of going to a bar, though, we stopped in at the Korean deli on the corner and got a six pack. Miguel explained that three nearby theaters were showing midnight films. The Saint Mark's was showing *Blade Runner,* the Eighth Street was showing *Rumble Fish*, and the Waverly was showing *Stop Making Sense*. Miguel knew Ian, the manager at the Eighth Street, so we could get in free. I didn't want to deal with Pepe, so we swigged beers and walked to the theater.

While watching the film, I wasn't sure if it was the beer or the picture but the image seemed liquidy and unsteady. Either I or the film was drunk. When it was over, we decided that we were both still thirsty.

After the beer, the walk, the joking, and then the film, I couldn't have guessed that our earlier argument might've still been raging in Miguel's mind. He led the way to a bar on Fourth Street called The Bar. Only when we entered did I realize that it was a gay bar. I don't know how well I disguised my apprehension, but it was the very first time I was ever in a gay bar. I immediately sensed that Miguel still wasn't convinced about my assumed sexuality.

After ordering beers, Miguel started with sidelong glances while assuming a well-trained unassuming posture. I kept my eyes on safe inanimate objects, the pool table, the wayward bottles, and so on. Finally I heard him utter, "What do you think of these two guys?"

"Real nice," I replied with no idea of where he was looking.

"Okay," he replied jokingly. "These two are ours."

"What?" I winced in disbelief.

"They are ours," he enunciated. I looked up and noticed his stare, deft and fixed like a matador's sword preparing for the final kill. He knew I was full of bull. It was time to either awkwardly laugh and tell him the truth or bluff it right to the end.

Miguel's upper lip was twisting and rolling now as if beset by Parkinson's disease. Following his line of vision, I saw two guys who looked like they were the result of the crossbreeding of storm troopers and surfing bums. Was there any escape route? I considered the plausibility of announcing some dreaded venereal ailment. But then Miguel probably wouldn't permit me to work. Slowly they stepped out from the screen of disbelief and started sauntering over.

"Hi," Miguel said smilingly.

"Hi," they said back. Everyone seemed familiar and, except for my sudden dumbfoundedness, the procedure seemed to be so gracefully lubricated that I wondered whether everyone already knew each other.

"Warm day, wasn't it?"

"Precious for a February."

"Spring's just around the corner."

"And summer's just around spring's corner." They sounded like placid-minded housewives leaning out on adjacent window sills.

"You should join us. We're going back out to the Golden State tomorrow."

"Gosh, I'm getting sweaty just thinking about it."

I stared at the ground and listened to everyone contribute a line to this potpourri conversation. It was a three-way dialogue that amounted to nothing more than a show of good faith; all meant well and were sane and shared common wants. Now Miguel started walking over to the bar with one of them. The remaining one, the hulkier of the two, was left standing with me. I maintained an autistic fixation of the filthy tiled floor, but evidently he found even that cute because he just kept gazing at me.

"Hi," he softly bellowed. I finally looked up. Tiny tributaries of sweat collected down the sharp part of his face, as if he had just arisen from a pool; apparently he had danced to an excess.

"What happened to your arm?" One couldn't help but notice the missing sleeve and the bandage.

"An accident," I quickly replied, hoping to avoid any sympathy that might turn into affection.

"Looks kinda cool." He touched the surrounding area, tenderly nudging my arm under a soft drop light. Lowering his nose to the spot, he sniffed it: a dirty bandage with a dry line of blood crusted along the exterior.

"You can have it when I'm done," I said, referring to the bandage. He accepted the offer and proposed buying drinks in return.

"I don't drink."

"How about a walk?"

If a walk meant what I suspected then I was a gimp. But all the while, I felt Miguel's microscopic stare haunting me for results. If I could just walk with this guy until after the bar closes; he wouldn't be able to return to make his report, then I could dump him. And since this guy was leaving tomorrow Miguel would never be able to confirm anything. He'd have to believe whatever I told him.

"Good idea, let's walk." He got his leather flight jacket, and we both gave farewell nods to our companions and left. All were right, it was a beautiful night, but it felt more like autumn than spring. The glacier of winter's cold was still ahead, not behind us. We walked without any destination, which was okay with me because to establish any destination in this vocabulary of clichés and euphemisms might sound like a commitment of some kind. For a New York night, the sky was clear. Aside from the many lighted skyscrapers, which were New York's consolation for having no visible constellations, I could make out the star, the big one in the northern sky. We strayed westward. And since we were only on Second Avenue there was a lot of westerliness before us.

The oddities of the night included a crab-like man hunching under a huge ghetto blaster angled on his shoulder and back. It was playing "Purple Rain." Turning north, we journeyed to the corner of Saint Mark's Place and Bowery, and as we passed the Transient Hotel, we were propositioned by a hooker who couldn't intuit our alleged longings. Passing Cooper Union, we walked around an array of garbage, which was street vendor merchandise, unsold and abandoned from earlier that day. Looking north on Fourth

Avenue, I saw the clock at the Metropolitan Life Building and the outline of the Empire State Building, an attractive view that was to be barred with the erection of the Zeckendorf Towers in '86. Walking through the parking lot on Astor Square, we swung south down Lafayette past the Public Theater. On Houston Street, we noticed a makeshift abode: an old table covered with boxes adjacent to an old sofa—an ingenious housing project for a group of derelicts. Making a right at Houston, we passed the NYU projects with the Picasso centerpiece. There, the wanton one initiated a conversation. "David Byrne lives in one of those apartments." I could think of no reply.

We turned south on West Broadway. There, through the store windows, we saw art. I wasn't sure whether or not he was making an advance, but as we were nearing Spring Street, the wordless one took out his penis and urinated against a metal pull-down gate that had the word BOONE painted on it. As the stream of urine trailed from the gate across the sidewalk and into the gutter, he mumbled with a grin, "Wanna taste?"

"I'm a believer in nice, slow courtships." To this he sighed tiredly.

"Then you should move to my old town," he replied. "That's why I left."

"And that's why you came here? For the more accelerated life?"

"Well, that and the culture."

"What do you mean, culture?"

"You know the opera, dance, Broadway. This is the center of culture. Isn't that the reason everyone comes here?"

"I came to New York for the roaches, the filth, the sense of intimidation, the foul odors, the violence and...oh yeah, the sky-rocket rents and the over-population, not to forget the freezing winters or the insanely hot summers."

"If you don't like it, why don't you leave?"

"Don't like it!" I replied. "But where else can I get all this?"

The guy wrinkled his nose boyishly and made a completely innocent expression that made me laugh. He was cute, handsome, and seemed like a decent, intelligent guy; it just wasn't my ballgame. I started to feel bad that I was just using him. It was a shame that he wasn't as cold as everyone else. I had no business being in this situation, but I wanted my theater job even if making this poor guy into a fool was the price. One loses a little bit of one-self with each cruel gain. I decided to limit the humiliation as much as possible. I gave the guy a sporting slap on the back. I noticed a clock in a store window, the bar was still open so we proceeded slowly south toward the dawn rising over Canal Street.

People were starting to come out of their little holes, a new day was stepping up to the mike. Soon, the bar would be safely closed, it was time to relieve the misery of this wounded yesterday. We cut a left on Canal and exchanged some notion of going to Chinatown.

"What time is your flight?" I asked, as we crossed Broadway.

"Three o'clock."

"Well mine is now," I replied and dashed down the flight of subway stairs. An R train fat with people was sitting in the station making awkward attempts at sliding its doors shut. The beach boy was tumbling down behind.

"Wait a second," he yelled. As he fumbled through his pockets for a token, I hurdled like a gazelle over the turnstile and shoved in just as the doors locked.

Looking through the plate glass on the subway door, I could see the panic in his eyes, like a lost child in the crowd rushing upstairs. I made rapid and meaningless gestures that tried to indicate concern and sorrow. As the train pulled out of the station, I regretted that this random guy had been made into my Exhibit "A" for Miguel. Slowly I made it back to Helmsley's.

SIX

I wearily walked up the stairs to Helmsley's apartment and found the door unlocked. When I opened it and flipped on a light, I wished I was back on the train. His house had been busted up. Clothing was tossed, dishes were broken. I noticed that some of his prized books had been damaged. No one was home. My first guess was that a struggle had occurred. Where the hell was Helmsley? Maybe he too had been brutalized.

His first German printing of Spengler's *The Decline of the West* had declined into shreds. His nineteenth century folio facsimile of Shakespeare's tragedies was tragic. His autographed first edition of *Being and Nothingness* was now the latter.

When most of the harvest was in, Helmsley walked through the door. Wordlessly he dropped onto the couch and threw his head back, closing his eyes. I immediately noticed that his reddened nose had a new angle to it, his hair was tousled and his old clothes were tugged and ripped.

"What the fuck happened?"

"I got into a fight," he replied with a nasal honk. He was a mess.

"Well, I'm back from work," I replied furiously. And putting a letter opener that might serve as a weapon in my pocket, I said, "Let's go kick some ass."

"We can't." There must have been too many of them.

"Then I'll call the police." I started dialing.

"Put it down—it was Angela," he said and didn't look at me. I didn't know what to say. I wrapped some ice in a towel, brought it to him, and inspected his nose. Considering his nose was broken and a chunk of his precious collection had been mauled, he seemed to be taking it well. Perhaps he was just fatigued.

"Well, I suppose that ends that relationship," I finally said, not knowing what else to say.

He looked to the ground and began whimpering that he didn't know how to deal with this. He tried discussing it rationally, but she had kept pounding at him. When he pulled his shirt off, I saw welts and bruises zebraed along his lower chest, his ribs bruised, probably cracked.

"Exactly what happened?"

"Well," he started, as his fingers ran across the lumps rising out of his scalp. "We were lying in bed this morning, just a couple hours ago, and she said that it was time for me to arise. I explained that there was no reason to get up, but she insisted that she wanted to go out for breakfast immediately. Maybe she's hypoglycemic."

"What happened next?"

"I said that I wanted to sleep for another hour."

"What happened next?"

"That's when she shoved me hard with her foot."

"And how did you respond?"

"I told her violence was the language of animals." I waited for him to tell me more, but he volunteered nothing. "What did you do next?"

"She laughed and made some weird reference to colleges and called me a wimp and that's when I told her to stop laughing, and she slapped me."

"Did you hit her back?" I yelled at him.

"Of course not. I told her that if she was angered over something it should be discussed."

"And was it discussed?"

"No, I told her she was acting like a simpleton."

"A simpleton, huh?"

"Yeah, that's when she started tearing up the books, and when I tried to stop her, she hit me on the nose with an ashtray." No wonder he didn't want to volunteer anything; what a pathetic tale.

"Maybe you should go to a hospital; I think you've got a broken rib."

"They don't tape ribs anymore."

"Your nose is bent to one side."

"I never cared for symmetry," he tried joking, "and it isn't worth seven hours in a waiting room to look harmonious. Just help me into bed."

I helped him into his room and laid him on his bed. Then silently I unknotted his shoes and helped him off with his clothes. He dropped the ice pack to the floor and laid quietly with his aches and pains.

"What happened to you?" He pointed to my shoulder from his supine position.

"Nothing, I'll tell you when we're awake," I replied and pulled down the shade, concealing the morning light. He quickly drifted off. I kicked my shoes off and laid on the couch. As the sun rose high in the Brooklyn sky, I listened to Helmsley's newly acquired snore, thanks to the newly angulared nose. I also thought of last night's silly date and slowly slipped into asleep.

When I awoke, it was pitch black outside; it was seriously late. Helmsley was still soundly sleeping. I tiptoed into the bathroom, where I showered and carefully peeled off my arm bandage. I should have insisted on stitches, because the scar was crisp and permanent. I prepared a new bandage, dressed, and left. It was about midnight and Brooklyn, unlike Manhattan, still had that old duration of time labelled "late." Places were closed and mass sleeping was in effect. People obeyed the sun's ebb. But I was now too corrupted by the irregular cycles of Manhattan time; I was irrevocably awake.

I dressed and went to the F train and paced the empty station. I looked along the tracks covered with filth and followed them as far as I could up the dark tunnel. Looking in the other direction, I could see the sky. At this stop the elevated track poured its rails purgatorially into the ground.

Waiting for a train in New York requires more than just patience; it also demands a defensive outlook. During the early eighties, the city cordoned off "designated waiting areas." They were encased in yellow overhead signs and usually they were within view of the token sellers, so if you were beaten to death within this section, your benefactors might have a good case at suing the city.

Despite the wolf-pack gangs and the doubtful worth of the overpriced token, I had nurtured a perverse pleasure in riding the subways. I would get a ninety-cent thrill out of pressing against the front unwashed window, leaning next to the conductor's booth and straining into the near darkness as the train whipped between the ribbed support beams through the enigmatic bowels of the great city. What subway riding in New York offers that far surpasses a train ride anywhere else is the wonderful relief upon arriving safely at your destination. I experienced this relief an hour later.

I got off at Fourteenth Street and walked across it, past the many cheap storefronts that were all covered with metal pull-down gates at night. Past the old Luchow's and the Palladium, I walked. From the corner of Third Avenue, I could see the Zeus Theater flag snapping in the wind. Why the theater had a proud flag, I wasn't sure. The theater lights were still on and I had no particular place to go, so I decided to stop in and see Miguel. When I got to the corner of Thirteenth Street, I noticed the crowd out front. But then I remembered, the vanguardists Hans and Grett were premiering their film tonight. As I approached the NYU film students and punks flocking outside, I waited as gaggles of gays slowly filtered through and out, and then I pushed in. Hans, who was acting as a doorman, let me in. I walked rapidly through the theater.

"Hey!" the Cambodian porter Thi yelled.

Accidentally I had stepped into a pile of condoms, Kleenex and tiny squeezed out tubes of KY-Jel. Thi had marshalled the garbage together with the blowing machine, which was strapped to his back. Quickly he shovelled the pile into a black multi-plied garbage bag and sealed it. In the office I found Miguel chatting with a bunch of skinheads. He greeted me with a lapse of silence. I felt compelled to say something managerial, so I asked, "How's business?"

He pointed thumbs down. "It must be the nice weather."

I nodded and left the office; I didn't mention that I had just seen enough gays exiting to start a gondolier's union; he had to be stealing money. I decided to keep hushed and wait. Soon, Miguel left his office, the skinheads scattered, and he joined me in the lobby. The crowd was now entering, and as the guests filed past the box office, Hans and Grett handed everyone a plastic cup filled with champagne.

"They sure must've put a lot of money into this," I mumbled to Miguel.

"No," Miguel confided, "a generic case of Astor Home Champagne on sale from the New Year's Eve surplus. Anyway you got to be a little zonked in order to truly relate to the full cinematic reality." He wasn't smiling, so I guess he was serious.

After all had entered, I started mingling with the crowd. There were several cute intellectual-type girls flapping about, but to judge the semiology of their then-pop semiology books, I feared an insincere impregnability. One girl, who came alone and also seemed to know nobody, seemed to be pretty prey. As I approached her, I noticed something that might give me some leverage; there was a green booger just above her nostril. I discreetly whispered this into her ear, feeling assured that she'd feel forever indebted for saving her much embarrassment.

"It's a jade nose ring, asshole!" And she marched into the theater, out of my life forever.

Slowly after all the free champagne was gone, all gravitated into the theater where they assumed seats. Even though all were ready, certain crucial professors and daring small independent producers had not yet arrived, so the boys were still delaying the screening.

Not knowing anyone and sensing that most people preferred it that way, I retreated up to the projectionist booth. Miguel was up there explaining to our projectionist the few idiosyncrasies that this screening would require; at certain moments the volume had to be turned up all the way, and on three occasions she had to sneak into the theater and whack cymbals together. He then gave her an envelope of money, which she quickly counted. Since our theater hours were what the projectionist union termed an "eleven hour" booth, and since Miguel didn't want Ox to detect the undesignated overtime on the payroll, Hans and Grett had to bear the projectionist's fee themselves. When all the details were ironed out, Miguel turned to me with a wide and mysterious grin asking, "So?"

"So what?"

"So how was it?"

"How was what?"

"I don't want to violate your space," he replied, "but last night you went home with one of the prize trophies off Muscle Beach."

All of last night fell back into my lap and accordingly I snickered and said, "I don't kiss and tell."

"It's not the kissing I want to hear about."

"Let me put it this way. I didn't get any sleep last night." That much I could say on any polygraph machine.

Suddenly the intercom buzzed. Grett announced that cinema history could no longer be delayed. The lights dimmed, the projector was started, and Miguel and I took seats among Han's and Grett's alumni. After the credits, which were thunderously applauded, a muddle of images and colors flooded the poor screen. Racing down the sound track came metallic screeches and oblong howls, and then an interjection of urgent radio news broadcast started crackling out of a wall of static, which was overlaid with quasi-images of the tumultuous and the tranquil. It was all carefully disjointed and painfully abstract. It ushered in a host of whispered yet supportive clichés, of which I could hear a couple behind me whispering: "Postexpressionistic...prehensile...atonal..."

Peeking about, I noticed Miguel was nowhere to be seen. Discreetly I abandoned my seat and slipped off to the office; maybe there'd be something painless on TV.

Opening the door, I saw Miguel seated at the desk, talking with two older guys. The air was thick with smoke. A cup that was torn into a makeshift ashtray was filled with Gitanes cigarette stubs.

"No, I don't think it's fair," said the more dashingly dressed NYU student. "You charged Hans a fraction of what you're charging me."

Miguel threw me a quick glance, and putting down the pizza he was eating, he replied, "Look, me and my partner simply don't feel that staying here for that length of time is profitable for any less than a hundred a piece." I was an instant partner in some leery deal.

"Well"—the young filmmaker arose—"I have only a hundred dollars budgeted to this screening. Beyond that I'll just have to look elsewhere."

Before he left, Miguel replied, "When you find that it gets no cheaper, swallow your pride and come back."

The young director left the office, and his sidekick closed the door behind him.

"Hungry?" Miguel took an angle of pizza from a cardboard box that was sitting on canisters behind him. "It has a whole wheat crust."

"What's going on?" I asked, and then bit into the slice.

"I'm supplementing our income a bit, is all."

"Well," I said as I gorged myself, "I don't want to play the devil's advocate, but can't you settle for a hundred less? I mean, a poor student like that can't have much more to spare."

"Trust me when I say that I know what I'm doing. I'm a sweetheart. In fact, I didn't charge Hans and Grett a cent. I just said that so I could get money out of this guy."

"What've you got against this kid? His film has got to be better than that...cinematic havoc now on the screen."

"Did you ever hear of the Owensfield Complex?" It sounded at first like a Freudian term, but I remembered reading about it. The Owensfield Complex was a glamorous group of midtown co-ops that had been in the news recently because they had remarkably reinterpreted certain building codes and zoning laws.

"Who is that guy?"

"Nigel Owensfield, grand-nephew to the tycoon-founder Clarel."

"The guy that just left here?" I inquired.

"Yep. Do you know the *Harrington Quarterly*?"

"I've heard about it." Helmsley had gotten stuff accepted there.

"What did you hear?"

"That it recently gained a lot of prestige, if that's what you're getting at."

"Prestige came with a cost. The only thing that separates mainstream culture from subculture is a budget. Owensfield bought an editor position and at the same time pulled the quarterly from the level of the *Sleazoid Express* and put it on rank with *The Hudson Review*."

"How do you know all this?"

"I heard," Miguel replied, lighting up another cigarette. "In short, he could spare another hundred bucks."

"Am I really your partner?"

"Oh, sure. I've been meaning to talk to you about it. I have a lot of connections and I need your help."

"Fifty-fifty split?"

"Well, sure," he replied benevolently, only to add, "but half of nothing is nothing, isn't it?"

"What exactly does Owensfield do at this magazine?"

"Part owner and some kind of editor. Why?"

"Just curious. You wouldn't mind if I talk to him alone, would you?"

"What are you going to say to him?"

"I'm not sure, but I promise I won't ask for a cent less than you want."

Miguel smiled and jumped out of his chair. He dashed through the theater, hunting for the heir-editor. I sat in the swivel chair and in another moment the heir was sitting alone with me in the office.

"I think I can deliver this place to you at the fee you want, but there are two provisos."

"Continue."

"Before I continue, I don't think we've been properly introduced." I told him my name and explained that I was an obscure visionary poet from the East Village.

"Another obscure visionary poet," he muttered bored.

"Not another," I corrected, "one that has control of a theater you need, and frankly I'm hoping to be less obscure."

"That would leave just the visionary."

"Right, and I envision that we can help each other."

"You're jesting." He quickly understood the direction in which I was heading.

"I've been writing poetry all my life and, other than in school, I've never been published. All I'm asking is that you look at a poem of mine. If you don't like it, nothing lost. But if you do like it, you gain a poet and a theater."

"Why in God's name do you think that I can get you published?"

"Everyone knows that you are to the *Harrington* what Delmore Schwartz was to the *Partisan Review,* what Mencken was to *American Mercury* and what Perkins was to Harper & Row."

"Perkins was with Scribner, and that wasn't a magazine."

"I thought Bartelby was with Scribner's."

"Oh, God!" He sighed and rose to go.

"Look! All we're talking about is a couple of well-crafted lines, one stanza that describes the mechanism of the East Village."

"The mechanism of the East Village?" He smiled. "What's your poem about, a car?"

"Call it what you will."

"Is this machine rhymed or free verse?"

"I rhyme, but..."

"Narrative, confessional, free association...?"

"Essentially narrative."

"Where is this sacred poem?" he asked. Apparently I had passed the multiple-choice part of the quiz.

"I'll have it for you in a week."

"A week! Tomorrow is our final editorial conference. Then we go to print. Next week is my first vacation in two years." He rose again and said, "That ends that."

"Wait a second." I stood up. "I can have it for you before the film ends."

"All right, fine," he replied, prepared to go.

"Then you'll do it?"

"I'll consider it if you get the poem here before the film ends, but I'll tell you right now, don't expect much." He opened the door to leave.

"One last thing," I requested before he departed. "Miguel's a bit of a barbarian. In order to get you your price I would like you to tell him that you're paying the whole two hundred. I'll cover the deficit."

"You mean *if* I accept your poem," he added. Then we shook hands, and he went back into the auditorium.

I swiftly went through the office collecting necessities to write poetry with, a beer from the fridge, a clock, two sharpened pencils, paper. Calling the projectionist, I asked her how long the film would last.

"Another reel, about twenty minutes," she replied, curiously free of any antagonism.

I snuck into the bathroom stall, and for the benefit of any curious eyes that might check the exposed underpart of the partition, I dropped my pants around my knees and sat.

I hadn't written a poem in years, and was not sure of why I was doing this. Occasionally opportunity was prompting enough. I thought hard about nonsense and started scribbling. First, I started just jotting out recollections of New York, but then I dashed down little slogans and aphorisms that I had heard over the past few months, then I rhymed them into a quick poem, while offering my own criticism in alternating verse:

Stop Aids not Gays.
It wasn't well rhymed
No entry for gentry
A graffitied wall chimed.
Only niggers pull triggers
There's a strong verse,
Drink, Drive and Die—Alliteratively terse
Mug and Goetz what's coming
A pale little pun.
I'll stick to free verse
Couplets are done!

But then I remembered that I specifically said it would be an East Village poem, so I started thinking about each street, from First to Fourteenth. I drew up a small map and noted every established hangout and local institution; the poem had to be short, cute, and simple. I sensed that this was all the silver-spooned editor could digest.

There were no revelations in that refuge for defecators and lovers. Sitting upon that unwashable and ancient toilet, I toiled, tinkered, and versified. When seated in that position too long, something is bound to fall out and soon the bowels moved; a cheap little stanza complete with all the squalid neighborhood emblems. For no clear reason, I entitled it "Cowboy Streets, Indian Avenues":

> *Third Street bikers*
> *At Seventh Street bars*
> *Met Twelth Street whores*
> *Screwed quick in cars*
> *Are busted by cops from Fifth Street way*
> *Who drive them all off toward Avenue A*

It was forced and trashy and I hoped that one day I would be a writer talented enough to repudiate it. Outside the stall, I could hear someone pacing, and then more feet. The film must have ended. After quickly writing a final draft, I flushed the toilet for effect and abdicated the chair.

Entering the theater in the middle of deafening applause and brightening lights, I saw no sign of Owensfield. But then I heard a bunch of giggly punk boys and girls and spotted the patron in their midst. Silently I watched them giggle and react to his every movement. Wealth, like fame, provided incredible leverage to one's character; an adequate mind seemed brilliant if it belonged to a star. Not-repulsive looks made a blue blood stunningly handsome; mild sensitivity catapulted one into heights of sexiness; basic decency made them rivals of Mister Christ. Owensfield and his lucky entourage were about to skip out the fire exit when I intercepted him.

"Here." I shoved the poem in his face. With nothing more than a rise of his eyebrows, his group was signaled to linger outside. As he mumbled the poem aloud, Miguel appeared from the other side of the theater and started approaching.

"Well," he uttered as he crinkled the page into his pocket, "to buy this much space as an advertisement would cost you about a hundred and fifty dollars and frankly we've published a lot worse."

"Is that an acceptance?"

"No, it's a deal."

"What's a deal?" Miguel entered in the middle of the conversation.

"Your friend drives a hard bargain." Owensfield seemed to yield. "He got what he was after."

"Wow!" Miguel marvelled as he looked at me.

"I've got people waiting," the well-to-doer replied. "We'll discuss all the bindings later. *Au revoir*." And he was gone.

"How the Tao did you do that?"

"I knew what appealed to him. It turned out I had read his latest piece, a study on Bobby Musil. We talked about that awhile, until the next thing I know we're both reliving Hapsburg, Vienna, Wittgenstein, Karl Kraus, and Saint Stephen's. My God, first we were in tears and then in stitches."

"What the hell are you talking about?"

"Kindred spirits!" I exclaimed. "Elective affinities. For the moment we were the same person. Hell, when I finally popped the request it was like I was asking myself for something."

"And you're telling me he just gave in."

"It was more like I gave it to me."

"Amazing. And I always thought the richer they were the poorer they were. I was ready to take his offer." Miguel looked perplexed. Only the speech pattern and mannerisms remained of the Miguel who was once the sincere earth child. The money and the vulgarity had made its breach;

Miguel knew he couldn't walk nude along the streets or hand out dandelions, and he knew that rhetoric was just rhetoric, but in his heart of hearts I think he really wanted to believe that the right words could precipitate the correct actions. He nodded, still perplexed, and went into his office.

People poured into the street, coagulated into lumps, which broke away and dissipated. I waited outside for Miguel to lock up. When he was finally done, a bunch of people had collected, waiting for him, or waiting for the few people who were waiting for him. I was about to bid him goodnight, when he asked me if I was hungry.

"Yeah, but I'm broke."

"I'll advance you," Miguel offered. "You made us a tidy bundle tonight."

So a group of us walked over to Second Avenue and south toward the Kiev where the cuisine was a mix of Eastern European and American greasy spoon, prepared by Indian short-order cooks. The waitress pulled together a bunch of small tables and after we took our seats, she quickly took our orders. I got a mixed pierogis with sour cream and a side of fries. Fragmented conversations started. I ate and listened to one group in front of me yapping about the film. When one guy called it "a low budget 2001," I turned to my left and started eavesdropping on snatches of conversation in that direction, "Elijah Muhammad, Malcolm X's mentor, was the one who had him assassinated...and when Mayor Laguardia died they found that all he had was eight thousand dollars in war bonds...I've heard that both Roddy MacDowell and Uncle Miltie have the largest penises in Hollywood..." Although the details were interesting, they were difficult to follow.

One guy that Miguel had casually introduced to me earlier that evening, an older, responsibly dressed fellow named Marty, was whispering excitedly to Miguel at my right. Keeping my eyes fixed on the bore who was talking about the film, I leaned into Marty's direction and listened:

"Well, he's only in the damned place like once every two months or so. Particularly now, since he's working in Paris."

"Do you think burglars were watching the place?"

"I'm sure of it. Anyway, it was all insured but now the premium is going through the roof."

"Well, I only wish I needed a place." Carefully I propped my right elbow up on the table so that my hand was against my right ear limiting the peripheral noise.

"It is too bad," Marty replied, "because you're just the right type. I only wish I was gay."

"Now what's this compulsion he has with gays? Is he?"

"No, it's just the opposite—he's an insecure heterosexual. Also I think he thinks they're clean or something."

"Well, I'm a pig myself." Miguel giggled. "What kind of rent is he charging?"

"I'm not sure, but it's not a money question."

"What are you guys talking about?"

"Nada," Miguel replied tiredly. "What's new with you?"

"Nothing, I've been spending all my free time apartment hunting, and it's really frustrating."

"Rents are ridiculous." Miguel replied.

"It's not that. Frankly I think that they've been deliberately restricting me because I'm gay."

Miguel glanced over to Marty.

"What exactly are you looking for?" Marty asked casually before taking a sip of his fruit compote.

"Oh, I'm not very selective. Heck, I don't even mind room-mating with someone so long as they're clean."

"It sounds preordained, Marty," Miguel said outright.

"Preordained?"

"I think I might be able to help you," Marty started.

"How?" I asked wide-eyed.

Marty told me in slow detail about a famous film director who was in his prime during the sixties but since then, due to a series of profitless films and subsequently a broken marriage, had been convalescing. Yet during the last five years or so, while hunting down backers, he had been slowly producing his last film, a real swan song.

"What's his name?" I asked. He didn't want to tell me just yet: this only whetted my appetite all the more.

"Orson Welles?" I asked, knowing that at the time Welles was desperately trying to make a swan song film and had trouble getting backing.

"No," Marty replied, only adding that the filmmaker had no immediate plans to live steadily in New York. The great director had lived his life in several countries and probably spent more time in lofty transit than anywhere else, keeping an operation center/bachelor pad in almost every glamorous world capital. In New York, for instance, he had purchased a spacious SoHo loft when lofts were still just warehouse space flooding the market. He stocked his large space with many valuables, captured after long and great safaris in endless auctions, galleries, boutiques, and curio shops.

"Is it Zeferelli?" I asked, knowing that he had a fear of wide open spaces.

"No," Marty replied, rambling on about how over the years the great director had fallen from lofty metaphysicist to staunch empiricist. Marty explained how other renegade materialists had appropriated his goods. In other words, he had been burglarized three times this year alone.

"Huston?" I asked.

"No."

"Kubrick?"

"No."

"Capra?"

"Capra? No!" Suddenly I felt Miguel nudging me under the table. My catlike curiosity was getting the better of me. I apologized and listened.

"He wants a house sitter. That's all you'll need to know now."

"What sort of rent range does he have in mind?"

"He'll probably only be asking for a nominal rent to see that you're responsible. But the catch is that occasionally he does come to the city, and during those few times he'll probably want the place to himself."

"You mean that he might just pop in at any moment and bang, I'll have to split?"

"Unfortunately."

"No matter what hour of the night?"

"It's not like that. He's extremely formal. If he comes to the city once a month, I'd be amazed. And actually I guarantee that he'll notify you well in advance."

"Sounds good."

"Good, but he'll have to meet you first. Understand that nothing will be in writing; all arrangements will be verbal."

"Which means I'll be unprotected. He'll be able to chuck me out any time."

"Unfortunately, yes, but Sergei is a decent guy." Eisenstein had died in the forties. What other great directors were named Sergei?

"Keep in mind," Marty continued, "that in essence you're getting something for nothing."

"What country is Sergei from?" I asked.

"I don't know. Listen," Marty continued. "This might sound a bit strange, but if you really want this place, a word of advice is look now."

"Now?"

"He's very taken by those who are very gay and very fashionable, very 'now.'"

"You do look more 'then.' For a posh loft," Miguel stated, "looking 'now' is a pretty small trade."

"All right," I replied, without the slightest notion of how I was supposed to transform into this ideal image. But if there was indeed an apartment in the balance I'd certainly try to tip the scale to my favor somehow. I agreed to find the proper attire, and then trying to contain the excitement amidst all the noise and cigarette smoke, I pardoned myself for a brief suck of air.

Although it was chilly outside, I slowly became intoxicated over the spectacular windfall. It was like winning a lotto without even waiting on the long line with losers; a poem published and a loft in SoHo. Standing in the iciness, outside looking in, a fanatical fantasy unfurled: palls of hashish and marijuana smoke streamed from the loft skylight, dust bunnies of cocaine gathered trembling in the chandelier. The permanent temperature of my abode would never breach above or below the mid-eighties so that nude bodies would never be made self-conscious by the cold. There would be no more hard or edgy surfaces to fall against. I: a sultan who had finally found his harem, a thick juicy nerve in search of well-deserved stimuli. Poetry would be written between orgasms. Tonight long-deserved rewards had finally toppled into my lap. I returned to the moment, reentered the restaurant and resumed my seat and pose.

"So who is my patron going to be?"

"Please don't ask me that," Marty responded.

"Why such a big secret about his identity?"

"Sergei is very nervous about his privacy being invaded."

"And what exactly is his need for a gay?"

"Well, other than the fact that he thinks they're cleaner, I think his girl-friend might be coming to town. I'm not sure. He might feel insecure about that."

"So he wants a court eunuch?"

"I guess so," Marty replied with a grin. "But you're gay, so all that is settled."

In his mind I was gay and in this instance that meant I was invincible. I could witness the interlocking of the sexes and remain unfettered. So after I had polished off my pierogis, Marty explained that the celebrated but inse-cure Sergei would be notified and we'd all have a meeting.

SEVEN

The long ride to Brooklyn that night seemed much shorter. When I got in, Helmsley was deep asleep. He had slept silently during my voyage to and from Manhattan. Silently I undressed and cuddled to sleep with the thought that this hard couch under me would soon be replaced by a king's bed. Sleep came quickly.

The lights were suddenly flipped on. Through squinted eyes I made out the figure of Angela.

"Hey! Turn off those lights," I moaned, and then pulled a pillow over my face.

"I oughta throw you the fuck outa here!" she yelled back drunkenly. "Who the fuck you think you are?"

"What is going on?" I heard Helmsley say, and looking up I could see him knotting a bathrobe over his pajamas.

"This cocksucker cursed me out and I'm gonna teach him who's dumb," Angela said, pointing at me.

"Christ, Helmsley, she's drunk." Looking into Helmsley's puzzled face, I knew he was in for a tough one.

"Ya just gonna stand there?" she addressed him.

"Look Angela, I didn't give you my key so that you could barge in here like a lunatic."

"You faggot! God wasted a dick on ya."

"Let's go to bed," he replied. Grabbing both her shoulders, he slowly tried to steer her into his room.

"I oughta get my brothers to kick the shit out of ya. That'd put hair on yer chest." In a moment Helmsley succeeded in enclosing her in his room, but several seconds later, I heard a scream—hers. A moment later, a cry, his, and once again the door smashed open and she reemerged, stopping before me.

"What's going on?" I asked.

"I want you out."

"This ain't your house," I replied.

"Don't tell me what the fuck house this is, I'll bash ya." Helmsley now limped out of his room, cupping his testicles over his pjs.

"Angela!" he winced. "Stop this now!"

But she was beyond him. Her eyes were targeted toward me now. Helmsley proved himself ineffective as a protectorate. I looked to the floor and saw my shoes and pants. Glancing toward the window, I noticed it was almost dawn.

"I want you out of this fuckin' house," she repeated as she stared at me.

"I ain't going."

"Please," Helmsley appealed. "Go."

"I ain't going."

"I'll give you money for a hotel," he implored.

"No."

"I'll get him out for you," Angela said, taking a step forward.

"No," Helmsley commanded.

"Then call the fucking police!" Angela yelled. Helmsley stood still and looked about miserably. She screamed louder this time, "Call the fucking police!"

Helmsley went over to the phone and looked at me pleadingly. "For God's sake, please go. Just for now."

"No, Helmsley," I replied. "If you can't rule your own house you should go into your room and let me handle it."

"YOU DIAL THE POLICE GODDAMN YOU!"

Helmsley snatched up the phone nervously and started dialing. As he did, a victorious sneer smeared over the bitch's face.

"I got your own friend calling the cops on yer, yer a pair of fucking faggots."

"I thought you were going to bash me," I taunted.

Her face started lacing back and tightening. Before I knew it, she jumped forward and tore the bandage off my right arm. When I stood up, she clipped me, a right cross to my head. Falling backwards, I reached out to grab her, trying to regain my balance. Accidentally I shoved her. She fell backwards right through the old oak coffee table. Now she was screaming and hollering.

"He hit me! The bastard hit me!"

"It was an accident," I replied as I tugged on my pants. Helmsley hurdled over his fallen lover and was punching me all over. He was bigger and stronger than I, so I tried running, but he pinned me down with his knees on my shoulders. All the anger that she had generated and he had stored was punching out on me. I tried to talk to him, but suddenly I felt the hem of my pants being pulled up. Catching a glimpse beyond Helmsley's anchored torso, I saw Angela drunkenly yanking up my bare leg, and I howled as her molars pierced deep into my calf.

Quickly and instinctively I kicked her in the face, catapulting her against the wall and onto the floor in a heap. She lay still now. Helmsley saw that she was badly hurt. He bolted off and attended his beloved maniac. Grabbing my shirt, shoes, and coat, I wobbled out the front door.

Several yuppies walking in an unintentional formation must have thought it a strange sight on their way to work, when they saw me wearing little else but pants, madly limping down Clinton Street. Suddenly a police car with sirens blaring turned a corner and screeched in front of Helmsley's door. The son of a bitch had actually called them. Goose pimples or not, I wasn't going to dress until I was a couple blocks clear of the serpent's love nest. I dressed in a doorway and inspected my leg. Both the upper and lower bridge of her teeth had sunk deeply into my calf. Upon careful inspection I noticed a tiny patch of flesh and sinew ripped off altogether. It was probably sitting in the bottom of Angela's leathery stomach. I tied a tourniquet around my knee and hobbled to the F. Not knowing where else to go, I got off at Broadway/Lafayette and walked up Broadway, finally ending up at the Loeb Student Center at NYU. I limped my way to a booth in the cafeteria downstairs. There, I recuperated over four cups of tea squeezed out of a single tea bag. My jaw had a deep bruise, my neck and chest pulsated and everything else swelled. But the bloodiest gem of my lacerations was the tear in my right leg. With napkins and rubber bands, I was able to sop up and control the ooze of blood, but I was still worried about infection.

I finally decided to go to one of the most merciless and dreaded places in the city, a hospital.

Since I owed Saint Vincent's money for repairing the cut arm, I started hobbling northeastward toward Beth Israel. As I walked, the wound reopened. I kept stopping and trying to curtail the bleeding.

I wasn't in pain, but by the time I reached Second Avenue I was numb and dizzy. I paused a moment in front of the Saint Mark's Cinema, just to catch my breath. I didn't recognize anyone inside. By the time I finally arrived at Beth Israel, the self-applied battle dressing along with the hem of my pants and right shoe were all soaked in blood. I staggered into the emergency ward. Quickly a novice nurse laid me on a gurney and started cutting away at the pants.

"He hasn't been admitted yet," I heard the head nurse remark. Someone questioned me, and then the young nurse returned to the wound. She cleaned it out and brought over an intern, a young Indian woman. She quickly stitched all the frayed flesh ends into an integrated calf, and dashed off to the next impatient patient. As a final fuck you to that wimp bastard, I told the hospital people I was Helmsley and gave his location as my billing address.

After a couple of hours of recuperation, it was time to go. The Zeus Theater was only a couple of blocks away, and it was already late afternoon, so I slowly staggered there for work.

I arrived a half hour before my scheduled time. Today was going to be my first solo flight. I was supposed to manage the theater alone. But when Miguel saw me his mouth fell open in disbelief.

"Are you a masochist?"

"No."

"What's with you? Every time I see you you've been wounded."

"Fate's a sadist."

Miguel offered to cover that night's shift, but I could tell that he was looking forward to having the night off. He had been working every night for the past two weeks, ever since the manager whom I was replacing had quit. I was equally eager to see if I could handle the job. He planted a thankful kiss on my cheek, promised to call, and left.

All I had that day was the watery tea at the NYU student center, so I appropriated some money from the petty cash drawer, and I went out to get some food. I went over to the Korean greengrocer, which had just opened a salad bar, and put together a complex salad. Then I hobbled back to the theater, and slowly ate it down. I began my first inspection of the theater. Toilet paper was stocked in the bathroom. All the fire codes were being observed. Checking the screen, I noticed that all the acts of fellatio and sodomy were correctly in focus and all the grunts and moans were distinctly audible. Along some of the seats, I saw the dark silhouettes of pleased patrons in rhythmical motions. Life was following art in the theater. I was about to dip back into the office when I heard someone address the box office lady, "Is Miguel here?"

"Miguel?" she replied. I turned to see the oily subway kid who was initially recommended the job by Tanya. Before the box office lady could tell him that M i g u e l wasn't here, I stepped up and spoke to him.

"Can I help you?"

"Are you Miguel?" he asked. Silently I went around to the turnstile and opened the door for him.

"Why?" I said.

"Tanya sent me for the manager's job."

"I needed someone a week ago. Where the hell were you?" I replied, and then concluded, "I filled the spot."

"Shit," he replied.

"Sorry," I replied. He vanished back into the night.

Proceeding back into the office, I took out the portable TV to forget the dirty deed. The kid shouldn't have taken so long. I turned on the TV.

The only time I had ever watched TV in the recent past was when I was depressed. After about five minutes of watching a sitcom, the funniest part of which was the laugh track, I lost reception.

Finding nothing else to do, I started cleaning the accumulations out of my pockets. Other than soiled tissues, I found a "Be A Cashier In Six Weeks" mail order coupon, which in my former unemployed despair I had pulled from a subway advertisement. The bottom of my pocket was impaled with broken toothpicks and lined with pulverized after-dinner mints that I had taken from the Italian restaurant where Helmsley had treated me, pre-Angela. Finally I came across an unknown phone number scribbled on a loose piece of paper. This I threw into the garbage with everything else. But no sooner did I drop it than I remembered that it belonged to the career woman I had met during the hold-up. I push-dialed her number, but got a recording mandating use of the newly implemented 718 area code. I remembered that she said she lived in Brooklyn Heights, and I dialed the number again, properly. This time I got a mellow "hello."

"Hi." I tried to sound at ease. "I hope this isn't a bad time to call."

"Who is this please?"

"I'm the guy you took to the hospital the other day, after the hold-up."

"The would-be poet."

"How did you know?"

"How did I know what?"

"That I got a poem published. You didn't see it in print, did you?"

"No," she replied. "I mean, I don't know. I only remember your mentioning Hart Crane. Where did you get a poem published?"

"In the *Harrington Quarterly,* the upcoming issue."

"Congratulations, best of luck with..." A clicking sound interrupted. "Oh excuse me, I've got call waiting."

She clicked her phone and talked to some other party for a while, giving me time to locate a target. I decided that I would ask her for lunch the next day.

"I'm sorry for keeping you," she finally said, "but I've got a long distance call on the other line, and I'm going to be a while, so I've got to go."

"One request. Can we go for lunch tomorrow?"

"Look, I'm about ten years your senior."

"Maybe, but you're a lot younger than your age and I'm a lot older than mine."

"Ten years is ten years."

"All it really means is that you'll have more to say than me."

She giggled and told me to give her a call in the mid-afternoon, and that ended the conversation. I toured around the theater a bit and returned to the little office. I tried watching TV again but soon lost reception again. Eventually I buzzed the projectionist booth and announced I was coming up. When I arrived, she swung open the door and asked what I wanted.

"Just checking to make sure everything's okay."

"Well I would have notified you otherwise, wouldn't I?" she replied.

"Sorry for bothering you," I said and turned to leave.

"Hold on there. There is one thing." She led me into a back room. "Look at this." She pointed out a large rusty pot filled with stagnant water.

"Why don't you dump it?" I replied, not knowing what else she might have wanted.

"Because the roof's leaking, stupid."

"Okay, I'll make a report of it." And again I turned to go.

"Hey stupid, how are you going to make a report on something you haven't seen?"

"Huh?"

"Don't you think you should check the roof? It might just be a leaky pipe or something."

"It's not necessary," I said. I didn't want to go up to the roof.

"Check the roof!" she insisted. Then she led me to a steel ladder that was bolted into the wall. I climbed up the ladder that led into darkness. In the darkness I realized that a metal hatchcover was tied down with thick hemp ropes. I undid the ropes, shoved up the hatch, and continued up to the roof. Outside it was dark and drizzling. I walked around the roof awhile. It was dirty and littered. I accidentally kicked through a rusty tar can. At the very rear of the roof I noticed a rattly old fire escape. But it was too dark to see any cracks in the tar so I climbed back down the ladder and reknotted the ropes.

"Yep," I told the projectionist, "there's definitely a leak."

"Well, get on the ball and fix it or expect a grievance from the union."

I hurried downstairs, away from the projectionist and out of her testy domain. It was a flash lesson in the value of warm secure boredom. When I went by the box office, the lady told me that I had two calls: one from Miguel checking to see that all was well, one from Marty. He left a number. When I dialed it, an older male with an accent answered. I introduced myself.

"This is Sergei," he only gave his given name. "So you are the young man whom Marty recommended."

"Yes."

"Well, when can we meet?"

"Whenever you like."

"Tomorrow at noon then."

"Perfect."

"Do you know Caramba?"

"On Broadway."

"Very good, brunch. It will be my treat."

"Wonderful."

"Oh," he suddenly exclaimed. "I'm looking at my appointment book and I realize that I have a conflict. Damn, damn. And that would have been perfect, too. Let's see..." I could hear him flipping through small pages. "Damn, I'm overbooked. Meet me at Caramba for a quick meal, and if we haven't resolved things you'll just have to accompany me on my next appointment."

"I don't mind," I replied, as if I'd been asked.

"Wonderful," he replied, and that was that; I still didn't know this "celebrity director." No sooner did I put down the phone than I realized the upcoming problems. I had no money, no clothes, and nowhere to spend the night. I had already borrowed what little petty cash could be spared for dinner, and I had already borrowed against my first paycheck from Miguel.

If worse came to worst, I could spend the night in the theater, on the office floor, and scrub my clothes clean in the sink so that I could look half-presentable tomorrow. But I was looking more and more raggedy. The right sleeve of my jacket and the left bottom leg of my pants were cut off.

Paradoxically all I could do to fight off the anxiety was flip through Miguel's *Village Voice*, a paradox because the *Voice* usually gave me anxieties. First, there were the cartoons, Feiffer's and Stan Mack's Real Life Funnies. Arthur Bell had just died and Musto had not yet put the edge to his column. With Newfield, Hamill, and Hentoff it had a solid crew of writers, but they usually left me feeling   politically incorrect.   Then there were the film reviews; this week both Sarris and Edelstein found something subtle to attack in blatantly bad films. And then the Literary Supplement and eventually you wound up in the classifieds. The personals were fun, but apartments were foremost in mind. If Sergei's apartment fell through, the only chance I would have of staying within a half-hour radius of the Village was a roommate situation. I quickly skimmed the prices, but even the shares were above my impoverished means. I did notice two relatively low rentals. But upon reading the specifications, I saw I didn't fit in. The first one read: "SWM 40 successful architect seeks SF age 20 to 32 to share bedroom of luxury West Village Condo, rent \$210/month. Send photo to P.O. Box 878..." The other went: "Companionship and good times, WM willing to share one bedroom upper West side low rent in exchange for light duties, candlelight breakfast for two." Getting an apartment in the city was serious business.

With the buzz of the intercom, I was informed by the box office lady that the last show had begun. It was time to calculate the final balance. In the box office she counted out the money in the till. It came to five hundred and twenty-four dollars. It was a good night.

Touching the stack of cash sent a jolt through me. Over the past two years, I had learned the fullest value of money. The American Dream for me wasn't leisure, just day-to-day survival. Soon I was told the film was over. I cosigned the cashier report, turned on the inside lights, turned off the front marquee lights, locked the turnstile, and said good night to the box office lady.

I took the cash into the office, locked the door and recounted it. It was then that I noticed the tremor in my hands. There was something very philosophical about money. I filled out a deposit slip, bound the whole thing together with a rubber band, and stuffed it into a night deposit bag. I was about to zip and lock the bag, but I couldn't bring myself to do it. I opened the bag and took out the money. It was tightly stacked and banded—it felt like a truncheon. I held it in my hand for a moment, just weighing the heaviness of it, the power. I unbanded the bills and put them in my pocket. It wasn't close enough to me. I put the money between my shirt and my chest. But then a sound or something awoke me. The money wasn't mine, it was a piece of costume. I took the money out of my shirt, rebanded it, and with the deposit slip zippered it back into the night deposit bag.

The automatic turnstile dial amount was framed in the wall; I transcribed the number and checked to make sure the amount was correct. Every time a patron entered the theater, through the turnstile, the digit increased one. A speck of dirt was caked over the tenth digit. Using my fingernail, I scratched off the dirt, the tiny square of glass moved just a bit. Jotting down the figure, I subtracted it from the matinee figure; it came to one hundred and thirty-one, the number of patrons that had come tonight. Multiplying that by four, the amount came out correctly to five hundred and twenty-four bucks.

What prevented me from taking that money? Or at least part of it? First, there were the Spanish-speaking cashiers, but their memories were always a clean slate the next day, never remembering or reporting anything of yester-day. The only real safeguard was that dial in the wall.

It started as a curiosity that crystallized into a hunch. When I scratched the tiny frame of glass and realized it was a little loose, I found that with a great deal of tedious angling the glass could slip up just fractions of an inch. But this was just enough space to wedge a straightened paper clip. The paper clip caught into the tiny teeth of the right cog. I flipped the clip up and the small dial turned back a digit. Each time it turned back a digit, it meant four dollars were mine. It was like turning back the very hands of time.

A sudden knock at the door shattered everything. "Who's there?"

"Day's done, see you tomorrow." It was the irate projectionist.

I realized that it was time to lock up the theater so I quickly inspected the place. Although no film was on the screen and the lights were turned up, there were still guys doing it downstairs and in the auditorium, so I turned the house lights up full and yelled that the theater was closing. I could hear pants being buckled and, slowly, guys filed out. After a moment, I checked the place again: empty. I turned off the lights, pulled down the drop gate in front of the theater, and locked the glass doors. I returned to the office and locked the office door.

With a tempting money supply before me, I needed something other than my own desire to calibrate the flow of cash into my pocket. On the day-to-day desk calendar it was procedure to dash down the amount of money we totalled each night. I spent the next hour summing up two averages. I summed up the average amount that we had brought in every night for the past month, next I figured out the average amount we took in every day this week. It took me about an hour before I realized that sitting in front of me was approximately two hundred dollars above the average amount earned each day that week, and approximately a hundred dollars above the average amount earned that month. I decided to pocket two hundred bucks, and dismiss it as an unprofitable night. I rewrote a new cashier's report, and reforged all the signatures. While in the middle of this, there was a soft knock at the door.

"Who is it?"

It was only Thi, the night porter, another false alarm. After leaving, I walked to the night deposit on Fourteenth and Broadway and made the drop. Heading up Broadway, I made a left on Twenty-third and walked over to the fashionable George Washington Hotel, just north of Gramercy Park. It was a far cry from either the filthy YMCA or Helmsley's hell house.

Even though rooms were cheaper by the week, I wasn't sure how long it would be before I could move into Sergei's house. Money was still a handicap, but I had recuperated much since earlier that evening. At the bar in the lounge, I had a couple of whisky sours and relaxed. After a while, I took the elevator to the tidy room; there I stripped and slipped between clean, cold sheets. I tried but couldn't sleep.

I thought about Helmsley and his twisted beloved one. Trains of thought jumped tracks while I waited for sleep. Eventually I ended up at that old and familiar terminus. I always ended up thinking about death. Looking up at the strange shadows along the clean ceiling, I thought about how one day my awareness and everything about me would be no more.

A moment later fresh morning light poured into the room, and I was aware only of being in a strange room. I had this sudden panic. I needed to know the time. I called downstairs and the desk clerk said it was nine A.M. While dressing, I considered the two appointments of the day. The first appointment was with the director, and then I had to try to get a lunch date with Glenn. The trick was looking both punkishly gay for Sergei, but afterwards older and responsible for Glenn, the career women. It was still early and I didn't have to evacuate the room until noon. I checked my key with the desk clerk and left to hunt for a punk wardrobe. In the clothing shops of Twenty-third Street, I purchased all those styles of clothes that I had always ridiculed—black, torn, tight, and aggressive looking. Even in the early eighties they were passé. I saw a line of male cosmetics while passing by a drugstore. The counter girl gave me profuse advise on what mascara to buy, then applied it thickly and held up a mirror before me. I looked like a vampire, but it was probably exactly what Sergei was looking for. She also sprayed me with a new body scent called Truce and put a touch of a cologne called Bondage gently behind my ears.

Hair was still one of the most important canvases of fashion, and in order to be convincing, I needed an authentic haircut. I got to a pay phone and called the Astor Place Hair Cutters; that was *the* haircut place. A couple of years ago, the Astor Place Hair Cutters was just a couple of older barbers going out of business like most other old-fashioned barbers, but apparently one of them snapped his fingers one morning and learned how to pander to the fashions. Some guy on the phone said they had an hour's waiting time. It was too long.

I walked around the area until I passed one salon, which had a sign in the window. It read, "Special, this week only, $25 for any fashion plus a free nipple piercing!" The walls of the place were lined with posters of punks, and all the barbers were ambisexual punks. Squeamishly I rubbed my chest and entered. Until now, I had only patronized the barber college on the Bowery where a haircut cost only three bucks. I put haircutting on the same parallel as fingernail clipping and tooth brushing. Twenty-five-buck haircuts seemed ludicrous, but I rationalized it as down payment for Sergei's apartment. I chose the flashiest barber, a guy who had the colors of the spectrum running down his mohawk and, sitting in his chair, I nervously asked him for his most daring concept.

"Daring concept?" he asked. "Heel and sit."

"I'm just a bit nervous," I confessed. He leaned the chair back and fitted my head into a sink. He shampooed my hair, wrapped it in a towel, patted it dry, and then started clipping. Initially I watched him in the mirror, but after a while, I couldn't bear it. I looked away at the shelf where he kept all his accessories. After about ten minutes, he started up his blow drier. Fashion, which I had neglected so long, was finally taking revenge on me.

"Finished," he finally said. "Now remove your shirt for the piercing."

It could have been worse. I looked like Billy Idol. My hair stood on end, electroshock style. All that junk he kept pouring into my scalp was peroxide. I was bleachy blond.

"Divine, no?" He displayed me to the other hair virtuoso who, due to the absence of any other clients, inspected.

"What about the nipple piercing? It comes free." With a tiny, long acupuncture-type needle he pointed to some kind of local anesthesia.

"No, thanks."

"How about a nose piercing?" He wanted to stab some part of my flesh. An ear piercing, I thought, would erase any final doubts Sergei might have in his terrified little mind. A dangling earring would be a banner of my fashion-at-all-expense attitude. "How about an ear pierce?"

"Fine."

"I'd like it done with a new needle," I requested.

"Course."

After the stylist numbed my ear, he took the needle to my lobe. I closed my eyes, bit my cheek and while counting to ten, felt a pinch. Then I opened my eyes again. He was swabbing away a drop of blood.

"We have a little training post. But what I want you to do, is clean your lobe tonight with soap and water."

"I will."

"Promise me."

"I swear," I assured him. I then put twenty-five bucks in his hand and picked up my bags.

"I accept tips you know," he said.

I gave him a dollar and left. I felt the tiny gold drop in my lobe and, passing by a cheap jewelry joint, I bought an earcuff from an Indian salesman. While trailing back to the hotel, I was aware of someone walking behind me staring. I blushed so hard that I felt feverish. Dashing into a department store, I bought a pair of sunglasses. When I went to the cash register to pay, I noticed a bunch of preteen girls giving me the eye. One of them finally said, "Hi there."

I wasn't sure if they felt my androgynous look was free of sexual threat, or if they regarded me as a child might regard a clown. I silently paid and left.

When I finally got back to the hotel, I asked the desk clerk for my key. His eyes widened and, he asked, "What the fuck happened to you?"

"How do you mean?"

"Nothing," he replied, retrieving my key. I indignantly grabbed the key and went up to my room, where I put on all the clothes and accessories. It was eleven o'clock. The trip downtown by cab would take no more than ten minutes. For about a half hour all I could do was stare gloomily at my new self in the bathroom mirror.

Finally, after my brooding fit, I went outside. A thrift store was across the street, so I popped in and purchased a cheap and heavy army coat that draped down to my knees. I also bought a black knit beanie that I could tug over my disastrous head and pierced earlobe. All that, with the sunglasses, erased all identity. The salesgirl shoved everything into a Unique shopping bag, where I also shoved my former clothes. I then hailed a cab and was let off at Great Jones and Broadway.

Before entering Caramba's, I noticed a black-stencilled message; it read: "People starve on this block." At the rear of the place, past all the yuppies around the bar, Marty and the director were seated, sipping aperitifs. The great director didn't bat a lash at my get-up. Apparently he expected it, but I could see Marty gently bite his bottom lip.

"Enchanted," I said, softly shaking the tips of Sergei's fingers. I didn't recognize him. I took a seat, shoved the Unique shopping bag under the table, and plopped a cloth napkin on my lap. "I'm famished."

"This is Sergei Ternevsky," Marty said, finally unveiling his last name, and allowed a pause for appreciation. I vaguely recalled drunkenly watching an experimental film that had showed one midnight at the Saint Mark's Cinema. It was a dumb satire about tools.

"As I suspected. I've seen your films and may I say that it is hard to imagine what cinema would be, were it not for your contribution."

"Moving along," Marty commenced. "Sergei would like to know something about your background."

"Well, it's probably going to bore you to tears. I was raised in Queens, the only son in a Jewish household. A passive father, and a domineering mother. After high school, I got accepted to the Fashion Institute, you know, FIT on Twenty-seventh? And well, here I am."

"What became of your last residence?" Ternevsky asked.

"It was a sub-sub-sublease that sunk. Currently I'm back with the folks."

Then a tenacious silence leapt on us like a hedgehog and gnawed away. They both just looked at me. I felt a gathering tautness, so I took the presumptions, "I came to terms with my sexuality at a relatively young age."

"I have no interest in that," Ternevsky replied, and then he added, "You say you've seen my films. Which ones exactly?"

"Well, I've always worshiped *Phillips and Flatedges*." This was the boring experimental film I'd sat through. It was done in the sixties and parodied documentaries. It was a history of the screwdriver.

"Sergei's in production on something similar currently," Marty mentioned.

"No, really!"

"It's an attempt to bring philosophy to the screen," Marty explained.

I nodded enthusiastically. I was about to say something like, "Bringing philosophy to the screen is a good thing," but decided against it.

The waitress came and put down hors d'oeuvres, a big bowl of chili with tortilla chips and virgin margaritas. Apparently Ternevsky had already ordered for all. It was while both Marty and I were munching away that Ternevsky chose to launch into his great soliloquy, a monologue that said little other than he was skillfully modest and modestly skilled. Occasionally his pet, Marty, would lick his hand with some compliment. He talked about others in Hollywood like Steven Spielberg who had benefited from his experiments in technique. Money was reserved for the quick and greedy, but history holds all the real laurels. Soon he brought his conversation around to the abode.

"It's kind of a private museum," he explained, "furnished with personal relics. All I'm going to ask is a mere one hundred dollars a month, a courtesy fee. But I won't be shy about one demand." His face tensed and he leaned over his chair toward me. "I don't want it to be a hangout, do you understand? This isn't some fuck pad for you and your friends. If I find anyone up there other than you, you're out, understand?" It was clear.

"Good," he replied, and suddenly rising to his feet he looked across the large dining area and yelled to the distant waiter, "Check!"

"Come on," Marty said to me as he put his own coat on, "Sergei has an important appointment."

The waiter was too slow, so Sergei dropped two twenties on the table to cover the appetizers and drinks.

Outside, Sergei vigorously walked to a Mercedes parked on Great Jones. Marty dashed ahead, and opened the door for the maestro. Grabbing the Unique shopping bag from my hand, Marty tossed it into the trunk and slammed the hood. Apparently Sergei was going to some fundraising gala at a new ritzy restaurant. It was crass to travel with any less than a party of three, so even though he and I had little else to say, Sergei desired my company. As Marty drove up Lafayette, Sergei explained that he was to meet a great star of record and music video. He mentioned a name that I didn't know. She had topped all the charts effortlessly, and now the only other place for her to go was motion pictures.

Lafayette turned into Fourth Avenue, and Fourth turned into Park Avenue South, and then into Park Avenue, dipping down into a sunken tunnel. Around the Grand Central/Pan Am Building mezzanine, we finally made a left on Fifty-seventh Street. We stopped in front of a place that had the rear end of what looked like a Caddy for a canopy: The Hard Rock Cafe. A doorman swung open the door, and a swarm of teenagers were screaming behind police barricades as we all entered. Marty took the liberty to explain that the gala was sponsored by the African Relief Fund, the same people that had organized the "We Are The World" song. But all that had occurred in L.A., and there was still an untapped resource on the East Coast. Of course, there were the constant strains of rock and roll songs. Screaming over the noise, Marty explained that these people were the movers and shakers of the record industry. Between them were divided a Roman Empire of the teenage world. Sergei quickly spotted his future movie queen and zipped off, leaving us to wander.

Video technicians were racing about, each filming his own excerpt. The bar was open so I downed a couple and just stared around. Under a large poster of a swollen-bellied African child, I believe I spotted Cindy Lauper sipping with Lionel Richie. Suddenly there was a stir in the crowd. Was it Michael Jackson? Mick Jagger? I heard someone mumble it was Bruce Springsteen. This was his first public appearance since his first marriage. Marty excused himself. He wanted to have a look at the Boss. I listened to clumps of people talking in small groups. They were talking "labels," and other studio jargon that eluded me.

I spotted Dr. Ruth Westheimer, the sexologist, all alone. Getting a glass of white wine, I started walking over to her. She looked at me with anticipation, but suddenly Marty grabbed my arm.

"Come on, we were about to leave without you."

"Perhaps we'll meet at some other benefit," I said to the sex doctor.

"Perhaps," she replied with that accent, and her entire face smiled.

Outside Sergei was petulantly pounding his fist on the roof of the Mercedes.

"What," I asked stupidly, "didn't you find your next star?"

"I wouldn't let her be a mutilated extra in a mass murder scene!" Marty quickly ushered Ternevsky into the back seat of the car. Dashing back out Marty handed me a set of keys and told me my new address. "You can move in tonight after ten. I'll pick up the monthly rent at the theater."

With that he jumped into the driver's seat, made a wild U-turn, and zoomed off down Fifty-seventh Street. It was then that I remembered that I had left my Unique bag, containing my overcoat and old clothes, in the trunk. Like Cinderella after midnight, my punk charm suddenly converted to embarrassment and self-disgust. Additionally it was three o'clock. I was supposed to try to finagle a date out of Glenn. Putting on the dark sunglasses, I walked north to Fifty-ninth Street and took the IRT local down to Astor Place. Fortunately I still had some pocket money.

EIGHT

Between Broadway and the Bowery along Astor Place, street vendors lined the south side of the street spreading out anything that could be sold. The sellers weren't franchised or affiliated with anything other than the garbage they'd collected or robbed, but occasionally they'd come across an item of worth or curiosity. I was able to buy a shirt and a pair of pants. I tried trading away articles of my punk clothes, but no one would take them. One vendor whom I had come to know, named Flowers, offered me a good deal on a leather waist jacket, so I bought it. Passing down Waverly Place, I noticed that there was no line in front of the Astor Place Hair Cutters. It was an off-peak hour. I quickly located one of the old Italian barbers in the fray and asked him to give me an old-style hair cut.

"The kind I'd give my kid, ya mean," he muttered, as he tried to salvage something. After ten minutes, my second haircut of the day was done. My hair was very short.

By four o'clock I was on a corner phone asking a secretary if I could speak to Glenn Roberts. While waiting on hold, a very young punk girl walked by wearing a bone in her nose. It reminded me I was still wearing an earring, which I removed and discarded.

"I'm sorry," the secretary returned to life, "Miss Roberts is presently indisposed. If you'd like to leave your name and number she'll try to get back to you."

That meant rejection; I was about to hang up wordlessly but I suddenly heard Glenn's voice interrupt, "It's okay Erica, I'll take it."

Erica hung up and I asked Glenn if she was available for any meals. She was silent for a moment, so I tried making it easier. "How about I bring up a cup of coffee to your office?"

In response I heard strange whiny sounds, and gradually I realized that Glenn was fighting back tears. I learned that her boyfriend—a big executive at a rival firm—had been having a torrid affair with his secretarial pool. Apparently one of the ambitious drips from this pool, a secretary to whom he had promised the world, got angry when he failed to deliver. She got her revenge by informing Glenn.

"You should go home. Do you have a friend?"

"He cheated on me," she replied, in complete control.

"You shouldn't be at work now."

"I have more appointments," she replied.

"So he didn't really mean anything to you?" I asked. She couldn't respond. I heard her crying, and thought about the fact that someone whom I really didn't know was crying on the phone to me.

"Do you really think you're in a condition for business?"

"No, but frankly I'm afraid of an empty house." I offered to join her. She then gave me her address and hung up. She lived in a brownstone, with ivy up the facade, on a quiet tree-lined street in Brooklyn Heights. Wordlessly she opened the door, still wearing her overcoat. She led me through the antique-filled house into an elegant living room. I sat in an armchair. She silently sat on a sofa across from me holding a glass of Chablis and staring intensely at nothing.

"How're you feeling?" I finally said after about five minutes.

"Fine," she replied softly, but added, "Let's not talk."

Which comes first, the moods or the thoughts? I focused on her lips, which looked hard and thin, but as I watched them they seemed to bloom and become increasingly more delicate. The slight gloss of her eyes seemed to increase. Devastation became her. We were in very different moods. Finally I arose and quietly sat down next to her on the sofa. First, conspicuously not touching. Gently I brought my fingers up, stroking along her collar.

"Don't do that," she replied tensely. "I don't feel right, now. I just want to get over this."

"He sounds like a real bastard."

"I don't want to talk about it. It might sound rude but I'm really tired."

"I am too."

"I have a spare bedroom you're welcome to use," she replied.

"I can leave if you like," I replied.

"Despite the fact that I don't know you," she began, "I don't really want to be left alone now, and few things seem more depressing than waking up at night all alone." Fine with me. She led me to one room and disappeared off into another. And then there was sleep. And then sounds awoke me. It was dark out, hours had passed. I dressed and joined her. She was making us some food, the TV was on, we watched. She still seemed dazed, preoccupied, violently silent. I got increasingly tired. After "Johnny Carson," "David Letterman," "Sally Jessie Raphael," and "Ben Casey," I drifted off to sleep.

"How dare you!" I bolted off the couch, expecting an Angela. It was light out.

"How fucking dare you!" she repeated, screaming into the telephone. "Ten years of all we've been through together! You little sleazebag! There's no reason for you to, cause I'm tearing up all your clothes! Some little bitch just out of secretarial school has to be the one to tell me!"

There was a tense pause. She held the phone to her ear. I awoke and realized she was speaking to him. This would be the interlude when he would be pleading, begging, wallowing, crying, punching his genitals, and quickly trying to hammer together a perspective that would minimize his crime: "I'm just a lonely middle-aged man whose life has amounted to a hill of beans. I started my first business day when I was twenty-one, fresh out of college, and now I'm forty-five, and that prototypical business day—right down to the one o'clock lunch with the boys—hasn't changed. Twenty of my most fertile years, Glenn, gone!" He might also bring up circumstantial and peripheral details, such as: they weren't married; his lies were indications of his concern for her; and all the boys have mistresses. But alternately, he might realize that this was a romantic case and not a judicial one; sometimes the best strategy is none at all. Suffer the pangs and continue on.

The longer Glenn held the phone and listened to his apology, the better his chances were. This clown made me feel bad for not fighting harder to keep Sarah. I should've let Sarah draw some blood. That would've evened the score. I figured that in another minute, Glenn would be cursing him and then tearing some of his clothes, but then he'd be on his way over, both in tears and renewing vows of their rediscovered love. I didn't care to witness any of it, so I tugged on my shoes, and tucked in my shirt. But then, without so much as a change in expression, Glenn hung up the phone.

"What's up?" I asked for the verdict.

"It's over."

"What did he say?"

"It doesn't matter. Nothing he can say can change any of it. He fucked everyone in that office that could type over ten words per minute."

I sensed that she didn't care to reexplore the event. Although she was in her mid-thirties, that morning, as the sun came into the window, after all the tears and sleeplessness, she looked fresh out of puberty. Her current frame of mind probably made the future seem bleak and lonely. She had suffered a slight death. So I got up from where I was sitting and sat down next to her. Gently I put my arm around her and gave her a peck on the cheek. She was icy cold and I held her paternally, but she just calmly pulled away. After a couple of minutes, when oxygen made its way back up to her brain, and when her lost blood had been replaced, she murmured, "What a schmuck."

I wasn't sure whether she was referring to me or the guy on the phone until she kissed me. I started softly kissing her face, along the ridge of her collarbone, undoing her blouse buttons, moving down along her breast. All the while I expected her at any moment to properly stop me. I wondered if perhaps I wasn't taking advantage of her at a vulnerable moment.

When she led me into her bedroom, I could see all the traces of him, the cologne on the bureau, his satin and monogrammed robe, and so on. She slowly massaged, rubbed and tickled over me in the course of the afternoon and early evening.

In the few days since I met her, I thought of her as neither promiscuous nor giving, but I had lucked out. It was all timing. I had won all the love sired by spite. I made attempts at reciprocating, but it had been so long since I had been on the receiving end that I couldn't bring myself to put an end to her outpouring.

When I awoke, it was afternoon the next day, I could feel her gently stirring against me, nude to nude. She opened her eyes slowly and then burst open her arms in a yawn. Through the lace curtains the sun softly speckled everything, and from the backyard beyond the windows, I could hear birds chirping. There were no sounds of sirens, pigeons or sidewalk crowds.

"I'm ravenous," she whispered, and the kissing started again. But just when she started loosening and I began stiffening, she broke off and led me off into her bathroom. It was the size of a studio apartment. A Jacuzzi was sunken into the floor and after it was filled and turned on, we slid in. Water of equatorial temperature whirled around us making creamy bubbles, and we made love again. Slowly towelling me off, she pampered me, first with a lotion and then with a powder. She then led me back into the bedroom. I felt a combination of rebirth and redevirgination. My skin was never silkier. We both began to dress, until she saw what I was wearing. "You can't wear those clothes."

Leading me to a deep closet filled with enough men's clothes to stock a store, she picked out an expensive suit, a new Armani shirt complete with cellophane wrappings, pins and the cardboard necking. She spent the longest time finding the exact tie. Everything was a little loose on me, but it was still pure extravagance. As I put it all on, I was grateful for the guy's vanity. We locked arms, and Glenn led me to a very classy "supper club" on Montague Street. It was too late for lunch so we had an early dinner; French cuisine with an excellent wine that the maître d' suggested. This was a whole new league for me.

The waiter, some young Pierre, brought over two silver platters with covers. When he opened the platters, the food was still sizzling. One plate was fish and the other was meat; both were nestled in unusual vegetables and sautéed in a terrific wine sauce. After two days of fucking and fasting, I was starving. Grabbing my utensils with both hands, I forked that food into my mouth faster than any farm boy ever flung hay. Soon Glenn was casting glances, and I could sense that she was resisting an urge to correct my slobbishness. I only ate with one hand and took a slurp of wine after every mouthful of food to pace myself. The gourmet banquet, the elegant abode, the discerning wardrobe, the panache of it all was making me giddy. For a sober instant I was paranoid: was she expecting me to treat her? I took a gulp of wine, and started wolfing down the food nervously again. I wanted to ask her who was picking up the tab, but I knew that she would regard it a vulgar question. She had to pay; my condition was obvious.

"Really, you should masticate your food," she commented.

"How are you going to pay for this?" I asked just to get the insecurity out of the way.

"With money," she replied. "I write dinners off as business expenses, why?"

I continued eating at her pace, and felt somewhat insecure by the security and control she had about everything. Her remark about the meal being a "business expense" had put everything in its proper framework: the last two days were nothing more than business. After dinner, the Pierre brought over a dessert tray. I picked out the most intricate structure of chocolate ever constructed. With it we had two reviving demitasses. Because she was a little low on paper, she paid the bill with plastic. We left the restaurant and walked down Montague Street toward the river. There, we strolled the promenade, which decked around Brooklyn Heights giving a humongous view of

Manhattan on its Nile. It was late afternoon, and although the sun was sinking early, it was the warmest day in the past week of frost. There was something autumnal about the day—the tiny, bony branches should have been
gently swaying with yellowing leaves. When we finally made it up the stately
steps of her brownstone, she said her first words since we left the restaurant:
"I don't know how I could've passed through this alone."

Once we entered her living room we took off our coats. While I exam-
ined my borrowed clothes in a full-length mirror, she explained that she
didn't want to be callous yet she needed to be alone for a while. If I liked,
she said, I could make use of the lower floors. Then she went to a cabinet,
where she took out a brass ring of keys. "If you want to go out, these are the
house keys. This is the key to the garage downstairs, and this is the key to
the Mercedes, if you drive. I don't."

"You're very kind," I said, grabbing the coat. "There's no need to feel like
you've got to pay me, I'll get going and call you in a day or so."

"Wait." She was suddenly distressed. "Where will you be going?"

"I don't know, why?"

"You can't go. I'm not just being polite. Would you do me a favor and
come back later?"

"What's the problem?"

"This might sound strange, but I know I'm going to be going through a
kind of roller coaster ride, and for a while it's going to be difficult to handle
things."

"What kind of things?"

"Sometimes...I lose track of life. Things lose their value. I become very
messy." Then she lapsed into an embarrassed silence.

I knew the feeling. I agreed to stick around. She thanked me and
retreated upstairs to her bedroom where I could hear her close the large oak

double doors that separated the upper half of the house from the lower half. The house was loaded with modern conveniences. Everything was either reconditioned antique or high tech.

Behind a set of panel doors in the living room, I opened up the RCA Entertainment Center—that was what the label read—that included a wide-screened color TV, at least twenty-five inches in length and a VCR. In an old bookshelf that had been built right into the wall and that probably once supported a classics library, VCR tapes were aligned. I picked out two films that never became too popular: *Cutter's Way* and *Wise Blood.*

It was just after five o'clock and while I was trying to get the VCR to work, I lost the sound on the TV. Both the VCR and the TV had separate remotes and while trying to make them cooperate, I watched a mechanical woman soundlessly broadcast the news.

Flashing across the TV for only an instant on a screen behind the Newsreadette was an old college yearbook photograph of Helmsley. By the time I cranked up the volume, I heard the Newsreadette say, "...was identified by a relative."

NINE

As I dashed out of the front door, I figured that I had a thirty-minute run ahead of me. Turning back before the front door swung shut, I raced downstairs to the garage on the ground floor. The Mercedes started right up. I zoomed out and down Court Street zipping through lights and cutting off other cars until I screeched to a stop at Helmsley's front door on President Street. I dashed up his steps and banged on the door. I heard some rustling inside, and then the peephole was filled with an eye, "Can I help you?"

"I'm a friend of Helmsley, please open up."

The door opened and a decrepit old lady appeared, her face was all droopy and crinkled, "Poor boy, mixing with trash."

"They killed him?"

"Well, I certainly believe so."

"How...what happened?"

"A Brody, he done. Right off the bridge. That's what they say, anyhow."

"When? Did they find who threw his body off the bridge?"

"I only know it was the Brooklyn Bridge," she mumbled as she disappeared into Helmsley's bedroom.

Looking about, I couldn't believe it. His books were thrown in stacks around the house. I arbitrarily picked up a cloth book yanked from its spine; *Das Kapital,* one of the earliest editions, in a three-volume set; it had been invaluable. I let it drop back to the floor. I remember him showing me one book that was singed brown. It was printed in Cyrillic. He explained that it had survived the 1812 torching of Moscow. So many of his books that had survived brutal tests of ages and centuries had finally met their end here. When I finally composed myself, I asked, "Did the police see this? Do they know who killed him?"

"Police?" squawked the old lady.

"'Course," I replied. "They should see this."

"What are you talking about?" she asked. "That's plain crazy talk."

"What do you mean crazy talk?" And then pointing to the floor I screamed, "Look at what those fucking wops did!"

"Wops!" she replied. "Who are you calling wops? His family's Polish."

"What?"

She explained that when the gang of relatives heard of Helmsley's demise, they came quickly to life. They descended upon his meager belongings. Their beaks tore into his body. As this pinhead standing before me, an old and straggling member of the herd, described the occurrence, I fought an urge to bang her over the head with a shovel. I walked from room to room, staring at the floor.

Greed has no patience, and there are no claims from beyond the grave. Apparently the landlord was eager to repossess Helmsley's rent-controlled hovel and had generously given entrance to anybody claiming relations to the deceased.

But I had the last laugh, these mindless insects were more attuned to consumption than taste; they thoughtlessly loaded up their shopping bags with shiny trinkets and tinsels. To them books were things to prop up air conditioners and hold open doors. They didn't know that the closest thing that Brooklyn could ever compare to a privately owned library of Alexandria was what they had been walking on. I discovered that when the many kin and cousins first rampaged earlier that day, a frenzy had occurred. The books had been shoddily cast into small miscellaneous heaps; the jackals had stripped the books from the shelves checking for any penny-ante treasure that might be stashed behind them. They didn't know that when Helmsley wanted to read a book, he would go to the library because the books he owned were treasures.

"Has anybody taken any of the books?" I asked the old lady.

"Naw," she replied, fishing through old pots and pans. "Super said his son's throwing them out tonight."

"May I take some?"

"Whatever," she replied.

For a moment my heart, my arms, everything opened and unfolded and rapture engulfed all; these books are mine! But as soon as I dashed into his bedroom—only then did it hit me. Helmsley: My mentor, that athlete of the mind whose passion was rivalled only by his logic, a minor twentieth century

New York philosopher who had unfailingly caught me whenever I dropped from my tightrope. He was dead.

I didn't have energy in me commensurate to the loss. I sat on his bed and carefully labored to conjure, summon, recollect, and synthesize all the nuances toward the identity of Helmsley Micinski; to address his distinctions, and why in a world of five billion he was indispensable, and how mankind somehow would never solidly complete its final purpose—whatever that might be—because of his robbed life. But most of all, I tried appraising how much of me was Helmsley: how much of my own thought syntax and spiritual matrix was traceable to him, was him? All of this stewed in that greasy pot of agony.

When I escaped to the city trying to shake free the stalking grief and heartache of my father's death, I learned that loss was life. Tears were inexperience. The shock was gradually absorbed, all emotional bodies eventually regained their proper orbit. The closest thing to relief was when I eventually perceived my father had always been dead. But now there was Helmsley and once again life was for mourning.

Once, as a teenager, I had believed that people could change themselves. Finally I realized that all one could ever hope was understanding one's filthy self better. I felt cleaner by realizing that more than anything in the world, I desired Helmsley's books. And far more than missing my friend, I felt sorry that I had lost my insurance of continued existence. Also, I had been closer to him than to any of these strangers. With all this in mind, I started making piles of books, first selecting the most valuable, such as a Shakespeare & Company signed edition of *Ulysses* that was still in mint condition. I wrapped most of his precious books in his old clothes and stacked them on the bed. I had nowhere near Helmsley's vast data bank of knowledge, and I sensed that I was ignorantly discarding volumes of priceless books, but I had neither the time nor the space. The super's son would execute his duty in a short couple of hours; I could only save as many as would fit in the car.

Once I had them sorted out, I ran downstairs and jumped in the car. I drove around the corner to a liquor store. Giving the owner five bucks, he gave me as many boxes as I could stuff into the back seat. I sped back to Helmsley's, raced up and down the stairs, up with the empties, and down with them filled. I ballasted that old Mercedes down like a freighter. The old lady watched in amazement as I ran by with the boxes. Finally she hollered, "If you want, I got a whole basement full of them Reader's Digest books."

"Thanks, no thanks," I yelled back when I was done. The chassis of the old Mercedes was almost rubbing against the tires. There wasn't room for another page. In a sweaty and exhausted mess, I went upstairs for the last time and asked through gasps, "You wouldn't know where Helmsley is now, would you?"

"You mean his body?"

"Right."

She gave me instructions to a funeral home. "Tonight's the last night of the wake, though, and if you see his cousin Elsa there, tell her I want the china teacups."

"China teacups, fine," I replied and was about to run out, but stopped short when I saw her poking on the couch. I had slept on that hard old couch endless nights. Mercifully I grabbed a steak knife in the kitchen, elbowed the old lady to one side, and slit open the upholstery, liberating those overwound springs.

"Hell's bells, what'd you do that for!" she screamed.

"Believe me I was doing both you and the couch a favor." I just couldn't bear to think of my old couch in one of their tacky Queens basement–living rooms with stucco walls and aluminum siding.

The Malio Family Funeral Home was handling the interment. As I pulled the car to the curb, I was amazed to see such a large group of mourners. They were all dressed loudly in black and they loudly crowded outside together. I parked in front of a hydrant and went in. There were three galleries for bereavement, and only when I entered Helmsley's display room did I realize that those strangers were only strangers.

In an adjacent room was laid out the dead body of some matriarchal grandmother; the wailing group hovering around were both direct and derivative members of her lecherous hatch. A closed coffin in an empty room was Helmsley's final salute. People avoided me. I heard someone mumble, "You don't go to a wake dressed like that!"

I went into his vacant room and pulled the door shut behind me. Helmsley wouldn't have cared about the filthy clothes, or the streaks of peroxide in my hair. I sat in the front chair that was closest to his box. As I listened to the rumble outside, I grew increasingly angry that no one else had come. They had mentioned his death on TV. His academic pals could have found out where he was. The crowd outside should've been Helmsley's crowd. No one had come to see him off, not even that slut Angela, who probably compelled his suicide. What had happened? I would've given anything to know. I didn't just want an account of the events leading up to him jumping off the bridge, but what he saw in her; why did he allow himself to be degraded by her? He was as handsome and intelligent and amusing and considerate as anyone I ever met. How could a lifetime of study and creation have come to such a forlorn end? I rose and paced back and forth in front of the closed lid.

All he asked me to do that early morning was to leave the house, just for a couple of hours, and I acted no better than his beast-lover, making it an issue of pride. After all the patience that I had demanded of him over the years, I suffered that I hadn't returned any.

Perhaps out of a compulsion to punish myself, but I think out of a macabre need for forgiveness, I opened Helmsley's casket. He was badly mangled, the bone of his right forearm was ledging out of the side, just below the skin.

Autopsy sutures that crisscrossed his face and body were thick and unconcealed. I ran my hand through his flaxen, still alive hair and I stared into his bluish face. Until there was a knock at the door, I didn't realize that time was passing. I quickly shut Helmsley's lid and threw open the door. A tall lanky man in a cheap dark suit, curly hair, and silly porkchop sideburns entered. He looked like a portrait Helmsley had of the poet Pushkin.

"You knew Helmsley?" I asked slowly, assuming, based upon his appearance, that he spoke a foreign language.

"No, I'm sorry, but the home is closing."

I thanked him and left. The mob of a family outside was gone. The Mercedes had a ticket on the windshield. Slowly I drove back to Glenn's house and carefully parked the Mercedes in her garage. After locking the garage door, I went back upstairs into the living room. I had forgotten to turn off the TV, so I used one of the two remotes to lower the volume. Then I quickly downed a double bourbon. About two minutes later, Glenn entered wearing a nightgown, and stretching her arms out, she declared, "I've had a refreshing nap."

"A refreshing nap?" I murmured, still picturing Helmsley drained of life, and locked in sleep. Her remark seemed to be a freakish contradiction. I started laughing, uncontrollably laughing at what she said. All that had occurred in the short period of her nap. She stood there and looked at me as if I were crazy. If I tried to explain all that had just happened she would have no doubt about my insanity. Instead, I pointed to the TV. "I'm sorry. I just watched 'The Odd Couple.' Boy, is that Felix unpredictable."

She had a drink and felt refreshed and talked about her boyfriend and how she was adjusting to the break up. So I filled my glass and kept up a polite expression.

"...as if my wings were clipped...you know, so what now? Well I'm not sure myself, just all the little things that I've always wanted to do, but he prevented me from doing. All I really know is I have this sudden sense of being free!"

She rambled on itemizing all the grievances and why she felt good about the break up. I just drank more and smiled more and nodded more. While she talked, I envisioned Helmsley in that closed book of a coffin in a dark room. As I got drunker, I thought more about the meaning of death. In this instance, most poignantly, it meant a potential unrealized. Reams of blank pages, unfilled. He truly intended to dedicate his life to writing. All the plays, the novels, the essays, the short stories, all those philosophical tracts that he would pretentiously talk about or those he actually had written: now, only I would know. He would have found life unbearable if he had known that he was going to die with virtually none of his plans achieved. It retroactively drained the meaning from his life; so why would he kill himself?

Suddenly I heard Glenn again. "The thing about my relationship with him was that I was in constant admiration of him. I used his language, I looked at things with his values, but I realize now it's because I was essentially intimidated by him deep down. That's why I really thank God that I've broken up with him, because now for the first time I can see what it is being myself..."

"But he gave you so much," I replied, applying her statement to my relationship with Helmsley, "can you really just forget about him like that?"

"He took so much more," she replied. "He was utterly demanding and selfish." I couldn't follow her here, because Helmsley asked for so little. It was as if we were passing on crisscrossing escalators, hers ascending and mine descending.

Soon we watched some TV and played a board game. Eventually after some persuasion on my part, and reluctance on hers, she told me a little about her first marriage: they were both too young. There seemed to be something more she kept restraining herself from saying, and I was too stretched out of shape to induce her any further. After a late night snack, we went to bed.

I lay next to her and quietly she slid under the sheet and tried to start up the engine. The combination of booze and dead Helmsley was too much. I just couldn't solidify. But she only reacted with greater determination. I wanted to tell her, but, like her, I too was restraining myself from getting emotionally entangled. Finally I tugged her off and told her that I just wasn't up to it, too much bourbon. She felt the chill, rolled over, and went to sleep.

I awoke the next morning in a sweat. I had dreamt that Helmsley had died, and so he had. Glenn wasn't lying next to me. I found a note on the night table, it read:

> Went to work. If you need any money, there's some on the cabinet. If you need the car, help yourself. One problem is I need to be alone tonight. I must work out some problems. But please, this is not meant to be a rejection. Call me tomorrow
>
> Glenn

The alarm clock had been set for seven; so she was up four hours ago. I went downstairs and fixed myself some breakfast. While eating, I kept thinking about Helmsley. I went downstairs and saw the Mercedes, loaded up to the ceiling with his books.

Without removing the books, I took the car out and drove back to Helmsley's neighborhood. I drove along streets that we had walked together just a week before. Finally I stopped in front of his house. There, next to a line of garbage cans, I saw all the remaining books loosely piled. They trumpeted: Helmsley is dead. I drove some more. When I passed the bar where I first met Angela, I parked the car, entered, and ordered a beer. It was a perpetually shaded room with old men just killing time. A placard over the bar read, Italian American Legion Post #118, Veterans of Foreign Wars. Carefully I looked around; there was no sign of her.

Eventually I got up the nerve to ask the old bartender, "Hey, you know anything about that guy that jumped off the bridge the other day?"

"Why?" he barked back. "You a snoop reporter?"

"I served with him in the 107th back in 'Nam," I replied Americanly, and then raising my beer mug toward the flag, I drank it down.

"You served with that guy?"

"Sure, he saved me when I got hit at the Diphthong Delta." And then taking the liberty, I kicked my leg up to a bar stool, rolled up the hem of my pant leg and showed him where Angela bit me the other day.

"The wound looks fresh," he commented.

"Some wounds heal faster than others."

"I can't believe that guy served."

"Hey pal, I don't know if you've ever been in combat, but you change afterwards."

"I know," he muttered pridefully, and without a request he gave me another draft.

"Look, that poor guy was here fighting with his girl that night."

"Did you know the girl?" I asked.

"Oh sure, she's a local girl."

"Angela? Was she with him when you saw him last?"

"No, he raced in here alone. It was about two nights ago. It was about midnight. He got loaded pretty quickly and just sat quietly for a while. He looked pretty roughed up."

"What do you mean roughed up?"

"Someone had beat up on him. You know, he had blood coming out of his nose and mouth. I had to clean up a whole pile of bloody napkins later."

"Then what?"

"Bar closed, he left, and that's all she wrote. I guess he went right to the bridge."

When Helmsley was sitting here, drinking his heart out, I was with Glenn, just a half mile away. If he went directly to the bridge, he would have had to walk right by the house, within twenty feet of where I was lavishing in splendors. If I had just looked out the window, I might've seen him walk by, a drunken and despondent shadow; I might've saved him.

"Have you seen Angela since then?" He shook his head no, walked to the other side of the bar, and there he poured a drink for someone.

"Do you have any idea where she might be?" I asked when the bartender passed by again. "I just want to talk with her."

"Sorry," he said. He didn't want to talk anymore. He knew he was treading the line; a snitch is the lowest form of life everywhere.

"Listen," I said finally. "When I got hit, I went down. My leg was a shred, the VC were hopping around us, finishing us off. That guy carried me out of there. Do you understand? Now I just want to find out what happened, and I'm gonna find Angela anyway."

"Try the OTB around 1:30," he said. "But listen, I didn't tell you dirt, all right?"

"Not a word," I replied and threw him a salute. Then I drove around the corner, put a quarter in the meter. I leaned up against the car across the street from the local betting place and waited. After fifteen minutes or so, I saw her enter with a group of guys. She was wearing a large cowboy hat and a wide-framed pair of dark sunglasses. Through the store-front glass, I watched her clown around awhile with the guys until they took out their racing papers, and chatted: "Devilrun's got bandages and is running on bute.... Yeah, but Breakingwind runs well on slop... Hippityhopity always comes from behind..." Soon everybody started placing bets. They all watched the horses run on the monitors then either ripped up their tickets or collected. Slowly the group she came in with mingled with others, and I casually entered the place and leaned up alongside of her. She was busily jotting notes on her racing form.

When there was no one around, I quickly grabbed her arm and muttered, "If you don't mind, I want to talk with you."

"Who the fuck are you?" She broke loose hollering. Out of nowhere a fat guy with a neck the size of my waist had me in a painful headlock.

"You want I should knock his teeth down his throat?" he asked Angela. I felt like a taxidermed head mounted above a fireplace, and as she slowly realized who I was, I impossibly tried to prepare myself for a great deal of suffering.

"What the fuck do you want?" she asked. "You're the little shit that broke my nose."

"And you killed my only friend," I hoarsely replied in the vice.

"What the fuck are you talking about?"

"You and your brothers."

"You want I should snap his neck?" the pizzeria owner asked.

"Let him go," she issued a reprieve. The guy let me drop and walked away.

"What the fuck are you talking about?"

"Who killed Helmsley?" I asked.

"He killed himself, the stupid shit." Then she lifted up her sunglasses and showed me a shining black eye. "Look what the little shit did to me."

"What happened?"

"We got into a fight and I decided that he was a fun fuck but it was all over. He wasn't a man. He was a pretty boy and I told him so, and I told him that it was all over."

"And then you beat him up to amuse yourself further."

"He was playing with me! Using me!"

"And you got even, didn't you?"

"I got hold of an ashtray and knocked the shit out of him till he dragged himself the fuck out...then I heard on the TV that he did himself in."

"Wonderful."

"Listen," Angela said, "I just want you to know that I let you talk like this because I respect you. I was drunk and you straightened me out. But I also want you to know that I ain't scared of you."

"Does it make any difference to you," I asked Angela, "that a person killed himself because he loved you?"

"Look, one night I was horny so I went to a bar and picked up a guy for a quick fuck, capisce? I never adopted him."

"But couldn't you..."

"Look pal," she interrupted, "you're talkin' to someone who was dropped more than a yo-yo, and got more final disconnection notices than anyone else alive." With that she returned to her racing forms and then the betting window. Guilt only affects the larger upright animals. I returned to the car and watched her for a moment from behind the dash. She watched the monitor and then went to a cash window.

I started the ignition and drove down Court, but I had nowhere to go. I didn't care to return to Glenn's home, so I just drove around. Driving in New

York was like a big game of bumper cars, people were cutting people off, stopping fast, accelerating just as fast. Until the day before, I had never driven in the city, and I didn't even have a valid license. I was tired and remembered that my new abode, Sergei's place, was now mine. I parked near the local F train stop and locked all the windows and doors. I realized that the value of all those books in the car exceeded fifty thousand dollars and possibly a hundred thousand dollars. The Mercedes already had its radio missing, but this was obscured by the boxes of books. Locating a piece of paper, I wrote: "RADIO ALREADY STOLEN, NOTHING OF VALUE IN CAR." I framed the note in the window track. Locking the door, I went to the subway and paid for a token.

TEN

While waiting for the subway, I scrutinized Helmsley's tragedy; unintentionally I had reduced Angela's guilt. She was brought up to see love as a weakness, whereas all Helmsley's books and needs had revealed love to him as a strength. Perhaps Helmsley's view was nobler, but in the end her vantage certainly proved more endurable. I got off the F train at Broadway and Lafayette, where all the beggars were congregated. One guy a little older than me asked for a quarter. I told him to get a job and kept going.

When I reached West Broadway, a bombshell struck; I suddenly realized that I was missing—had missed—Helmsley's burial. I kicked the ground and yanked my hair. He was being buried unaccompanied. The dead were so helpless, and being buried seemed like such a humiliating act. I could picture the grave diggers spitting as they shovelled the dirt into the hole.

With each step, the synonyms of his death whirled by: he's gone, he's cold, he's still.... It really wouldn't have mattered if I pursued the box into the earth. On West Broadway, I turned left, retracing those same streets that I had walked on my fraudulent gay date. By daylight, the area seemed quite different, large ponderous buildings with fancy storefronts, warehouse chic. I located my new apartment. A security system realistically evaluated the menace of Manhattan; locks were everywhere. First, a front door lock, then a key-operated elevator, two locks to the floor, and finally a lock to shut off the burglar alarm. Inside, it was one spacious industrial room, constructed for machines. Modern apartments pressed people into small, enclosed cubicles. In Sergei's place the machines had long since vanished. Along the two walls bordering the width of the place were laminated posters of Ternevsky's film experiments. Between these walls were juggled objects of technology and antiquity, much like Glenn's. Apparently the rich either go for the very new or the very old. To imagine this stage as a one-time sweat shop cast with anemic seamstresses speaking in Yiddish was now nearly inconceivable.

As I sat on a large circular water bed in the middle of the floor, I heard a metallic clinking sound. Leather straps were fastened to both the heads and tails of the bed frame; they must have been part of Sergei's insecurity. Spending most of his life in an Iron Curtain country must have given him a totalitarian sex drive. As the tide rippled across the mattress, I floated toward the quaint night table, where I found a rustic remote control switch. I turned on the TV. I flipped the TV back off and got off the bed. Persian rugs and Empire-style furniture juxtaposed with Dutch Nouveau. A state-of-the-art sound system was hidden below a long antique chest of drawers. There was also a panel of dimmers and rheostats that could more subtly vary the lights and shadows than Rembrandt himself.

A note written on a large empty bulletin board announced: "The cabinet by Napoleon is yours." Sure enough, across the room on an old ionic pedestal was a marble bust of the great French general. Next to it, below an original Warhol silk-screen, was a beautiful rosewood chest of drawers. On the top shelf sat my Unique bag containing my single-sleeved shirt and single-legged pants. The few clothes that I had taken from Sarah's and stashed at Helmsley's had apparently been snatched up with the rest of his things by his grab bag relatives. Now my entire wardrobe consisted only of the suit that Glenn had given me. I carefully folded the suit jacket and placed it in the top drawer of my cabinet, I folded my suit pants in another drawer, and the shirt took up residence in the bottom drawer. I resumed my tour of the apartment in my underpants.

Bathrooms are where a truly rich mentality distinguishes itself. Sergei's bathroom had no door. Tiny terra-cotta mosaics lined the room from floor to ceiling. Under the dimmer switch were two knobs—one was a thermostat that modified the water temperature, and the other dial heated up the tiles on the ceiling. On a glass shelf above the sink were many soaps, clay packs, lotions, and other miracle cures, aimed at restoring skin to the sacred state of youthfulness. Claiming over half the bathroom floor was the deeply sunken bathtub. In it was a white stone bench chiselled with reliefs. A huge porcelain faucet shaped like a small fire hydrant was fixed over the tub, urban architecture that Ternevsky probably found droll. I opened the hydrant all the way and set the water thermostat at a hundred degrees. While it filled up I took a dump and only afterwards did I realize that there was no toilet paper. I was contemplating despoiling one of the monogrammed hand towels when I noticed a small foot pedal. I hit down on the accelerator and a jet stream of hot water bull's-eyed my butt. I'd heard about bidets but that was the first time I was ever abused by one. Turning off the faucet-hydrant, I eased myself onto a kind of shelf alongside the submerged stone bench. The water was bliss. I paddled about a bit and soon relaxed, drifting into that state of deliverance. A carrot simmering in a large stew. Between shades of wakefulness and waves of unconsciousness. Slowly a gentle noise signaled from above. My eyes opened, but I was still asleep. Before me—behold! stood a bath nymph; an angel had escaped from the myths of my dreams. I watched as the divine guide rummaged through my underwear, which I had casually tossed on the toilet seat. Although I knew at once she was real I took my time before addressing her.

"May I help you?" I whispered graciously. She emitted a penetrating scream as she backed away.

"What's the matter!" I jumped out of the tub, concealing my drippy genitals with a monogrammed washcloth. I followed her out to the living room.

"Who the fuck are you?" Her vocal cords were high-strung and fearful. She lamely offered a vase as a weapon.

"Sergei Ternevsky sublet this place to me. You must be the girlfriend." With little else to offer, I extended a hand.

"Well, he told me nothing of it," she replied. Even while threatened she stood captivating and captive, a vital beauty in the blonde Harlow/Monroe tradition.

"I wouldn't break into the place just to take a bath. Call Ternevsky and ask him!"

"He's out of town. If you subletted this place, you would know that."

"Call Marty." I was shivering cold and dripping a puddle in the center of his lacquered, polished floor.

"Marty, right!" She went over to the phone and while she dialed I dried off and put on my underpants. While getting my pants from the rosewood cabinet, I heard her appealing, "Christ, Marty, why would he do this to me? What did I do? What haven't I done?"

When she turned around and saw me standing there listening, her voice dropped to a whisper and she walked away. The extra long telephone wire uncurled until I could only grasp segments, "How am I suppose to...so what the fuck am I..." I started getting terrified; losing one's residency meant losing everything. I went into the bathroom and sat on the toilet seat, waiting in suspense for some kind of verdict.

Finally I heard her exclaim, "He is! You're sure?!" After a while longer, she walked back into the living room with the phone. Then I heard her put the phone on the hook and waited for her to make a move. After a couple minutes, she approached the bathroom door frame, said, "Knock, knock."

"I hope everything's been straightened out," I said. She only looked at me with a smile, and I quickly realized that Marty had informed her that I was gay. I half resented it, but in compliance with my agreement, I offered a stereotypically slackened posture.

"Sorry for being so rude," she said.

"It's okay."

"You must understand, I was quite terrified by your being here. No one told me a thing about it."

"Me neither," I replied and took a seat. I folded my right knee over my left and bent my head up slightly. I wasn't sure how long I could maintain this position. "No one explained to me that someone else was living here."

"Well I had been living here, mainly as a favor to Ternevsky. I guess he now sees fit to replace me," she said.

"I could never replace you," I complimented with a smile. "Sergei told me that he just wanted me to watch over things because of the burglaries. He was probably worried about you being alone here."

"Knowing Sergei, he was probably worried that I was stealing his stuff."

"That's absurd," I laughed with a flair.

With no prompting at all she divulged her entire Sergei file: They first met at an uptown gallery opening. He announced up front that she had sexually stimulated him and would very much like to besmirch her. In gratitude for this, he added—she imitated his accent a bit—"Janus dear, I must confess, I have little time for commitment, but I could compensate for this by granting you full use of my place and within reason I might be able to assist you by extending some of my connections in the trade." She was a hopeful artist.

"We don't have sex that much, he's a rotten lover." I commented on the straps at the four corners of the circular bed. She claimed they were just for show.

She went on to say that at times she felt ashamed. "It's the closest I've ever come to prostitution."

"If you feel that way, why did you do it?"

"He had me at a disadvantage." She then started to elaborate. She had arrived in New York after graduating from an all-girl's school. It was a small college town where the bulk of her colleagues were farmer's daughters. Her actual education began in New York and after studying the present state of art she put down the brush, folded up the easel, sent the model home, and adopted the conceptual philosophy. But a female artist from out of town trying to break into the SoHo art scene was farcical. It seemed only those who were artists could be artists, no new ones were permitted. Until she met Sergei.

"What did he do for you?"

"He got one of my works accepted to a group exhibit."

"Oh really, is it here?" I asked surveying all the expensive junk in the large room.

"No," she laughed, "the curator threw it out."

"Threw it out! It must have crushed you."

"No, thank God he did; it was a disposable installation."

"What?"

"It was a rotting mess." She then went on to describe the piece: a human torso made from the organs and muscles of dead animals that had been sewn together.

"My God! Where did you get dead animals, what were they?"

"Oh, the kind of stuff you'd find in any old meat department; pork, beef, chicken, fish, all the cheapest cuts."

"Cooked?"

"No raw, but cooking it could be a future reinterpretation." She rambled on further about her life, expectations, and personal affairs.

"Tell me about you, now," she said upon conclusion.

After touching on the sketchy details that I had fabricated for Ternevsky, I mimicked the master trying to suggest a talent and modesty that I completely lacked. I told her, among other things, that I had dropped out of medical school after three years to write poetry.

"Oh really." She bit the bait. "Have you ever published?"

"As a matter of fact, I just got something accepted in the upcoming issue of the *Harrington.*" If she had any doubts as to my vast sea of lies, she could refer to this one drop of truth.

"Really. I get a subscription to the *Harrington,* I mean Sergei does."

"Good, then we'll read it together when it arrives."

"Oh," she said, suddenly looking at her watch. "My Swatch says five. Gotta run." She explained while grabbing her coat that she had a class at

Parsons. I too had to run; work was waiting. Putting on the rest of my suit, I locked the locks and left. The sun was setting early as I walked through the rush of homebound people. As I walked, I realized that today was the first time that I had a stable address in a while. I also realized that today was the first day that Helmsley would be facing an infinity of decay. Glenn was probably home alone now, perhaps wishing I was more accessible. Angela, who by now had probably lost more money than she had started out with at the OTB, was probably semi-drunk at that American Legion Post bar, looking for a new victim.

These were the songs playing on the Sony Walkman of my mind, tunes suddenly halted when I stepped into the lobby. Miguel was standing there awaiting me, dragging indifferently on an herbal cigarette and looking at me expressionlessly as I entered.

"How's tricks?" I asked casually.

Pointing expressionlessly toward the office, he wanted to talk in seclusion. Could I have shut off a wrong circuit? Did I accidentally permit school children entry? Perhaps the cantankerous projectionist had complained.

When we finally sat together in that cramped office with the door closed, he began, "Do you feel it?"

"Do I feel what?"

"It's lying between us like an age-old sequoia, look at it! Can't you see it?" He pointed to the empty safe. He had discovered that I had participated in a crime that he had exclusive rights to.

"You mean the fact that we're both stealing money," I replied.

He snubbed his cigarette and sat so silently that all I could hear was the buzz of the fluorescent lighting overhead.

"Look, I don't find it shameful. You shouldn't either," I said offering him a way out. He sighed and smiled and laughed.

"All right." He looked up at me and included, "Honor between thieves. You're not pissed are you?"

"Why should I be pissed?"

"Because I would've been pissed if you confronted me with it. I mean, I didn't know that you knew about me. I was about to fire you, but now I feel like a regular Judas."

"Well, I'll always be straight with you," I said, not intending any puns on my sexual preference. "If you ever find it otherwise, just prove it to me and hey, I'll quit."

"Thank you," he said almost spiritually. Leaning over in his chair, he gave me a gripping handshake. Then, leaning back, he looked unblinkingly at me. I sensed he was struggling to bring all this to a graceful conclusion, so I decided to give him a hand.

"By the amount Ox pays us, all he buys is my presence. Loyalty costs a lot more."

A smile broke on his face. "I felt bad before, 'cause I was going to fire you just to preserve my own facade of honesty. But now I even feel like more of a hypocrite. See I never have been entirely honest with you, but maybe I can make it up."

"What are you talking about?"

"Well, let me first ask you, how did you figure that I was stealing?"

"By comparing the amount the theater made on the days you did work with the days you didn't."

"I figured that would be the only way that I could be discovered, and I couldn't do anything about it. Because the old manager who I used to work with was such an asshole. But now you're here, and I need a partner," he said.

"What are you proposing?"

"Let me present a speculative prospectus." The hippie had collapsed away to the businessman. I leaned back and listened. He talked about raising capital. Then he talked about leverage, interest rates, credit rating and finally investments; the future. I had no idea what he was getting at. He sounded like one of those sleazy guys who buys time on syndicated TV to hype something. Finally, though, he started talking about specifics.

"Hoboken is dying as a blue-collar community. But it is slowly returning as a white-collar, yuppie neighborhood. Now I located a place, an old garage that could easily be converted into a theater. I've got an independent contractor who already has plans. I've even got two used thirty-five millimeter projector heads. All I would need are lamp houses, and I'll have the projectors."

He talked suspensefully for another two hours, telling me about everything from the fold-down chairs and emergency lights to the hiring of ushers. But he kept me wondering about where I entered in this picture. I think he wanted me to approach him, but I decided to sit back and let him make the offer; he wouldn't take the chance of telling me about all this if he didn't want something. Deciding to show him that I was no school boy, I started arguing about all the possible bugs. "How about the projectionist wage? How long could you sustain that if you don't break even quickly?"

"Hoboken's a non-union town. We can exploit some kid."

"How many other theaters are there?"

"Just one duplex in the entire town, the real competition will come from the five or six video stores."

"How about a distributor?"

"If it can be done," he said, "we can do it."

"That's the second time you've said 'we.' What do you mean, 'we'?" I'd have done anything for the chance of getting in on the ground floor of any kind of deal.

"Here's where you come in. If I can scrape together ten grand by this June, then this place will soon be ours. But we have to keep on a rigid payment schedule."

He wouldn't involve me in this if he didn't absolutely need to. "Who exactly owns this place now and why won't they let you just put something down and extend the payments?"

"We can make the amount together by June," he said, not volunteering anything else. "But we can only do it if we do it together. How about it?"

"Let me ask you two questions. First, where exactly will I stand in this Hoboken theater?"

"Well, this would really depend on how much you're willing to participate. Would you like to work at the theater full time?"

"Absolutely."

"Well, a seventy-thirty split on what we clear, with possible options to a larger share when you have more money, that would be my rough estimate. What's the second question?"

"How much will we have to steal from here each night, on the average, to reach the deadline date?"

"We'll need to average a little more than a hundred-and-eighty a night."

"We might be able to get away with it," I replied, "if we don't get caught by the checkers." They were people hired by the production and distribution companies to check against what we were doing.

"Well, that's the risk. How about it?"

I thought about it. I could discreetly take in half of the prescribed amount and still live high on the hog. Or I could agree to a partnership, steal an incriminating sum each night, risk getting caught and live on a pittance. More than any other word, America meant ownership and by that definition I was a patriot. "Okay."

"Okay, fine. I've already arranged for another account at the bank we deposit the theater's money. Every night, fill out a deposit slip to this other account and zip it into the same night bag, understand?"

"Isn't that playing it a little close?"

"Everything'll be fine." Apparently one of the bank officers was in on the deal.

We both gave a final shake on the deal and then he left. While considering his offer, I'd scratched my calf. When feeling moisture along my fingertips, I noticed blood and quickly realized that I'd accidentally torn open the Angela bite scab. I cleaned the wound and taped a napkin to it. I then checked my arm wound, which seemed to be healing. I then thought about Glenn. She seemed so strong and infallible during the day of that hold up. I walked in on her life at a bad time, and watched her deteriorate. I, on the other hand, had remained consistently in shambles.

She was undoubtedly waiting for something better, so I decided at that moment to bring it to an end. Taking out a piece of paper, I wrote:

> Dear Glenn,
>
> What we had was short lived but sincere and to try to con-
> tinue it any longer would be prolonging a natural end. I don't
> want you to see this as a rejection, but what we have is neither
> a relationship nor a friendship. All this can lead to is prevent-
> ing a more important person from entering either of our lives.
> Enclosed, I'm returning the keys that you entrusted me with.
> Take care.

I signed it and then reread it. She wouldn't mind breaking up with me as much as being dumped I figured. So I wrote the phone number of the theater allowing her the option of formally dumping me.

I then taped her house key and the car keys to the letter. I put it in a stamped envelope and sealed it. Glenn was actually quite a find, but the decision seemed noble and wise—occasionally those decisions also turn out to bring the most gain. It was only when I stuffed the letter into my jacket pocket that I remembered all of Helmsley's books I had left in the Mercedes. What Helmsley would have liked me to do with the books was the next float in the parade of questions. I didn't think he'd forgive me if I just sold them and bought leisure gear with the proceeds. I could probably donate the whole mess to the New York Public Library on Forty-second Street. Perhaps I could stipulate that there would be some established title honoring him: The Helmsley Collection. It had a nice ring to it. Anyway all this meant I couldn't break up with Glenn yet, so I called her. Answering the phone, she sounded calm, "Where are you?"

"I'm at work. Why, what's wrong?"

"I thought you promised that you'd be in the vicinity?"

"You said you wanted to spend the evening alone and I had to work."

"I suppose so," she said.

"The theater doesn't close for another half hour or so. Would you like me to come by then?"

"Do you want to?" she asked.

"Sure," I replied, lying. I had to take the books to the library tomorrow anyway. This way it looked like I was doing her the favor.

"See you, then," she said and hung up. With jittery hands, I counted out the nightly sum of money and prepared Miguel's cut. As soon as I had finished turning back the gauge, establishing Miguel's cut, flipping off the lights, locking the theater, and dropping the money in the night drop, I hailed a southbound cab on Third Avenue. It went down the Bowery, over the bridge, right on Tillary, left on Court, and on Pierrepont it halted. I dropped a five-dollar bill in the front seat, dashed up the brownstone steps, and knocked softly on her front door.

She opened the door. As soon as I entered, she hugged me and dissolved on my shoulder, crying, "It's all a mess!"

"What happened?"

"I saw Adolphe."

"You mean, like Hitler?"

She was too far in tears to reply. "What mother would name her son Adolphe?" Through sobs came broken phrases, "He's so sorry...right now he needs...he says he loves me...he needs me so...." She couldn't stop crying, and I couldn't make heads or tails of what she was saying.

"Space!" she finally barked. "The jerk needs space..."

"I can understand that," I replied, trying to be understanding.

"Oh? So what are you saying. It's okay to cheat on someone, long as you get away with it?"

"No, I just meant that everyone needs some space."

"What are you saying? That I'm difficult to be around?"

"Not at all..."

"Do you feel uncomfortable around me?"

"No...no, I'm just saying that everyone needs some space. Of course I feel comfortable around you." We talked some more along the same shaky and halting lines until she yawned and said she was tired. The nervousness was too much and I vowed that first thing tomorrow I would unload the books, park the Mercedes in the basement, and bail out of whatever I had gotten involved in. We lay together without touching. I could feel her fidgeting in the darkness and wasn't certain what she wanted. She seemed very tense and it made me nervous and sweaty. Somehow, eventually, we fell asleep.

When I awoke the next morning, I found myself alone again; I had been awakened by the front door buzzing. I wrapped myself in a sheet and grabbed a note that Glenn had left for me. I read it as I headed for the front door:

> Sorry about last night. This is obviously a very unstable time for me. I'm not like this at all. I really don't even know you and I feel disgusting dragging you through this. I'm willing to make an effort though.
>
> Yours,
> Glenn

When I finally went downstairs, I hesitated at the door. Suppose it was Adolphe wanting to scorch the earth. Peeking through the Venetian blinds, I checked out a youth standing on the front stoop with a knapsack that said, *Rolling Stone Magazine*. I watched him waving good-bye to a passing group of kids and then he rang the doorbell again. I figured that he was peddling subscriptions.

"We don't want any," I yelled though the door.

"Neither do I," he yelled back. Opening the front door, he quickly marched in. He was in his early teens, wearing a Sid Vicious T-shirt, tight black pants, and combat boots. He didn't seem surprised by my improvised toga.

"What are you selling?" I asked.

"I was about to ask you the same thing. I'm Tom, where's Adolphe?"

"Glenn isn't getting along with him just now," I informed him.

"She's getting along with you, isn't she? My mom must have warned you about me."

"What's your mother's name?"

"Glenn. Who do you think?"

"You're lying," I replied. There was no way that Glenn could have engendered this kid.

He dropped his bag to the floor, still retaining the straps in his fingers, "My mother is a young cutie named Glenda, she had me when she was just a teenybopper."

"I never...she never even..."

"That Glenn's quite a card, ain't she?"

"Aren't you supposed to be in school?" I asked with a slight parental condescension.

"I was about to ask you the same question," he replied. Then he tugged the bag back up to his shoulder and mounted the stairs, three steps at a time.

I couldn't deal with this, so I quickly got dressed and left. On the subway I realized that I had completely overlooked the purpose of the day: dump the books, the car, and the relationship.

ELEVEN

By the time I got back to Manhattan, I had calmed down. While looking for the key standing outside Ternevsky's loft, I heard a high voice speaking against a musical beat. Looking toward the large bay window, I could see Janus exercising intensely before the TV, she was wearing a very scanty bathing suit. Her tanned body was glistening with sweat as she bent and stretched, unaware of my presence. Quietly I backed out the door into the hall and reentered making a deliberate ruckus. This time when I entered the living room, she was aware of my presence, but she didn't break her pace. Bending in different directions, she exposed the most intimate parts of that wonderful body only made more seductive by the scanty bathing suit. Finally she paused and calmly said, "I had to finish my 'Jane Fonda Workout.'"

"Oh," I replied while staring at the Napoleon bust to avoid staring at hers. The general's eyes were chiselled permanently forward.

"I'm a wreck if I don't do it at least once a day," she said as she turned off the VCR, and then she stretched out on the sofa. Sunlight flooded over her and she made no effort to save herself from it. I retreated to the bathroom where I drew a bath. While the tub filled up I hunted up a towel, and I tried to keep to myself, but, whenever permissible, I looked hungrily at her. Since the house had virtually no walls, I saw a lot of her. Finally, just when I found one of those monogrammed towels, she spoke: "You probably think I'm odd trying to get a tan in the winter and all, but I'm always back in Nice when I feel the rays on my body." She then peeked open one eye and glanced at me.

"I empathize completely," I replied, not trying to make her feel at all threatened by me. The magnet was slow but powerful. I could only get closer, not further away. When she squeezed a dab of Aloe Vera Sunscreen into her palm, my unblinking eyes helped her hands rub it in. I was so excited that I couldn't even get a hard-on. I tried to remind myself that I was being tested, a Job to her "Jehovess." Closing my eyes, I concentrated: move away from the kryptonite, Superman.

With eyes still fastened shut, I pointed to the bathroom and declared, "My bath is ready." I sat in the deep tub. With the hose attachment I ran icy cold water over my head and felt myself shrink. Then, opening my eyes, I saw her through a series of remarkably angled mirrors. She stood before the hall mirror, apparently unaware that she was in my line of vision. I started growing again. She was doing some kind of aerobic stretch. I ran the water over my head again.

My hands were trembling as I watched her under that freezing rain water.

Temptation was a spreading malignancy; schemes and deceptions were blistering out from the inventive half of my brain. Pulling the plug out of the drain hole, I arose and dressed. I pulled my pants and stretched my shirt over wet skin. Towelling myself off required too much patience. Socklessly I yanked on my shoes and marched past her without a word and right out the door.

Even though it was a clear and sunny day, it was chilly outside. I still had seven hours to kill before work. I walked up to the Loeb Student Center on Fourth and there I rested on one of those long sofas in the student lounge. I squeezed my jacket into a pillow and felt warm and secure and watched the lowlife huddling together outside in Washington Square Park. No sooner did I shut my eyes than did I hear, "Hey buddy boy."

I opened my eyes to a large guard's uniform with a visor for a face. "Break out the ID," the security guard bullied.

"It's at the dorm."

"Then sleep at the dorm, son."

"Come on, I pay your salary. I don't tell on you guys when you sleep on the job."

"Out," he pointed with his club. I went out and crossed the street to the big NYU library that looks like a prison block. There, I fixed the collar of my filthy shirt and pinched my cheeks for some color; I tried to acquire that guarded NYU look. Slapping some student newspaper under my arm, I filed in closely behind a bunch of coeds.

"Can I help you?" a guard individualized me.

"No," I replied, trying to continue, but he blocked my way through the little turnstile with his damned club.

I left and with nowhere else to go I joined the lowlife across the street, at Washington Square Park. Taking an empty bench, I curled up like a cat against the cold and tried to sleep, but the chill was too much. When I got to my feet, fifteen minutes later, my body was numb. Walking down Fourth, I made a left up Lafayette and turned on Astor Place. Looking about as I crossed that empty parking lot, I saw that the peddlers were out with their shit trying to get what they could for it. A bunch of assholes from Jersey were trying to spin the black rotating cube, a revolving sculpture located in the middle of Astor Square. I quickly checked out the vendors. While inspecting some antique lighters spread out on a blanket, the vendor suddenly rolled the whole operation before my eyes. A police car had pulled up and cops were impounding the merchandise. I walked over to Cooper Union and tried to enter, but they were even more thorough than NYU. So I went back to Astor Place. It was only a couple minutes later, but apparently the cops had left because just like pigeons after a loud noise, all the vendors had returned and were selling.

Soon I tagged along Saint Mark's Place. By the time I finally found shelter at the Saint Mark's Bookstore, I was freezing. After a while of just lounging, I asked a bearded old guy named Dudley, who looked like an old oak, whether this month's *Harrington Review* was on sale yet. Not missing a puff of his deeply bellied pipe, he frowned and shook his head. The interval had warmed me, so I returned to the street.

Passing the Saint Mark's Theater, I spotted Eunice. She didn't spot me. I watched her for a moment. She was talking with one of the ushers, an NYU kid. Pepe appeared and ordered the guy back into the theater, but before he vanished I saw Eunice give him a kiss. When the guy was out of sight, I watched as Pepe gave her a kiss. What exactly had the Mormons taught her? Sparing myself further torment, I resumed my trek up to my new theater.

The evening there was regular, everything ran smoothly. At the end of the night after carefully skimming the proper amount, I was about to leave the theater for the night deposit drop when Ox arrived. When he pounded on the door, I bolted up.

"Who is it?"

"Open the fucking door." I knew it was him. In a panic, I shoved the loot down the front of my pants and located the night deposit slip to the private fund. I started shredding and stuffing it into the garbage. Before I was entirely done, I heard keys in the lock. I shoved the remainder into the garbage just as he opened the door.

"What the fuck is wrong with you?! Why you no open the door?"

"I...I was about to."

"Why didn't you?"

"I was dressing."

"Huh?"

"I was hot so I took my clothes off."

"Naked?" He looked at me and didn't say a thing. When I was aware of him looking in my lap for a lengthy period, I glimpsed a look. The load of cash was shoved up in my pants like an erection. He seemed to sniff things. His eyes fixed for a moment on a soiled tissue I had blown my nose with earlier. After a long pause, he spoke again, "You're the new guy, huh?"

"Yes."

"What?"

"Yes."

"What?!"

"Yes, I am he—the new guy."

"So you the new guy," he said, and just stood there awhile glaring. I felt compelled to reply, "The night ran by quickly."

"Who ran by?"

"The night."

"What the fuck does this mean?" he growled.

"It's, you know...a pleasantry." I was jittery.

"In the future don't tell me things like that, okay?"

"Okay."

"How'd we do tonight?"

"Oh, it was real peachy." I froze, something had gone screwy with my pitch of words tonight.

"What the hell does that mean? In the future, if I ask you how we did, you tell me how much money we made and that's all!"

"Okay."

Picking up the day-to-day calendar he looked at the final amounts, and then he gave me a hard stare. I hardened up like a board, and he let the silence concentrate. Suddenly, like a spring releasing the both of us, the phone rang, and I sprang to answer it, but he was quicker on the draw. He had it to his ear first, "Yeah." He listened a minute and then silently handed it to me. Putting the phone to my ear all I could hear was sobbing.

"Hello Glenn," I whispered.

"Please...right away...get over here...." It was the phrases-through-anguish method of communication.

"So who the fuck worked last night?" Ox asked, impervious to the fact that I was on the phone. He stared at last night's tally sheet.

"Miguel," I replied to him, covering the mouthpiece, and then murmured to her, "Look honey, I wanted to tell you last night, but I really think we ought to break up."

"Hang up the phone," Ox directed.

"Just get right over. We can talk about it," Glenn pleaded.

"We've got to end this," I said, pulling away the keystone that released an avalanche of sobs.

"Anything! I'll give you anything you want but not that! I love you, I need you...." She was freaking out now, so I was about to concede and tell her that I was on my way, when Ox grabbed the phone from my hand and hung it up.

"What the fuck you think you're pulling, huh? When I say hang up the phone, I mean hang up." Instantly the phone started ringing.

"Let it ring," Ox said, and then holding up yesterday's tally sheet he asked, "Why is this?"

"What?"

"Why isn't this signed?"

"I don't know. I guess Miguel forgot to sign it."

"What the fuck is the matter with you people? You take your clothes off like you're at home. You speak to your friends all night! All you got to do is sign the fucking sheet and you can't even do that right!"

"I'll sign it," I replied, hoping to end the grousing. He put the tally sheet on the desk in front of me, and I signed in the vacant space.

"I don't know what's wrong with you fucking people," he said as I signed.

"Sorry," I said meaninglessly.

"Hey, what the fuck's the matter with you? Don't you ever say sorry to me."

"Sorry," I replied thoughtlessly.

"Hey," he growled. Grabbing the tally sheet, he stormed out the door. During the entire duration, the phone had been ringing. Soon as he walked out, I picked it up. "Sorry, Glenn."

"I know things were uncomfortable the other night," she quickly jumped in, anticipating whatever my complaints might be.

"I just think we're not really right for each other," I quickly replied.

"You can't leave me now! You can't just abandon me!" She pushed things into extremes.

"I'm not abandoning anyone, just calm down. All I'm saying is that I think it would be better for both of us this way."

"No, it would only be better for you. Just be here with me tonight. We don't have to have sex or even talk. I just need someone here tonight."

"Glenn, I just don't think it'd end there. I think it'll lead to an unhealthy dependency."

"No, it won't! I swear!"

"You've got to learn how to deal with depression."

"No!"

"I'll call you first thing in the morning."

"No, no, wait a second. I can handle depression! I just can't handle him." Now I understood. She was referring to the surprise son who had materialized from behind the front door.

"What do you expect me to do?"

"I need help. Usually Adolphe controls him."

"I can't control anything."

"Just listen to me," she started hyperventilating and again only phrases could escape, "a lot of savings..."

"Calm down."

"Alimony...child support...a stock portfolio..."

"What are you talking about?"

"MONEY! You could use the money!"

"For what?"

"Controlling him."

"What do you want me to do—adopt him?"

"No," she sobbed, "I just want him to see that I'm not alone, that there's a male presence."

"If I come by tonight I'm not spending the night, just coming by. I'll pound my chest a little, pee standing up, and then out the door. No more of this."

"I swear it," she started simmering down.

"You really should have told me you had a kid."

"I know, I'm sorry, I swear."

"Okay. I'll be there soon as the theater closes."

After the last film had ended and Ox had left, I made a new deposit slip for the purloined proceeds and dropped off the ziplocked bag. Afterwards, I went to a corner bar for a double bourbon. At twenty-three I never before had to play a surrogate father figure. In the course of the subway ride, the bourbon nullified all worries. But when I reached her corner all that changed. From there I could hear the thumping woofers of rock and roll; it was spilling out from the upper floor of the house. Other than that, it was all routine by now; up the stately steps, knock on the large oak door, and out comes the lady with the crocodile tears. Politely, she took my coat before submitting her complaints.

"I don't blame you for hating me," she said instead of hello, "but I'm in a real crisis."

"Relax," I replied and closed the door behind me.

"I must be a burden."

"You seem to think I'm the norm and you're ill. My life is no picnic. You know nothing about me."

"You seem like a nice guy, but you are too young. Maybe we can try to work something out, some kind of relationship."

"I think all our relationship does is cure symptoms, not problems."

"What's wrong with curing symptoms?"

"In just the short period of time that we've been together a dangerous routine has started," I replied.

"What kind of routine?"

"Don't you see it? First you feel lonely because your boyfriend dumped you. Then you call me. Then we make love. Then you begin to realize that you're an attractive young career lady with prestige and wealth and I'm a kid ten years younger living from pillar to post. And you feel embarrassed and ashamed so you need to be alone until it all starts again."

"So?" she replied. "Is it my fault that we live in a lonely, pathetic world? What the hell am I supposed to do?"

As I reached for my jacket, which she had seized from me, all I could think of saying was, "I'm sorry."

"Just one final request," she asked with a curious sobriety.

"What is it?"

"My son."

"Yeah, he really has that stereo too loud. I could hear it all the way down the block."

"I know. His father sent him here for the week, and I can't deal with him."

"Why don't you talk to him?"

"Believe me I tried, I tried to interest him, but when I asked him what was new, he said, 'your boyfriend.'"

"He's probably just a little jealous. I'm sure it'll pass."

"I can't even speak to him. When I asked him to lower that damned thing he slammed the door in my face. And the entire upper floor reeks of marijuana."

"Well, there is a limit. Perhaps you should consider some stern disciplining."

She looked at me fearfully for a moment and then out of the silence she asked, "Would you do it?"

"Without a second thought."

"He's up there now."

"You go right up there and show him who's boss," I pepped.

"You just said you would."

"Pardon?"

"You said you would do it for me."

"Me! Are you kidding?"

"You just said you would."

"I meant I would discipline my child if it came to it."

She looked at me maternally for a minute, "I'll give you fifty dollars."

"Surely you jest," I replied sincerely.

"It has got to be done; you said so."

"You're the mother," I replied. "If you do it he'll respect you. If anybody else does it, he'll hate you for a lifetime."

"I'll take care of that."

"Well, I'm not going to do it. It's out of the question."

"The boy's out of control, and I can't do it."

"I ain't doing it, period."

Suddenly she put on the poker face and upped the ante from fifty to a hundred, and then a hundred and fifty and then three hundred and then six hundred dollars. Just as quickly as she offered, I refused each sum.

"Look, I'm not just a pacifist, I'm also a coward. I freeze up in violent situations, it's a psychological thing. Some people can get instantly mad. I get quiet and terrified." Before the farce could continue, I grabbed for the door-knob.

"Leave here and I'll call the police," she screamed.

"Good, have them do it."

"I'll call them on you! There is a law against stealing a car."

"What?"

"Where's my Mercedes?" She pulled her final trump. I shut the front door.

"The car's old. I don't need it. I don't need the money. If you do this little deed, I'll sign over the title to you. Do you understand? You'll own it."

To own a Mercedes Benz: it sounded wonderfully unreal. For the first
time I realized how Glenn was capable of being a merciless businesswoman.
A Mercedes Benz, one of the classic status symbols of wealth—a working
Mercedes that could legally be my own. Where I came from, you were what
you drove. Typically, for the wrong reason, I meekly accepted her offer.
Before any reprieves of thought could occur, she raced over to her file cabinet, located the car's title, opened a fountain pen, and dramatically signed on
the dotted line, explaining, "I'll mail this in just as soon as the job is done."

As I climbed the steps, I came to realize the new low to which I was sinking—quid pro quo: thrashing a kid for a Mercedes. I envisioned Helmsley's
eyes glancing down on me sadly. I couldn't believe it. I paused on the landing, but as I listened to that heavy metal music, I decided that he wasn't
exactly a kid and I wasn't exactly an assassin.

I knocked on his door authoritatively and waited. I decided that I would
give reason a chance before brutality. I knocked again and heard a giggle,
and then a splashy sound and finally, "Oh, fuck."

"Open this minute," I yelled, and trying the knob, I opened the door.

Junior was on his knees, carefully searching the carpeted floor.
Apparently he had dropped his bong and was looking for the small wire
screen filled with grass.

"Man, you made me drop my shit."

"That's illegal you know."

He laughed and kept searching for the screen, which was probably the
same thing I would've done in his position. Locating the grass-packed mesh,
he restored it to the bong and after lighting up and holding it in, he extended
it toward me.

"Want a hit?" he creaked, not employing his smoke filled lungs.

"I'd like to talk," I replied as I walked across the room and lowered the volume of the stereo. I then squatted on the floor next to him.

"Shoot," he said, exhaling and then took another hit from the bong.

"Well, this is difficult to say, but I was informed that you were rather disrespectful to your mother."

I waited for him to reply, but he only exhaled and inhaled another hit.

"Ideally, I'd like you to apologize to your mother." He exhaled his lungful of smoke into my face and shook his head no with a big grin. I would've done the same thing.

"Get this through your head," I replied sternly. "You are going to apologize to her."

"Look coach, why don't you let her give you a blow job and calm down." Then peacefully he started on another hit. When I heard the bubbles gurgling in his bong, I decided that there were no short cuts, I slapped the bong out of his hands.

"YOU MOTHERFUCKER!!!" he hollered at the top of his lungs and jumped to his feet looking at the dead bong.

"I want you to apologize to your mother."

"Get the hell out of my house!" he yelled back. "My father bought this house! Get out and fuck off!" He started walking across the room to pick up his bong when I grabbed him by his thin neck and threw him on his bed. "Now listen to me. You are going to apologize, understand?"

"What the hell do you care?" he asked quickly, quelling his anger, which he might've realized was pointless.

"I love her," I lied angrily. "I want you to apologize to her."

"Well, that's the biggest lie I've ever heard, 'cause she can't love. You better get that straight, right off."

"Just apologize to her. We'll let it go at that."

"No, I can't," he replied. "I'm not as much of a liar as you or her. So the both of you can just go fuck each other."

The kid no longer reminded me of me. He was far more principled. I stood there a moment wondering whether he would apologize to her if I gave him a hundred dollars. But I didn't think he'd accept it. Besides, I didn't have a hundred dollars. After a silent moment, I decided that I still wanted the car and this kid's pride, which stood in the way, was just too weak a thing. "Are you going to apologize?"

Mimicking me, he stood up, crossed his arms, inhaled, and replied with an assumed lisp, "For the last time, coach, no!" I couldn't just hit him. I partly admired him. So I walked right up to him and shoved him onto the bed. He bounced off it and lunged at me. I had about fifty pounds on him, so I shoved him to the floor, pinned his arms around his back and held him there. "Are you going to apologize?"

"I'm gonna kill you," he seethed with the little air he could muster. I didn't want to hurt him but I had to break him.

"HELP!" he started screaming. I clenched his arms behind his back with one hand and with my other hand I gently covered his mouth so that he wouldn't yell.

"I want you to nod yes when you're ready to apologize," I explained carefully as he squirmed.

He twisted and kicked and tried biting my hand. With the hand that I had used to gag him, I clamped tightly over his mouth. Desperately he tried breathing through his nose. Leisurely I got around to pinching his nostrils. Then I wheeled my body around so that I was fully on top of his collapsing and ethical lungs. I could see a drowning look in his eyes as his body writhed and twisted. As his smothered face turned redder and redder, I felt my conscience shrivelling tightly until it was just a dry little pit inside of me. Time slowly passed, and I realized that there was no worse sound than gagged pain. Finally his head whipped up and down; he was ready to apologize. I helped him up to the edge of the bed where he caught his breath and stared despondently at the floor like someone who had just been violated. After a moment, I watched him calmly rise and tug off his shirt, then he opened the top drawer of his cabinet. I thought he was replacing his sweaty T-shirt, but then he suddenly turned around. His arm was over his head and a long knife was plunging down.

"You're dead," he said and dove dizzily at me. Snatching a pillow off his bed, I shoved it out and felt a stabbing deep in the cushion, which I think he did deliberately for effect. Before he could recoil, I grabbed his elbow and twisted it behind his back. The impaled pillow fell to the floor, and I kicked it across the room next to the bong. He looked up at me calmly, probably expecting me to be civilized about the whole thing. But in a single rehearsed football motion, I bowed low, grabbed him around the knees, hoisted him in the air then threw him headlong onto the floor. After the big bang, he curled up in the corner and started crying painfully. Yanking him out to the middle of the floor, I shoved him on his back, uncurled his arms and sat on his chest.

"Get the fuck off me!" he screamed. I hit him and hit him again and again and again, and soon I was frenzied and couldn't stop. The screams and cries for pity, the begging and blood, all that background crap didn't obstruct that lustful lava of cruelty that spewed out. I lost control and didn't stop until my hands were moist and my arms trembled.

In complete exhaustion, he was cowering, trying to shove his head under the bed frame, holding his hands over his face. I pulled him out and saw his nose bleeding; both his eyes were swelling and I thought I broke his nose.

"Apologize, yes?"

"No. Fuck no!"

Taking several deep hard breaths, I jumped on him and swung him to the floor. He obeyed all force without resistance. I held his arms in a full nelson and rested my mouth just above his ear. Calmly, in a throaty whisper, I said, "When I'm done and out of here, you're going to spend the rest of your life trying to forgive yourself for what you let me do now..."

"ALL RIGHT! I'm sorry, I'm sorry, I'm sorry, I'm sorry..." He started screaming and flaying his arms and legs so convulsively that I thought he was having a convulsion. I jumped off him, terrified that I had done something irreversible. But when he rolled under the bed, I realized that he was even more petrified than I.

Grabbing the kid by his collar, I pulled him out, led him into the bathroom, and said, "Wash." Now that the problem had been repaired, I was returning the goods nice and clean. All that remained were the red marks that by tomorrow would be swollen into blue and black bruises and then they would fade. I took some nice clothes out of his closet and put them on the bed. When he came out of the bathroom cleaned, I pointed at the attire and said, "Dress." He moved clumsily and drunkenly. Holding his collar, as if I were walking a big dog, I took him downstairs to his inspector.

"Glenn," I casually called out when we hit the bottom landing. "Your son would like to have a word with you." I plopped him down on the sofa next to me.

"One second," she called back from out of the kitchen, completely unaware of the pain and violence that had occurred.

While waiting for her, I took a cigarette from a crystal bowl sitting on an end table. Clipping it with my lips, I realized that the cigarettes in the jar were only part of the decor, like a bowl of wax fruit, offering only the illusion of generosity. I smoked the stale tobacco nonetheless and exhaled the smoke over the kid. He sat painfully straight, a pride to his trainer. Soon the mom entered and looked at her boy, "Yes?"

"Go ahead," I prompted him.

"I'm sorry."

"All right," she replied curtly.

He rose to go but I quickly caught him. I wanted Glenn to get her money's worth. "Sit down," I told him. "What are you sorry for?"

"For being mean to my mother."

"And now are things going to change around here?"

"I'm going to do as she says from now on."

"Good boy. Now say good night to your mother and run along."

"Good night, Mom."

Glenn arose and gave her son a proper peck on the cheek. "I don't like having to go through this. We're going through tough times, both in our own way, and both have certain rules to obey. All I ask is to be treated with the same respect that I give you. Is that unreasonable?"

"No," he shook his head expressionlessly. Nothing she could ask would be too unreasonable after our reality session upstairs. I watched him return to his room and I couldn't imagine what he would do once he got up there. When the Romans destroyed Carthage, leveled its buildings and enthralled its people, they founded a final form of peace. However, when Napoleon dictated terms at Tilsit, peace only lasted until one side was strong enough to overpower the other. I wasn't sure which kind of peace this would be, but that wasn't my job. The real bruises wouldn't be fully visible until tomorrow, and by then I'd be long gone. I had earned a nice automobile, Glenn would have to worry about the rest. As soon as all was still and I was sitting across from Glenn, I stubbed the decayed cigarette and announced, "Now if you'll just give me the title, I'll be on my way."

"What do you mean?"

"I mean I'm getting the hell out of here. I did what I agreed to do and now I'm leaving."

"Look, I insist that you at least have a drink." While speaking, she arose and went behind the bar and poured some wine. Soft music was audible and the lighting was indirect. She had a drink and handed me one.

"It's a Chardonnay from Sonoma Valley," she said, and I watched her take a tiny sip. I downed the drink, went over to her rolltop desk and started searching for the signed title.

"What are you doing?" she asked, but I think she knew.

When I found it, I realized that she hadn't signed my name to it, she had only gone through the motion.

"What the fuck is going on, Glenn?"

She snatched the title out of my hand, shoved it down into her bra, and childishly hid behind the sofa. I jumped over the sofa and pushed her up against the wall. "What the fuck is the matter with you?"

"Nothing," she replied. "I just want you to stay."

"I didn't tell you this, but a friend of mine, his name was Helmsley, he committed suicide the other day by jumping off the Brooklyn Bridge."

She didn't say a word, then she pulled the title out of her bra. Going to the desk, she signed it and handed it over to me. "I'll give you two hundred dollars to spend the night. You can sleep in your own room."

"You know that guy, Adolphe, who was cheating on you? I'm no better than him," I replied. "I cheated on my girlfriend. Her name was Sarah and she threw me out of the house." Silence, and then resignation. When she finally gave me the title, I grabbed my jacket and left the house.

TWELVE

At night you have to wait forever for a train, so I took a cab over the bridge, up Church Street, and through West Broadway. Janus wasn't home, so I went over to Ternevsky's bar looking for a sufficient cure. Nothing was as potent as his ashtray, which was filled with Thai stick. I lit up and faded away.

The next morning, I had this strange and tender dream; it was actually more of a sensation. I was slipping through a warm, slimy ooze and although I could breathe I was entirely immersed. There was no claustrophobia. In fact, I felt as if I was speeding toward some strange liberation. I was rising high and higher, fast and faster.... Laughter interrupted me: I was laughing and slowly pulling out of my subconscious state, the oozy warmth was part of me: I was ejaculating into Janus's hand.

I slithered out of bed. As I dressed, she watched me with eyes so clear. "I honestly like you and I'm attracted to you. When I saw you this morning, you were tossing and turning; I just wanted to comfort you."

"You don't do that to a person."

"It's not like that. I felt close to you from the first."

"That's not even the point. You just don't do that to a person."

"Well, Sergei says that there's no better way to be awakened."

"Well, not me," I replied and cleaned up, dressed, and left to go to a nearby coffee shop. As I drank coffee at the counter, squeezed next to a couple eating their breakfast, I wondered how I was going to spend the next couple of hours before work.

"Do you smell a water buffalo?" the girl sitting next to me asked her companion, loudly. Her boyfriend, who seemed embarrassed, tried changing the topic, but she persisted. I supposed she was right. Tight places are plentiful in New York and lately while in elevators, subways, and even bars, I had become aware of a recent hostility from strangers. I abandoned my coffee and left to a pharmaceutical discount outlet. There, I purchased generic bottles of mouthwash, underarm deodorant, toothpaste, dental floss, and other hygienic offerings to society. Noticing a box of prelubed Trojans, I thought about Ternevsky's darling. She was gorgeous.

Crossing Astor Place, the vendors were out in full force. After a quick browse, I bought a baggy old sharkskin suit for five bucks and a new pair of shoes. Then I bought dinner, pizza on Third Avenue, and a sixteen-ounce can of Bud. I feasted on the corner of Saint Mark's and the Bowery under the Optima cigar sign while watching the punks, whores, addicts, and sightseers all clogging eastward. By the time a bunch of Jersey kids asked me where McSorley's Bar was, I had finished the crust and decided to go to the Zeus.

I turned on the night lights and picked up the drops from the box office. As the closing time rolled around, I carefully rolled back the counter, stole the required sum, and waited to go. As I flipped through the *Voice,* I thought about Ternevsky's chick. I had to go back there, and I wasn't sure how to deal with her. I went to the bathroom where I utilized my body aids. I brushed my teeth, flossed, used a mousse, combed my hair, sprayed on underarm deodorant, gargled and, taking off my cheesy socks, applied foot deodorant. Then I changed into the sharkskin suit that I had purchased earlier that day. Some young buck that was cruising the lobby kept dipping into the john, leering as I was transforming. I then went back into the office, where I looked at myself in the mirror and tried to rehearse an imaginary dialogue with Janus.

But it was ridiculous. I was jeopardizing my living situation. Enough time had passed to heal the tear between me and Sarah. She would be saddened to hear about Helmsley. She'd known what he meant to me and would want to console me. I decided to dial her. After three rings, the answering machine gave a message. Her voice sounded bouncy and far happier than I had ever made her. I could never make her as happy as she now sounded on the recording so I hung up before the beep. Looking through my shirt pocket, I found some loose change and the wrinkled title to the Mercedes. I picked up the phone and held it awhile. Who could I call? Thoughtlessly I dialled some familiar digits and listened to the recorded announcement, "the number you dialled is out of service at this time, please check the number and..." I had dialled Helmsley.

Soon the film was over and the guys went home. I locked up the theater and made the night drop. As I walked back down Third Avenue, I felt an increasing pain in my leg, a stabbing from a metal barb. I pulled the contents out of my pocket and found a bunch of loose change and a big ring of keys. Examining the keys, I recognized the two keys to Helmsley's house and a lump arose in my throat. I had never even noticed them before and now they were all that was left. I let them slip through my open fingers, clinking onto the pavement. The locks they once opened had probably already been replaced. Glenn's house key was the next key under scrutiny, and as I walked the next block, I relived each punch and kick of the previous night. I held the keys to the Mercedes, her garage, and front door. I threw all three keys into Third Avenue traffic. By tomorrow they would all be irretrievably ironed into the tar. All the six remaining keys were still active, four were for Ternevsky, and two were for the theater. I halted and of course turned back. Waiting until the light turned green, I ran into the street and searched until I found the key to the car. Tiredly I made it back to Ternevsky's place.

When I entered, Janus was wearing headphones, lying on the director's circular bed watching his VCR. I quietly went to the most distant part of the place, the reading area. I sat in the great director's reading chair, which was adjacent to his great custom-made magazine rack filled floor to roof with great periodicals. If we were what we read then Ternevsky was a voyeur, a connoisseur, a bodybuilder, a midget wrestler, a numismatist, a philologist, and there I stopped. Most of the magazines were current, and even though they were broad in scope, most of them were crisply unread.

I glanced at an old copy of the *SoHo Weekly News,* which had gone out of business, and then a copy of the *East Village Eye.* I didn't want any confrontation with Janus. I just wanted to go to sleep. Finally curiosity conquered and I peeked over at her. Her back was toward me. With headphones on, she watched the large-screen TV. When I glimpsed past her to the TV, I realized that she was watching something pornographic. I discreetly watched it awhile; it was actually some kind of avant-garde film. Something caught my eye in one of the many vanity mirrors. I realized that she was watching, studying me. I looked away, back at the magazine rack.

She rose to her feet and I could hear her walking a bit.

"Want anything?" She was standing over at the bar, pouring herself a drink.

"Thanks no."

"What you up to?" she asked.

"Just reading the magazines."

"We just got a copy of *New York Native*. See it there?"

"No, but it's all right."

"Aren't you gay?"

"Not right now." I replied, not caring for any tongue-in-cheek crap. Why couldn't she just leave me alone. I gazed at the lingerie ads in one of the many woman's fashion magazines.

"What is your problem?" she finally asked.

"You."

"What'd I do?"

"I feel as if you're testing me."

"What are you talking about?"

"What the hell was that handjob this morning?"

"You looked as if you could use it."

"And now you're watching porno when you're just watching me, asking me if I want to read the *Native*, all of it."

"All right," she finally conceded. "You're right, and I'll tell you why, I think you're a goddamned fraud and the thing that bugs me is that you don't have to be."

"If I am a fraud," I nibbled, "why don't I have to be?"

"Because," was all she said for a moment, and then she elaborated. "You kind of remind me of me." She paused awhile, but I still wasn't going to show any cards. She had to show more than that.

"If you think that I gave you a handjob just to prove that you're straight, well, please, I'm not that disgusting. But you are straight."

"How the fuck can you be so certain. Why can't I be gay?"

"Well, first of all, I've known gays all my life. My father was gay, and you just don't act gay. Also you behave with this kind of repressed quality; you lurk. You're afraid that if you let yourself go, I'll see the truth. And you're always looking at me in this way. And lastly because I'm really attracted to you."

"So what now? I mean assuming I am straight. Are you going to tell Ternevsky?"

"If I wanted you out of here, it wouldn't matter if you were gay or not. All I would have to do is say that I don't like you."

"So is that what you're going to do?"

"No, don't you understand. I'd like to become friends..."

"Friends? Like how?"

"Well"—she moved alongside me and put her hand on mine—"Ternevsky's a great accommodator. But he's greasy, slimy and unromantic and he makes me feel ugly and cheap."

"All right." All her cards seemed on the table; if she wanted me out, all she would have to do is tell the maestro that I made a move on her. It would take a whole lot less than a handjob.

"All right?" she replied.

"All right, I'm not gay. Now what?"

"Why are you asking me?"

"I'm tired," I said nervously, waiting to see whether I had been trapped or not.

"Me too. Why don't you join me. I've rented a pretty good film."

"That porn film."

"It's an art film," she replied. So I got on the bed and she poured us both a drink and we watched this dirty art film, and slowly we got closer and when I started mimicking the film—kissy, touchy, feely—she didn't stop me.

When I awoke late the next morning, she was still in my arms, something I had never experienced with Glenn, or for that matter most lovers. I felt hot and sweaty, so I carefully pried myself loose and started a bath. While the water ran, I put on a pot of coffee and got the *New York Times* that had been slid under the locked elevator door. In the bath I aristocratically downed the coffee and English muffins while reading the newspaper. Soon Janus joined me in the massive tub, and we giggled and splashed around like toddlers.

The beginning of a relationship is always the prime cut of the affair. I was in love. That night, post-coitally, I asked Janus, "Do you think we're taking a risk by sleeping together?"

"No," Janus continued, "even if he did come unannounced, he'd come in the evening after a daylight flight."

"How self-assured," I replied. "You sound like you've done this sort of thing before."

She smiled and kissed me. "You're jealous already."

"Well, I'll overcome that. But I'm still nervous about him coming in and catching us. If he was so damn thorough about having a homosexual in residence, then he's obviously the jealous type. And it'd be a high price to pay if we got caught."

She agreed and carefully we established certain safeguards. The next day, we went out and bought our own linen, which Janus would put on the bed each night and replace with the normal circular sheets the next morning. Also she warned that we should never be seen in public, as the eminent director had a network of opportunists hoping for jobs in his films, doing anything they could to ingratiate themselves to him. Additionally she would distance us by indicating that I was too effeminate for her liking.

One evening, arriving late at work, I opened the office door and found Miguel sitting at his desk with a smile on his face. He didn't say a word. When I asked him what was up, he took two paper cups from out of the desk drawer and then a small frosted bottle of Cordon Negro from out of the dwarf refrigerator. Popping the cork, he announced, "We got it."

"Got what?"

"I just got the mortgage on the Jersey place."

"But it's nowhere near June."

"No, but we got enough in our account to get a loan from the bank. I got it away from the loan shark. If we miss a payment, I won't get killed."

We toasted and drank, and he explained that we had several more months of embezzling at the standard pace.

"But even then, we've got to leave here gracefully or they'll become suspicious." We toasted some more and got more enthusiastic. "By the by," he interrupted himself, "Owensfield called."

"About his screening?" I remembered that he was supposed to be finished with his film soon.

"Well, he mentioned it, but do you remember that conversation you guys had about Vienna or something?"

"Yeah."

"Apparently you really did impress him. He asked me to invite you to his contributor's party celebrating some new issue of his magazine."

"Why would he invite me?"

"Actually, he invited both of us."

"When?"

"This Friday."

"Not this Friday?"

"Yeah, why?"

"I'll be in Arcadia this Friday with lover boy." If we went to this *Harrington* party together, Miguel would discover my scam to get published. And although it was no money out of his pocket, I didn't want him to consider his future business partner so deceitful so soon.

"What is the name of this alleged beloved?"

"Donny," I selected randomly.

"Like Donny Osmond."

"More like Adonis."

"They're all Adonis," he replied, and grabbing his jacket he bid me good night and left.

After all the spins of the turnstile and the backward spins of stolen money, I locked up, made my night drops, and went to Ternevsky's. I opened the elevator door and stared at the house. It looked like a small tornado had hit. Janus was sitting on the bed. Silently she handed me the postcard that Ternevsky had sent saying that he had concluded all business on the continent and he would be home by the time she got this postcard.

The night was too grim to make love. The next morning we changed the sheets, and waited nervously for Ternevsky's grand entrance. Although neither of us wanted it, our great love was instantly turned into a protracted one-night stand. Janus even helped me apply some of Ternevsky's male cosmetics; transforming into a swank gay in season. As evening thickened so did our anxieties. We wandered around the house like strangers. I didn't have any work that night, so I pointlessly tried to console Janus. But we became increasingly depressed. She commented that we were just property of Ternevsky and finally suggested that it would be wiser if we were apart when Ternevsky arrived. I agreed and left.

I walked around the neighborhood, finally checking out the street vendors on Second Avenue. On the display blanket of one vendor I noticed an
old Hamilton wristwatch in fair condition.

"How much?"

"Five bucks," the seller said. He was a poorly dressed black man in his
sixties.

"How about three bucks?" I held out the dollars in front of him.

"Look, them extra two bucks means I eat."

"Hey, I'm no different than you," I replied. "It means the same thing for
me."

"Well, I don't see you selling your shit to stay fed."

"You want the money or no?"

"Four bucks," he finally replied. It wasn't poverty that compelled me to
haggle. I just liked the sport of it. Actually, I had this week's pay on me, two
hundred and fifteen bucks. I gave him the three and an extra dollar in
change and put the old watch with the elastic band around my wrist. I then
proceeded up First Avenue. If Ternevsky was back for good he was probably
going to ask me to move. The party was over; he was probably screwing
Janus right now.

"Hey," someone yelled as I was crossing Ninth Street. It was Angel, an
usher I had worked with at the Saint Mark's Cinema. We talked a bit, and he
asked me whether I had heard a rumor that the Saint Mark's Cinema was
going out of business.

"No way," I replied.

"I heard it was going to turn it into some kind of yuppie mall."

"I wish I was a yuppie," I said.

"Why?"

"They're young and they have money, the winning combination."

"Well, you're still young—halfway there. You're not looking for any coke, are you?"

"I'm just out for a walk," I replied.

"I can give you a good deal on some coke. Have a taste." And he unfolded a small packet of aluminum foil, dabbed a little on the end of his long-grown pinky nail, and held it up to my nose. I snorted and felt the tingle rise and spread.

"Wait one second," I said and went to the pay phone where I called Janus. I told her that I would be home soon with a parting gift.

"How much is it?" I asked the ex-usher.

"I'm freezing out here," he replied and gave me a great deal; two grams for two hundred bucks. I went home quickly and showed it to a grim Janus.

"Tonight," I said, "let's go out in style."

We went out to a nearby restaurant for dinner and then came home and watched some TV. Initially we were able to forget the impending return, but when we remembered it was additionally painful. We tried to be intimate but it wasn't working; we couldn't ignore the sword dangling over our heads. Finally she declared, "This is bullshit."

"Let's pack up and just leave," I suggested. But then there was a new silence.

She eventually broke it with her explanation, "I can't work forty hours a week just to live in a ten-floor walk up on Avenue C. I've lived with rats and roaches and I don't want to, ever again."

"I've lived like that too, but it doesn't have to be like that. Right now I'm involved in something and if all goes well, I'll co-own a movie theater in Jersey. It'll only bring in a modest salary at first, but there are still some nice places in Hoboken and Jersey City, and you can move in with me."

"Well, if that happens, great. But let's only count on what we got: Where's the coke?" I took out the envelope and she took down a small glass frame from the wall. It was the New York Film Series Award citing Ternevsky for Best Cinematic Effort of 1973. She placed the coke on it. Taking a letter opener from his desk, she plowed through the pile, creating fine lines of white powder. I watched with a silent smile as she quickly got a small piece of aquarium tubing from Ternevsky's top desk drawer and handed me one. She was an expert, there was no fumbling or improvising.

She smiled, kissed me and started up her nose siphoning.

Quickly a small fireworks ignited in the sinuses soared into the brain. Her eyes became glassy and we both started giggling. The celebration had begun. Half past a gram, the phone rang. Whoever it was, I wasn't worried. It was night and Ternevsky, the daytime vampire, couldn't catch us until tomorrow's afternoon light.

Answering the phone, I found someone in desperate need of Henry, a wrong number. An anonymous male voice had misdialed. From my drugged perspective, this was absolutely hilarious. But a moment after the phone was back on the receiver, it rang again.

"I need to talk to Henry," the voice pleaded, and once again I couldn't stop laughing until I hung up. Again the phone rang. This time I instructed Janus, "When the Igor asks for Henry, hand me the phone." She did so, and when the older male voice asked me if I was Henry, I made an affirmative mumble.

"Henry," he started sobbing, "Dad is dead." Janus was restraining laughs. This guy was sobbing and, coke notwithstanding, I was suddenly pushed face to face with an old familiar mood.

I hung up, unplugged the phone and chucked it across the room. Grabbing the aquarium tubing, I started snorting away from the caller and all the pathetic associations, snort exalting up into that cocaine cosmos.

Janus began undoing my clothes and I started stripping her. She brought me over to the big round bed. And everything was done, nothing was shameful, nor vulgar, nor squeamish, nor could be, everything was mustful. Energy launched and abounded; muscles bulged, bunched and loosened again. Nothing retained. Everything was a blastoff-moonwalk-splashdown, shameless sin before the expulsion. Each single sensation was on its own, soaking up itself, every second was lifefull and there was no nothingness, until my liquid concentrate diluted and then sinking forever deep, deep, deep....

THIRTEEN

Awaking to the sensation of a clench, I blinked through the gushing sunlight of those bay windows. I could make out Ternevsky standing over me with Marty entering behind him, hauling in luggage. I jumped to my weak feet.

"Doesn't anyone answer the phone?" asked the still-ignorant Marty, who was just stepping out of the elevator. Realizing my nudity, he dropped his bag and asked, "What the fuck is going on?"

"Your little faggot's dick!" Ternevsky screamed. "It was in my little girl—that's what!"

Ternevsky grabbed a vase of roses and poured it on the bed, splashing over Janus and myself. I shoved into my pants and shirt and she bolted up.

"What the fuck are you doing here?" she asked, immediately grabbing the situation.

"I've always suspected this, you little bitch. Now I want you and your things out of my house." Ternevsky, poor actor that he was, lost his exotic accent in his fit of anger.

"Sergei, I can explain."

"Don't explain," I yelled, as I zipped up my pants. "Come with me."

She looked at me angrily, making no attempts to conceal her nudity. She jumped to her feet before him and dropped to her knees, looking up at her master. She started crying into the loose legs of his trousers. After a moment of this, she pointed to me and started with the accusations, "It was that monster! He did it to me!"

Ternevsky looked at me with wild and widened eyes and since he was nearer to the kitchen than any other part of the house, he seized an electric can opener shaped like the Starship Enterprise and swung it dramatically in the air.

"Wait a fucking second! She's lying!"

"He did it to me," she yelled back. I dressed even quicker. As I squeezed my shoes on, Marty's hands fell softly on my back, not attempting to restrain me, but letting me know that he was prepared to.

"What exactly did he do?" Ternevsky asked her paternally. She looked up into my eyes with absolute terror. Instantly in those pupils I saw tiny saucers of that terror: overpriced rat-infested tenements, dull and underpaying nine-to-five jobs.

Pushing Marty onto the bed, I dashed into the elevator, which was held open by one of Ternevsky's bags. I kicked it out of the way and yanked the door shut, and as the elevator sank away, I could hear Sergei scream, "Quick, call the police!"

Outside it was a sunny but chilly day as I wandered unsteadily toward the northwest, still hungover by last night's baby powder. Janus had supplied me with a good time, and if there was anything that she could salvage out of the wreck, even at my expense, she was welcome to give it a try, no hard feelings.

Finally, twisting along Bleecker, I arrived at Abingdon Square. There, I joined the collection of young mothers, children, old folks, bums, monkey bars, and swings. I wish I had grabbed more of my clothes, once again I had only escaped with the things on my back. Checking my pockets, I realized I had just about blown all my money on last night's coke. So, without any immediate prospects, I just sat there awhile, waiting for something to come and for something else to pass. I watched a bag lady feeding pigeons and teenage kids wearing designer jeans.

I bought a candy bar, called it breakfast, and chewed it down as I walked through the West Village toward the F train. Passing the old restaurant where I had first met Sarah about a year before, I realized how quickly I had descended. I finally got to Fourteenth Street where I paid a token and realized as I walked down that long uriney tunnel connecting the IRT with the IND trains that the last time I had passed through this tunnel was when I went with Helmsley up to the Columbia University party. You know you've been in a place too long when every other locale serves as a reference for some sad recollection.

When I got to the F train platform, it was bare, so I figured I just missed one. Looking down into the dirty tunnel, I spotted a distant light. The train was on its way. But after a while when still nothing arrived, I checked the tunnel again and realized that it was only the flickering of an incandescent bulb deep in the tunnel's filth. After about twenty minutes of waiting, a garbled announcement came over the loudspeaker. All I could make out was "an alternative route..." I walked back through the long uriney tunnel. While waiting another small chunk of eternity for the IRT, I thought about how I had grown to tolerate almost all of New York's degradations. Reality now seemed authentic only with a certain degree of anxiety and humiliation. But I decided that it would be a sad day when I didn't mind riding the subway.

When a train finally arrived, there was a copy of yesterday's *New York Post* on one of the seats. After reading the gossip on "Page Six," I reached Boro Hall. As I walked toward Glenn's house, I started pulling together some bullshit tale to tell her.

Up the front steps, I rang the door bell and kept ringing it for about five minutes. No one answered. When I took a couple of steps back and looked up at the front of the house, I thought I saw one of the drapes moving. Could she be hiding? I sat on the stoop unsuspecting and waited for the career lady to return from her career.

After about forty minutes of sitting and rereading yesterday's *Post,* a van slowly pulled up. Suddenly I heard Glenn's door behind me swing open. Junior leaped out with a baseball bat and screamed, "That's him!"

The side door of the van slid open and out plopped a harmless-looking fat kid who fell on his face, but stumbling behind him was a little league team. I dropped everything and ran down the street toward the river. I had at least a half a block lead, which they closed by the time I reached the promenade. Jumping over the encircling gate, I moved through the shrubs and trees and tried squeezing through a fence into a private backyard, but I was too hefty. Through the foliage I could see nothing but running feet. They seemed to be all around me so I squatted low in the thicket and waited. I could hear them yelling between each other, "Is he up there?"

"No—did he jump over there?"

"He couldn't, either the fall or the cars would've killed him."

"Well he was around here a second ago."

"He couldn't've escaped. Spread out."

They were defoliating the bushes and shrubs, and I knew that in a minute they would be on me, so I chose a direction and waited for my big chance. A hard boot suddenly kicked me square in the center of my back, throwing me flat on my face.

"Found him!" one large guy was screaming. "He's right here."

"Grab him, grab him!" I could feel the thuds of approaching feet running toward me. I tried to rise but a shower of needles seemed to radiate from my spine. Then the hailstorm started. Feet and fists smashed up and down along my arms and legs. I curled into a ball and tried to get up.

"Hold his arms! Kick out his teeth!" I heard someone ranting orders, and a paddle wheel of shoes started on my head and neck.

"Stop it!" I suddenly made out Junior's voice. "Just hold him flat!" And a group of hands and arms weaved into a straight jacket holding me flat on my back. "Mama's gonna need a new lover."

Through the throbbing headache, puffy eyes, and loud ringing, I watched him pull that Afghan knife out of his pants. When I saw him snap open the shiny blade, it was like snapping open a capsule of smelling salts and inhaling. Convulsing up with all my might, he quickly gored his knife into my right inner thigh. When I started bleeding, they weakened their grip and I pulled to my feet and dashed through the bramble. As I hurtled back over the gated area, they pursued. A cop car was slowly patrolling the far end of the promenade and nothing was obstructing its view. One of the officers must've seen me dashing by with Spanky's gang close behind, but apparently it didn't warrant further investigation.

Running off the promenade at the exit with the flag pole, I made it about a quarter of the block up Montague Street before the fastest kid in the group grabbed me. A baby-faced monster with good sneakers, kicked me in the back of my knees. I went down. It was just the two of us. I lunged forward, putting him in a quick half-nelson, and fumbled through his pocket. Just as Junior and the tallest lad bolted forth, I found a Bic ballpoint pen which I placed right in the corner of his right eye.

"A step closer and skinny's a cyclops, I swear it." Junior caught the rest of the kids as they came huffing and tumbling out of the park. They encircled me and then Junior made a proposal.

"Let him go, and we'll let you go."

"There's no way you can guarantee that," I said.

"What do you want?"

"Just stay put," I replied as I backed up the block holding the hostage boy in one hand and the pen in the other. A retroactive pain was regrouping throughout parts of my body, a limp had caught up with me and bent me over. Neither cab nor cop came by.

As the pain settled, it became harder to hold balance, and when I finally tripped on the consistently broken pavement, dropping the pen, my leash was gone. Skinny broke lose and the dog pack was set free. In an excruciating limp, I dashed into the nearest open store, a Häagen Dazs ice cream parlor.

I pushed two people aside and jumped over the counter. When the kids dashed in one by one, each at his own pace, someone yelled, "There's a line!"

Running around the counter, they reached down and restarted with the kicks and wallops. I felt a tooth break in my mouth and fists pounding on my skull and chest. Suddenly, like a piece of furniture, I was lifted into the air for removal and disposal.

"Let him go!" A middle-aged lady wearing a red Häagen Dazs T-shirt cocked a small revolver at the group.

"He beat up our friend," one replied, the one who had first caught me in the bushes. "We're taking him to the police."

"No!" I whined pitifully, as I wiggled myself to my feet. Hands started gripping me tightly. "I was disciplining him for his mother."

In an unharmonious chorus they all started disagreeing with me, each supplying his own renditions.

"Shut up!" she yelled, pointing her gun. "I'll call the police here and solve the matter for everyone."

"Hell no," Junior replied. "We're not letting him go."

"Get the hell out of my store!" The lady spoke with a full maternal authority. Abruptly it felt like an anvil dropped on my head. I was dropped flat on my back and resisted passing out. The lady walked over and stood between me and the pack. Pointing the revolver at Junior, sternly she said, "Get the hell out of my store this instant."

"Fine," Junior said with a smile, and then addressing me he added, "We'll wait for you outside, coach."

Out they filed, one by one, waiting for me just beyond the door. She quickly had one of the employees lock the door and instructed the other one to call the police and an ambulance. She then helped me to a comfortable position and with a wet napkin she started wiping off blood. Judging from the sorrowful expression on her face, I must've been a mess.

"Thanks," I blurted.

"It ain't even loaded," she whispered while dabbing my face with a wet napkin. I tried to rise, but pain had replaced all senses.

"Just lie still." She looked at me intently. "Can you see me?"

"Yeah, why."

"There's blood in your eyes." There was blood oozing from everywhere, and soon, to the tune of sirens, I drifted. Through a heavenly fog I heard the queries: Why did they attack you? Who were they? Who's your nearest living relative? It was a reenactment of the Blimpie's aftermath weeks earlier only this time I had advanced from secondary character to lead victim. After a long wait, lying numbly in a gurney in the emergency ward of Long Island College Hospital, I was stripped, cleaned, bandaged, X-rayed, given a skull series, spine tapped, and ready to roll again. A calm doctor itemized my bill; I had a slight concussion, several broken ribs, a broken nose, a deep knife wound in my right thigh, and a large side order of bruises and abrasions. Then I was injected with some antibiotics and a local anesthetic. The bones were realigned and the thigh stitched up. When they found out I was financially unprotected, I was ready to roll yet again, this time to the overcrowded charity ward where I spent the night. I no longer got as many miles to the gallon but I still had some tread left.

A charity ward is not a quiet place, and the next morning when I awoke, a cliché was sitting in the visitor's chair at my right. I knew he was a cliché because he looked like every detective I had ever seen on TV from "Dragnet" through "Hawaii Five-0" to "Barney Miller." He wore the bland suit and had the badge hanging out of his outer jacket pocket. A wheeled curtain was pulled tightly around my bed; privacy.

"How are you?"

"Fine, thank you."

"What happened?"

"An altercation."

"It looks like someone altercated the hell out of you. Wanna tell me who did it?"

I asked the cliché if he would pour me a cup of water. He did and I quickly considered the situation. I had beaten on Junior pretty brutally, and I wasn't a particularly bitter person. Although he didn't succeed in either maiming or blinding me, he had broken a front tooth. But none of the injuries were really debilitating. Perhaps I realized that despite the pain and agony I was pretty lucky and it was a good time to cash my chips in and vamoose.

"I don't want to press any charges."

"Pardon me?"

"What good would it do?"

"What good? I'll arrest him, stick him behind bars."

"Can you arrest his mother's loneliness? Or put my greed behind bars? Can you arrest his father's neglect? 'Cause they were all accomplices."

"Spare me the melodrama. I get that in court," he said and then as if I didn't know, the cop explained. "This kid pounded the shit out of you. Now, why don't you tell me who it was and I'll make sure he doesn't do this again."

"He'll never do this again. He's actually a pretty decent kid."

"I don't believe this..." the officer pressed further. He wanted righteous outrage, but I was tired. He pressed until I feigned a massive headache, and only then did he go away. The rest of the day I spent asleep; I was still pretty drugged out. The next evening, I was allowed to make a local call. I called the theater. As soon as Miguel recognized my voice he hollered, "What the hell's going on?"

"What do you mean?"

"Marty called and the police came by here. Where are you? What the fuck is going on?"

"What did he tell you?" In other words, do you know the truth?

"No one would tell me a thing. Marty said you raped somebody. But then he hung up and said he'd call me back later."

"I accidentally slept with Ternevsky's girlfriend."

"Jumping Jesus!"

"But I didn't rape anybody. She was just as high as I was. I'll deal with it."

"Where are you anyway?"

"I'm at the hospital, I got banged up a bit."

"Which hospital?"

"Beth Israel, why?"

He then paused, and I thought I heard someone whispering to him, and then he asked, "What happened?"

"I got mugged."

"Well, are you okay?"

"Slightly busted up, but I'll recover."

"It's not at all related to the Ternevsky episode, is it?"

"No, 'course not."

"Well, how long will you be out?"

"I should be coming by soon. First I'm gonna straighten things out and then I'm going to be staying a bit with Donny."

"Listen, what's your number? I'll call you right back."

"I'm at a public phone in the hall and there are people waiting for it. I'll call you later." Quickly I hung up and dialled Ternevsky. I didn't mind helping Janus out, but there was no way that I was going to end up in prison over it.

"Hello." I heard that cute little voice of hers.

"Janus, thank God I got you. What the fuck is going on?"

"Sorry, but there's no Henry here, you must have the wrong number."

"Don't fuck with me. I'll tell Ternevsky the truth."

"Absolutely."

"Is he there?" I asked.

"Exactly."

"Do I have any reason to be worried?"

"None at all." She kept her delightful tone.

"I'm at Long Island College Hospital in Brooklyn. I got busted up pretty badly and..."

"Fine, sorry, bye." And she hung up. An attendant wheeled me back to my room. For the next twenty-four hours, sleep was pills and wakefulness was pain. Finally, on the third day, the nurse woke me with a paper cup filled with pills of different colors. I spent that morning thinking about Miguel. Incipient anxieties took a paranoid turn for the worse. Gradually each of his reasonable questions seemed to have a duplicitous underside. For the first time I realized that Miguel had all my money. Questions blistered: Who was the other voice in the room? Why did he want my number? Why did he want to know how long I was going to be away? When the doctor made his morning rounds, I asked him what time I'd be able to check out.

"Hopefully, in another week or two."

"Another week or two! You don't understand, I've got to go today."

"Today's out of the question."

"Look this isn't a prison, and I can heal at home for free."

"You're in a charity ward. You're not paying a cent."

"I might lose a lot more than you can imagine."

"The X-rays show that your skull was fractured. But the brain is much softer and far more delicate, and there is a short grace period between the time we can detect damage and the time the damage becomes fatal."

"As soon as I feel faint I'll hop in a cab and rush right over."

"You're still here for observation. We haven't even made a full diagnosis yet. For all we know, you have a hemorrhage and if the inter-cranial pressure gets too great, and we're not there to operate immediately, you could die."

"Doctor, I know that you've got my interest at heart, but if I stick around here I'm definitely going to lose my business and I won't have any life to return to."

"Would you rather have the luxuries or the life to enjoy them with?"

"Let me put it this way: I'd rather live a short high-quality life than a long bitter existence to mock myself with."

When he started nodding his head in resignation, I replied, "I'll make you a deal. As soon as I secure all my loose ends, I'll check back in."

"This isn't a hotel. The bed space in the charity ward is always in short supply. If you leave here, I can't guarantee a return ticket."

"Look, don't try to scare me. I got to go. This is my life."

"Fine," said he, and was gone in a huff. A few seconds later the nurse came in with a clipboard. On it was a form freeing the hospital of all liabilities. She said I had to sign it before I could go. I signed it, and for the last time, she sponged me, redressed my bandages, and got my clothes. As I slowly dressed, she asked the name of the recipient picking me up. It was for the records.

"Irving R. Towers," I replied, "but he's as shy as the moon in the daytime, and he's probably waiting in his car around the corner."

"Fine."

She was gone. The doctor returned and handed me a small menu of prescriptions. He quickly reviewed the particulars of how, when, and why each pill should be taken. I didn't listen because I couldn't even afford a cough drop. I was issued a cane, but then helped into a wheelchair and the hospital attendant quickly wheeled me out to the front lobby. Slowly I angled my bulk between my legs and cane and wobbled down Atlantic Avenue.

Everything reflected my aches. The sky was overcast. The air was still cold and uncirculated. The streets were still filthy and hard. The people were still bitter and ugly. The entire city of New York was sick and in desperate need of a vacation. Turning down Court Street, I finally found my old and undiscriminating friend Irving, a.k.a. the IRT. After the patient wait came the not-empty train. I took the closest seat and counted each stop with a silent scream. As the train screeched into the stations, the metal bar jawed my foot-stomped ribs, taking sharp bites out of my lungs. Quickly I thought of a game plan. First, I had to secure my holdings with Miguel, and next I had to go somewhere and recuperate. In order to check into the YMCA, I remembered that I needed money and ID. I could borrow the money but I'd lost my ID ages ago.

FOURTEEN

I got off at Union Square and slowly caned it over to the Zeus. The office door was unlocked, but the office was empty. Miguel was probably coming right back. Opening the lost-and-found drawer in the desk, I saw there were a bunch of wallets. Pickpockets usually worked the theaters; swiftly they'd grab the money and dispose of the evidence and we'd be too lazy to call the dispossessed. Looking at his ID, I realized my name today was Sven Cohen. Suddenly Miguel opened the door.

"What the fuck happened to you?" he gasped. Then, helping me into his swivel chair, he mumbled, "You poor baby."

"Nothing happened! I got into a fight. I'm better now." I shoved the wallet into my pocket.

"Are you sure Marty or Ternevsky had nothing to do with this?"

"Yes."

He glared at me with such dismay that I was curious to see myself. Looking into the small wall mirror, I saw my face filled with Halloween colors and inflated like a balloon. The streaks of blood in the pupils of my eyes accented the nightmarish effect. It hurt me when I laughed.

"You really should go to a hospital."

"I just checked out of one." I held up my wrist to show him the plastic ID bracelet.

"They should've been able to do a lot more for you than this," he pointed to my face, a case in point.

"They wanted me to stay for a week."

"Why didn't you?"

I stared at him for a moment until he looked away. He probably sensed my worry, my distrust of him. "I'll be ready to work tomorrow."

"Don't be silly. You'll scare people away."

"Miguel, how close are we to finishing up here?"

"Huh?"

"Toward Hoboken."

"Real soon."

"I'd like you to sign some kind of document stating that I have at least twenty-five percent of this business."

"If I signed something like that it might imply our little situation here." He pointed to the gauge.

"I'm completely unprotected. If I can't get some kind of documentation, I want my share of the money."

"Even if I did try to screw you, all you'd have to do is turn me in. That's pretty good insurance."

"Yeah, but after all this is done…"

"Look, there's still a lot of time before we're finished here, and you'll see the title of the place in your name by then."

"Listen," I replied, using his line of reasoning against him, "if you can trust me about this little secret then you can certainly trust me not to turn you in. Besides, if I turned you in, I sure as hell don't gain anything by it."

"All right!" he finally said, and sitting at the desk he took out a piece of paper and said, "Now, what would you have me write?"

I dictated some feeble statement saying that he owed me thirty percent of any movie theater he might buy and operate. He signed and dated the document and gave it to me. I knew that it and a nickel couldn't get me a ride on the Staten Island Ferry. But it offered some psychological comfort.

"I'm sorry," he finally said. "I don't know what prompted all this, but I've been a little edgy lately."

"Why are you edgy?"

"Because I saw someone in a car across the street most of yesterday."

"Probably some pimp."

"Maybe, but I figure that the only way they can catch us is by counting exactly how many people come in over the course of a day and then checking it with our figures."

"Maybe we should stop for a while."

"Well, you can if you want, but we're very close and time's getting shorter. I'm making a dash for the finish line."

"Then I'm with you."

"Well, you're no use to me like this. Straighten things out with Ternevsky, heal some, and then I'll give you your shifts back."

"Fine."

"Oh, by the way," he concluded, "I heard that Tanya's going to be back in town in a couple days."

"Who?"

"Tanya," he said and then I remembered how I had fraudulently gotten the job. "We'll all get together."

"Great," I replied blandly. I had enough to sweat over for the time being. I told Miguel I was staying with the fictitious Donny, but that I was broke and needed a couple bucks. Miguel opened the petty cash box, and counted out five twenty dollar bills. If memory served, that much should be able to float me for the better part of the week if I ate shitty food and checked into the Sloane House on Thirty-fourth. Even though it was a bleak outlook, I thanked him and told him all would be fine. I'd be well soon and wouldn't disappoint his faith in me. With one hand on the cane and the other on the unclaimed documentation in my pocket, I made my way out of the theater.

It was now about five, rush hour, and the recurrent nightmare of a packed subway seemed unbearable. I took a cab to the Sloane House; my bruised body begged for that one indulgence. But the cabby knew only two speeds: accelerate like a rocket and stop on a dime. After all the potholes, I felt like a golf ball after a tournament. Abandoning the cab on Thirty-fourth and Eighth, I breached through the repeated breakers of retreating commuters heading toward Penn Station and aimed my cane toward a cheap deli with blinking Christmas lights circling a big poster in the window written in day-glow pink, "Cold cut sandwiches, only $1!" I went in and asked for a dozen sandwiches.

"What kind?" a drab Arab asked.

"Bologna, liverwurst, salami, and ham—all on rye with mustard." All the processed meats looked alike, but didn't look like anything resembling meat. For dessert, I got two boxes of Entenmann's chocolate chip cookies and a big bag of Wise potato chips. It was enough to convert someone to anorexia. They shoved the shit in a white plastic bag and it came to eighteen bucks. I walked over to the Sloane House. The front desk was thronged with a group of foreign students passing through New York for a couple days or so. I stayed closely behind them. Then came my turn, "Where are you from?"

"Here."

"I'm sorry, but the Sloane House is only for people from out of town." I quickly took out the bogus wallet. Sven had a New Jersey driver's license. "I'm sorry, I thought you said where was I presently. I'm from"—I checked the address—"Fort Lee."

"Why don't you go home?"

"I want to visit for a while."

"May I see your ID?" I showed her Sven's driver's license.

"You don't look anywhere near thirty-six."

"Thank you. The living's been easy," I said, hunching over my cane. She let me sign; she then told me more rules and details and said I could either pay up front or pay on a day-to-day basis. I paid for four days in advance, which left me with about ten bucks to rebuild my life after I had recovered.

"Don't you have any luggage?" the desk clerk asked. I held up my white bag of groceries and explained that I travelled lightly. She made me sign a small white piece of paper and gave me a room on the eleventh floor. I waited for the elevator, which took forever, and soon found my tiny room and locked the door behind me. The narrow view of a courtyard emptying into a parking lot could make a Salvation Army Band suicidal. Tying a knot around my food bag, I let it dangle out the window in order to keep it preserved during the length of my convalescence.

A towel was provided by the hotel, so I stripped down to my bruises and bandages for a shower. With my right hand gripping the towel and the cane in my left, I limped out through the hall to the communal bathroom. Passing the stalls and sinks I moved toward the rear, approaching a racket of babbling voices, but I couldn't make out a single word. The shower room was tiled water-tight with a single large drain in the center of the floor. Everything tilted toward the center. Grouped around the drain was a crew of Indian-looking sailors who were squatting naked scrubbing their salty uniforms against the rough floor just as their fathers probably had. Under the spout furthest away from them, I carefully washed away all the caked pus and dried blood. As the water jetted against my skin, I felt increasingly more sensitive. I figured that pain killers had to be among the dose of pills I was given at the hospital that morning. When their effects began to taper, agony slowly replaced it. As I stuck my face under the stream of water, the dull pain reminded me that my nose was broken. The pain started getting worse and aside from feeling faint I realized that the hot water was making the bruises swell and the unhealed scabs were reopening. Nodding farewell to the crew, I returned to the front part of the bathroom.

Gingerly I dried off and found dabs of blood on the towel. Relying increasingly on the cane, I slowly made it back to my room and locked the door. It was dark out and I didn't turn on the lights. Slowly, carefully, I balanced myself on the hard bed. It reminded me of Helmsley's hard couch and that reminded me of Helmsley. As I got tangled in the skein of memories I slipped toward sleep. Still in that intermediary state, I suddenly saw all those boots raining down on me and bolted up painfully into a seated position, wide awake. Slowly I angled up and with the cane moved over to the window. Only the city lights were visible, and over low roof tops, and through that empty lot in the distance, I could see tiny cars flowing down some avenue. A black sky of night crushed the scene. I hated long views of life when the infinite overwhelms the finite subjects. Not even forever lasts forever, and again I thought no matter what I do, someday I'd be nothing.

Aside from all the bad luck, I was a shamelessly ordinary guy, wholly dispensable. Counterparts of me must have inhabited all times and places. Packs of me must have malingered through the Mayan, the Minoan and Babylonian civilizations—societies that flourished and spanned centuries with vast cities, expansive domains, and great armies—now even those great cultures were barely known. Once again, I felt entirely severed from old mankind and needed some kind of distraction. I thought of all the little comforting thoughts that Helmsley had passed along to me, with the help of Plato and the greats: "Beauty is truth" and crap like that.

But Helmsley had committed suicide, so he must've been wrong somewhere in the addition. For tentative peace and sedation, I ended up abusing the sacred memories of a young, leggy girl that I had known years ago back home. Then I took another stab at sleep and, after bolting up once more with the boots dream, I finally punctured through into hard sleep.

A tearing pain awoke me almost twenty-four hours later when I tried turning my head. A steady ooze of blood and other humors that had loosened during the shower had solidified and fused my head with the pillow. My sinuses felt sealed as if by cement. I felt like I had just awakened from a coma. Other pains, new and great, trumpeted as I tried to move.

The regress report: My back was a shattered windshield with nerves, the stitches in my thigh were cold and sticky. The right side of my rib cage, which looked as if it had boot-shaped tattoos, was not the same shape it was when I went to sleep, the loose bones had shifted. All the medication was gone from my system and now the vultures were descending. Still lying supine, I slowly worked the pillow out from the pillow case and wrapped it around my head like a turban. I limped naked through the hall, clinging to my cane, and passed a group of fascinated Europeans en route to the bathroom. Under a warm shower I slowly peeled the pillow case off my face and head. I could hear the Europeans in the adjacent toilets; wonderful people—free of hangups, like shitting together.

I limped back, dripping through the hall, too much in pain to mind the cold. Back in my room I locked the door and dried off. I ate one of the ledge sandwiches, lay down, and went back to sleep without a pillow.

For the next three days or so, I slept without a pillow and awoke to increasing pain. The ledge sandwiches, which slowly filtered the New York air, tasted more and more like car fumes. The slow persistent pain made sleep increasingly shallow, until it dwindled into just a constant dazed state of repose. On the morning of the fourth day I awoke exhausted to a knock at the door.

"Sven Cohen," asked a voice behind the door.

"Who is it?" I called from the bed.

"You're paid up until noon today. If you wish to continue your visit please come down to the front desk and re-register."

Convalescence was over. In the space of the next hour or so I tried to get up; my back and the other conspiring pains limited my moves. The aching and pulsating muscles were too swollen for the tight skin. Rising in order to get the last ledge sandwich was excruciating. As I chewed it down, I hungrily remembered the menu of prescriptions that I tossed out upon release from the hospital, pain killers probably among them. Checking through the pockets of my pants, I found ten dollars and fifty-three cents. My body was a study in pain. In order to limit the suffering, I sat very still at the bed's edge. With little else to do, I differentiated the pain into three levels. First, there were the sharp sporadic stabs that dug deep through my lower back without warning. This pain was the worst and I could find no remedy for it. Next, there was the blunt throbbing, which was like having a toothache in my arms and legs. I found that lying very still could limit the throbbing, but in exchange I had uncontrollable twitches. Lastly, there were the scabs, which probably masked most of my face and head. There was a fiery sensation like a very bad sunburn, but next to the two other, more aggressive, pains this was only a trifle and was soothed by the cool air.

Spiritually the only difference between dying and healing is the energy to resist. I was running dangerously low on this energy. The doctor was right, I never should have left that hospital and if I didn't get into one soon, I could conceivably die.

I spent the remaining hour dressing, and then with the help of my cane, which was my only luggage, I hobbled over to the elevator and down to the front desk. Upon returning my room key and signing out, I asked him where the nearest hospital was.

"Probably Saint Vincent's over on Twelfth." But I already had an outstanding balance there, which I couldn't pay.

"Do you know of any other hospital? Aside from that one and Beth Israel," I had already gotten my calf sewn together there.

"Boy, you're picky. Roosevelt, I suppose, over on Fifty-ninth and Eighth."

I thanked him, left, and waited on the corner for a cab to Roosevelt Hospital. I was down to six dollars when I finally, slowly got out of that cab in front of the Emergency entrance.

I used that cane to the fullest as I hobbled through a full waiting room to the nurse sitting behind a wall with a sliding glass. I saw gurneys in the hall behind her with still bodies on them. Realizing that I had to compete with all this suffering, I dramatically moaned and rasped about my sufferings. With minimal eye contact, she asked me several academic questions and told me to have a seat. Most of the people were just sitting quietly. It was hard at first glance to guess why they were there. I took the last available seat, next to the quietest inmate, an old guy who was very still and very white. A Puerto Rican child sitting on his mother's knee was holding her with both arms, whining in a sustained key. His mother was pressing a rag against his bleeding forehead and rocking him back and forth. Another man was quietly contorting his face in order to restrain his pain. As time tortured on, the little things took greater proportion; more people came, few left. The still, white man was stiller and whiter. The bleeding child required another rag and his plaintive cry dropped an octave. The facial contortionist was now venting his woe in twisting his arms and limbs; I sensed that his pains were abdominal.

I tried not to look at the new people. We had waited longer and I wasn't going to empathize with any new suffering. At one point, one of the recent entries started crying aloud. He was a black infant, and his mother started rocking him, but finally put her hand over his mouth in order to silence him. People appeared guilty and ashamed that they were sick and weak. I closed my eyes and tried to think about only nice things until I heard something disgusting. It was a rattling sound, phlegm deep in someone's throat. Above me a young guy was leaning against the wall. He was well-dressed, wearing a three-piece suit; his tie was slack around his neck and the top buttons of his shirt were undone. I could see that his T-shirt was covered with sweat. His eyes were closed and I watched him concentrating on breathing, accepting only the little pockets of oxygen his lungs permitted. He looked about my age. I knew he was going through an asthmatic attack because my sister had had asthma. I rose and steered him into my seat. With his eyes closed he took it. All his energy was focused on the breaths.

"Would you like some water?" I asked.

He nodded yes. I went over to the fountain. Filling a Dixie cup, I limped back over and gave it to him. Then I walked over to the nurse and asked her whether or not she had forgotten about me.

"There are people in front of you."

"Okay, did you forget about them?"

"Look, we're understaffed and overloaded. I'm here on mandatory overtime myself." Before she could continue, someone started hollering from down the corridor behind her. A gurney had appeared at the ambulance entrance. She ran over, joining a group in white who were working on the body as they wheeled it in. Turning into a side room, I watched through a door ajar as they stuck tubes into the body and cut off the clothes. Then the door was closed.

Pain or no, it cost too much to stay there. I couldn't compete. In fact, I felt stronger witnessing how much farther others had ventured into agony, realizing how much farther I could go. As I walked down Eighth Avenue, under the twilight sky, street lights slowly started flipping on automatically. The sidewalk was empty, but the street was crowded with cars racing homebound. For no apparent reason, I suddenly remembered that tonight was the night of the contributor's party for the *Harrington*. If Miguel went to the party, he'd discover my deceit in getting published. When he added that to the Ternevsky scandal, Miguel might begin piecing together what kind of person I was: someone not to be trusted. While thinking about Ternevsky, I remembered that I was still an outlaw and only Janus could issue clemency. At a corner public phone, I dialled her and put my finger to the clicker; if any male voice answered I was ready to hang up, but she did answer.

"Can you speak?"

"Yes, and I'm so happy. Ternevsky's proposed to me. We're going to Europe and there we'll be married."

"Just tell me one thing," I interrupted. "Am I still being hunted by the cops?"

"No, not anymore. When Sergei calmed down, I reexplained it. I told him we both got drunk, but he threw out your clothes just the same. He made me take an AIDS test."

"All my clothes are gone?"

"Yeah, then we both cried and he proposed to me. Isn't it wonderful? I'm now Mrs. Ternevsky. God, I am so pleased. I wanted this all along."

"All along?" I asked.

"Sure, I now feel some legitimacy."

"But he's old enough to be your father, and you said yourself that he's a horrible lover and he just uses you."

"I said we use each other."

"How about us?" I asked.

"We had a wonderful time and now it's over."

"But if I had the same amount of money and all…"

"Shit," she suddenly whispered, "I just heard the elevator, I've got to go."

"Good luck," I replied, and hung up slowly.

I searched through my pockets for another quarter in order to call Miguel and see what developments had occurred in the last four days. But I couldn't find another quarter. After the conversation with Janus, I had this overwhelming fear. In my back pocket, crumpled up, I found the legal document he signed stating my interest in his company. With cane in hand, and pain in back, I went over to Columbus Circle and caught the IRT number one to Fourteenth. I then hobbled down the long uriney tunnel to the L, which I took to Third Avenue. Walking up to the box office window, I saw the face of a young white lady, which was a race we'd never hired before in filling this post. I smiled at her.

"Four dollars," she commanded rather aggressively.

"Be careful," I replied. "You never know when you might be talking to an employer."

"Four dollars!" she repeated with added hostility.

"I'm the other manager," I replied and tried to grin. "Is Miguel in?"

"Who?"

"Miguel?"

"Miguel, oh yes Miguel. Yes, I was told about you, one second." Miguel had hired a dope I decided as I walked through the center door and down the corridor to the office. Opening the door was a two-way shock. I jumped back a bit and a nerdy guy leaning back in the manager's chair bolted upright. Miguel replaced me, was the first thought that entered my head.

"Where's Miguel?" I demanded angrily.

"Oh yes, Miguel. One second, I'll get him." He rose. "Please take a seat, I'll be back in a moment." He dashed out and I leaned back in his swivel chair. But immediately I felt something strange. The surroundings had been altered. Where the hell was the Yin Yang calendar? Gone too were the refrigerator and the TV. A lot of little things were missing, items that epitomized Miguel's personality. There were neither granola crumbs along the desk top, nor herbal cigarette butts rubbed out in an improvised ashtray. Who the hell was the new box office girl? Where was everybody?

In front of me, piled up high on the desk, was a stack of files and the theater's financial records spanning the last five years. Pushing them to one side, and seeing the wall behind it, only then did the mystery vaporize. A new digital dial system was encased in recently packed plaster. They must have caught Miguel, and I was next. I noticed that one of the buttons on the business phone was lit up. The nerd was probably notifying Ox on the extension in the box office. I slipped into the darkness of the theater. I was being captured by the new manager and his white box office woman standing near the exit. The only way out was across the roof. I limped up the steps to the projectionist booth and banged quickly.

"Who the fuck is it?"

I announced myself and she opened. "We went through this before. You're supposed to call up in advance."

"Sorry, I forgot." I entered quickly and shut the door behind me.

"What do you want?" she said. And then inspecting my enfeebled state, asked, "What the fuck happened to you?"

"I slipped while breakdancing," I replied. "What happened to Miguel?"

"I think that he was ripping off money. All I know is that there were a bunch of police cars and they closed the theater yesterday and apparently fired everyone. They even requested a new projectionist, but the union stood behind me all the way. I'm surprised they didn't fire you." Poor Miguel, was all I could think.

"You didn't turn him in did you?" she asked me.

"Of course not."

"Then why didn't they fire you?"

"They're probably going to soon. I think they just want me to break in the new managers."

"Why then did you have to ask me what happened to Miguel?"

"I wasn't here yesterday—you were. I just said that they asked me to break this new guy in."

"It's all a damned shame. See what happens when you don't have a union to protect you? By the way, be sure to fill them in on the union contract and my rights in dealing with them."

"It's already done. Listen, I'm a little busy right now and I've got a lot to do."

"Like what?"

"They're waiting for a report on the condition of the roof."

"Oh, they've finally got around to wanting to fix that, and you're probably going to take all the credit."

"What credit?"

"I was the one that told you that roof was leaking. That's what credit."

"Calm down. I mentioned you in my preliminary report." As I started climbing up the metal ladder, she kept hollering things up to me. While I undid the binding ropes and pushed the hatch free, I heard her nagging about the new manager looking like a repressed homophobe. What the hell did she want me to do, convert him? Despite my pains, I scrambled up and got beyond hearing distance. I wasn't sure if eccentric people became projectionists or if the job made them that way. I supposed long hours in closed quarters would effect anybody. Looking out the front of the theater, under the flapping "Zeus" flag, I saw a cop car double parked. Next to it, another car pulled up and a fat little guy plopped out. It was Ox. Then the passenger door opened and a slim young male figure got out. He looked just like Miguel. Both of them quickly went into the theater. What the fuck was Miguel doing down there? He was supposed to be in jail.

Quickly I limped around old tar cans and other debris toward the back of the building. I slowly worked my way down the rusty, rickety fire escape. It ended in the pitch blackness of some alley. I tossed down my cane. It took too long to hit bottom; I estimated a drop of about eight feet. Stretching myself from the bottom rung, I released and hit the ground on all fours. I painfully started to move. The fall awakened pains that had been napping. I picked up my cane and slapped it against the ground like a blind man. Following the alley to a large cyclone fence, I realized that the street was over this wiry hindrance.

I tossed my cane over the fence and then started up painfully. The wire dug deep into my skin and when I got to the top I felt a tiny stab. The top was meshed with barbed wire.

Slowly working my way through the darkness, I went as far as I could go before having to commit blood. Grabbing onto barbed wire and cutting yourself wasn't easy. It was one of those things that you simply couldn't order yourself to do, like trying to hold your breath unto death. So I just hung there and made a bunch of false starts, until I heard those walkie talkies in the distance. That meant that the cops had combed through the theater and finally bumped into the obnoxious projectionist, who probably demanded to know, "What the hell is going on? This goes against all union rules." And finally someone filled her in and she explained that the culprit was on the roof. In two minutes they would be here on this cyclone fence.

Pain upon pain, gash into scars into bruise through cloth and flesh. And then came the hope and then the chance and with strength, will, fear, anger—all I could muster—despite the barbs hooking into just-sealed scabs, I shoved everything into that puncture of a chance. I heard the sound of feet scampering down the fire escape so I dropped hard over the fence to the street. I grabbed my cane lying next to me and started limp/hop/running over to Fourth Avenue where I hailed a God-sent cab and was delivered.

FIFTEEN

"Where to?" the cabbie asked after I sat silently as he drove for a couple blocks.

"Just away," I replied quietly.

"But where?" the cabbie asked. The cab whizzed up Fourth Avenue until it turned into Park Avenue South.

"Thirty-eighth and Broadway." I randomly picked the coordinates so at least the cab had somewhere to go. But where was I going to go? What was left? When I realized that three dollars and fourteen cents were left, I had the cabbie stop when the red digits on the meter came to two eighty-five and gave him all my money. I got off at Thirty-first and Madison.

All I had was a cane and a worthless piece of paper declaring that I owned one third of a theater in Hoboken. My entire life was one ridiculous mirage after another, and after all these surefire plans of success sitting on the back burner, all I could do was rip that fucking paper to tiny bits. I limped along those streets, cold and depressed, my clothes shredded, with paranoia setting in like rigor mortis. Did Miguel get out of the car with the Ox? If so, why?

While backtracking to remember how I happened to remember to call Miguel, I realized it was due to the *Harrington* party. By elimination, it was the last place to go. So I limped over to a public phone and called information and got the locale. The office was on Twenty-third and Third Avenue.

By the time I limped over there it was ten o'clock, early for a Friday night party. I felt increasingly depressed with each limp. What was I going to do after the party? Where was I going to go? The offices were located in a renovated brownstone across from the School of Visual Arts and they must have been banking on some big bucks, because they hired an adorable little door/valet girl who for a single instant let me forget all my woes. She had an adolescent face and a body in full bloom, a unique distortion of perfection. She sat on a fold-out chair reading *Lolita* with a bored expression, just waiting to be devoured. My heart swelled to its bloody capacity as I got closer. But when filthy and broken old me finally hobbled up she scowled. Still holding the book she asked, "What do you want?"

"I'm a contributor."

"Bullshit."

I held my cane hard. There was only love at first sight, beyond that disillusion, pain, and death. I told her my name and she looked on the list, but couldn't find it. Then I told her Miguel's name, since Owensfield gave him the invitation, and apparently she located it.

"One second," she said and addressing the intercom had Owensfield paged. In a tux and with a longstem goblet of sparkling apple cider, Owens-field eventually arrived.

"What the hell happened to you?" He sounded so paternal.

"Well, Pop, I crashed the car on the way to the prom. I hope you don't mind driving Mom's car awhile."

He led me in past the bored beauty. I could hear the music upstairs. It sounded like a live salsa band, but he led me to a side room downstairs. Flipping on a light switch, a bathroom was revealed.

"There's a razor and a lot of nice-smelling things in the medicine chest. And also take a shower. If you need anything else..."

"Actually, if you can spare a shirt..."

He said he'd be back in a minute. Taking my coat off was like wrestling a cougar from my back. It was too painful to undress, and since my shirt was already shredded up, it was easier to tear it off. The shower curtains had an *I Love New York* motif, the temperature of water obeyed the commands of the knobs, and there were no sailors scrubbing their uniforms. But all the old pains were still in effect, and there was the same runoff of blood and filth. Owensfield knocked at the door and swiftly put some clothes on a hook. He told me to try them on after I was well cleaned.

"I'll come down and check on you in a while."

I thanked him and made use of all the hospitalities. A half hour later I was ready, but no matter how hard I washed I couldn't wash away bruises. I was still stuck in the same battered body. I sat on the toilet seat and tried to control the pain until Owensfield appeared and looked me over. He applied some medication and some cosmetics and when he could do no more he said, "Okay, let's go."

He led me upstairs to a large open area, which was an office space during the day. It was filled with cavorting, money-heavy people who didn't limp, and had a place to go afterwards, people who had never been wanted by the police and always had a destination when they got into a cab.

I felt immensely self-conscious, a beetle in a beehive, only these drones had no stingers so I just kept to myself. To combat all the nervousness and irritations, I quickly located the bar. The bartender, some little preppie trying to make points in the real world, gave me one measured shot of vodka. When I asked him for a second, he gave me a nasty look. When I asked for a third, he took his time about it, and when I swallowed that and asked for a fourth, he said no.

I went behind the bar and poured myself a generous glass of vodka. He tried grabbing the bottle out of my hand, but I yanked it away.

"You are not permitted behind the bar," he declared. In reply I downed the glass and opened a virgin bottle of Glenlivet. "You're not permitted here. What are you, stupid?"

I was in one of those shit-faced moods that drunks get into when they suddenly see everyone equal in the eyes of God, and they realize that they were sent to distribute His wealth. I decided that the only way I was leaving from behind the bar was by being physically removed. Considering the condition that I was in, that wouldn't have taken much. The novice bartender, though, approached Owensfield, who, in the middle of a conversation, swatted him away. I stayed put, and soon the kid realized that there was no one else to appeal to. He returned, pissed and silent. I started drinking more heavily just to spite him.

After about twenty minutes, I could no longer keep balance, so with the use of the cane I tried balancing myself. But a cane is only as sober as its master. I flopped down on some people sitting on the couch. One lady got indignant and threw her booze on me. As I hobbled away a young lady with a beautiful face mumbled to me, "Good for you, serves the bitch right." I nodded in agreement, but I didn't want to talk to anybody.

"What's your name anyway?" she asked.

"*Je ne parle pas anglais.*"

"*Je parle français.*"

"*Je ne parle* anything."

"Fuck you, too," the beautiful face said. Now she could link up with the first bitch, and they could both discuss what a bastard I was. I drank more alcohol. The figurative seems to become the literal when drunk. My sails swelled, my keel rose and dipped, the winds blew, and the waves pounded over my decks. A drunken vertigo spun me, the booze was a typhoon, a whirlpool, and ultimately a tidal wave. Drinking more and more and more, I vomited in an ice bucket behind the bar and drank more. I could batten my hatches no longer and tried to go to the bathroom. I stumbled through the party to a smaller room in the back, which seemed to have a haystack of coats. Upon them I collapsed, forgot about the toilet and dug a foxhole in the cloth and furs and fell deep asleep.

"Where's my coat? Where's my wrap? Where's my jacket?" Questions bombarded my little sleep, but the drunkenness provided extra cover. Slowly people plucked at the haystack of clothes. Gradually I got cold and began to shiver.

"Where the hell is my boa?" I heard some whiny Queens accent screaming. "Where's my boa...where's my coat...where's my..."

"Fuck your where!" I mumbled.

"Who is that!" she hollered. "Irving, there's a human being under that stole."

Someone removed the thing above me and my face was exposed. Through squinty eyes I saw a blurry Helmsley. "Helmsley? Is that really you?"

"You know this guy?" Helmsley asked Owensfield.

"Helmsley?" Owensfield asked. "You mean Helmsley Micinski? I heard he committed suicide."

"You know Helmsley?"

"I knew of him. We published some translations of his. He was a good translator."

"Why didn't you publish any of his poetry?"

"Get off the lady's wrap," the guy who looked like Helmsley said. Helmsley was dead.

"Please get off the lady's wrap," Owensfield corrected the fellow.

"Why didn't you publish any of his poetry?" I asked Owensfield.

"What poetry?"

"Get the hell off the coat," the Helmsley look-alike said. This time he grabbed me by my shoulder and wheeled me around onto my feet.

"Helmsley was constantly sending out poetry. He had a file full of form rejections from the *Harrington*."

"I never saw one poem from Helmsley Micinski."

"He wrote more than anyone I knew."

"Well, he never sent me a thing. I heard he wrote some decent poems back in the sixties, when he was just a kid in his teens. Word was that he was finished. Now please, the party's winding down, try sobering up a bit."

I slowly made my way over to the bathroom and peed my guts out while wondering whether Helmsley had lied to me. Maybe lie is a harsh word since he was his own victim. Writing was everything to him and maybe he couldn't write. He was always preparing, making notes, making tedious outlines, doing subtle character studies, forever sharpening the knife that, if he never truly used, he would one day have to turn on himself. To come to terms with the fact that he was burnt out at thirty would be devastating. As I drunkenly thought this, the squawking lady's words were still echoing in my ears, Where's this, where's that? I sat on the toilet seat and murmured, "Where?" The word seemed to be a philosophy unto itself, and all the implications right down to the homonyms seemed to embrace Helmsley:

> When your
>> ware
>> wear
>> where
>>> from there?

I then pulled my pants up and did the buckle and belt and rejoined the party. Lying on the bar was a pen and napkin. I scribbled down the little poem and stuck it in my pocket. Retreating back to the couch, I reclined in a pain-minimizing posture and napped a bit until I started feeling the earth rumbling. I awoke to a bunch of people hauling the couch I was on. They were clearing the room to dance. I rolled off the moving couch and landed on the floor: pain. Owensfield came over and after he helped me to my feet, I asked him, "When is my poem being published?"

"In this issue."

"When is that making its debut."

"What do you think this party is all about?"

"It's out?"

"Eureka!" From thin air he seemed to produce a copy. I grabbed it and thumbed to the table of contents, no name. I skimmed the magazine, but I couldn't find my name anywhere. Snatching it back, he quickly turned to the poem and handed it to me. I recited it proudly and drunkenly. Then I noticed the byline and started worrying, "Thi... who? Who is that?"

"That's you, remember."

"Like hell it is." It was a bizarre name—Thi Doc Sun. It was as approximate to my name as Cassius Clay was to Muhammad Ali. He took the magazine, pronounced the name aloud and asked, "Isn't that you?"

"No, but maybe I should change my name to that." Thi? I drunkenly recalled the name from somewhere, and then I remembered; it was the Cambodian night porter.

"God, I'm sorry. I promise you, I'll print an errata in the next issue."

"It doesn't even matter," I laughed. "The only reason I wanted to do it in the first place was to impress Helmsley." But it did matter. I thought for a minute about Janus and Glenn, I proudly told them both about my getting published. Now, if they bothered to check, they'd find out I was a fraud. Poetic justice.

Owensfield brought me over to the bar and secured a very expensive bottle of booze, which he uncorked and poured into shot glasses, "This is my favorite."

He poured more drinks and we talked awhile. Finally he mentioned that he had heard several people compliment my poem. He summed it up, saying, "For thirty-four words it offers a raw glimpse into gutter-level East Village."

"Glad you liked it. You know, I've just completed another poem. It's only a couple of words really." I took out the napkin and gave it to him. He mumbled it aloud.

"When your ware wear, where from there." He thought about it a moment and said, "There's not a word here about East Village."

"I have a broad sweep."

"When we want a broad sweep we get a broom." He handed me the napkin back. He was bored with me and he walked away, mingling with others. I chuckled drunkenly, considering that I had been fired from the theater and there was no way Owensfield would ever get his film presented. I remained loyal to the bar. The preppie bartender apparently had abandoned it and people were helping themselves. I was so drunk that I was somebody else, but that person was still conscious, so there was still something left to liquidate. A blur of bottles and glasses, somebody was reading poetry, but all I could recall was a couple lines of white dust.

SIXTEEN

I've never been able to recollect going to sleep, but I'll never forget waking up the next morning. I had had my unrestrained go at the drugs and alcohol, and now they had their go at me. I don't know the clinical terms, but the result was some kind of partial amnesia which lasted for the next couple of weeks. My memory of those weeks to come remains choppy. I vividly remember waking that pivotal morning because of several foreboding images and sensations which I made into dreams. The first "dream" was being back in a hospital, perhaps Roosevelt Hospital, and sitting very still next to someone, perhaps that poor Yuppie, because he was coughing and hacking uncontrollably. I just heard the constant groaning sounds, but I never saw a doctor or a nurse. Perhaps we were all just put in some kind of quarantine ward. The next dream was the earthquake, a long snake-like torso that kept sinking downward. Then I dreamt that I was in Ternevsky's hot tub, and then I got very cold and itchy.

When I reached down through the haze to scratch, I realized that I was drenched. Slowly I slithered out from under that colossal mudslide of sleep. I kicked down that wet sheet, pried my body out of the bed, and rotated to a sitting position. Instinctively I groped for my cane, but it was nowhere bedside. The drunken dome of my skull was feverish, and my eyes were hot gel. Although I had a basic control, simple logic, and partial recall, I had not yet detoxified. The gravitational pull was never stronger, inertia never more tempting, but slowly I assembled a whole picture. Old men on double decker cots were regimented tightly around the room so that it held a maximum capacity. I had peed in the underside of one such cot, I was naked and wet; slowly all these details dripped onto the sizzling hot frying pan of my brain. On my hands and knees, I felt for my clothes, but I found nothing. I was sure of only the floor. This I pursued to a wall and got to my feet and fumbled around the double beds, only able to open my eyes for long blinks. I was cold but it didn't matter. Hand over hand, I moved along the rough wall toward a distant door frame of light from which I heard a groaning sound.

When I finally got to the door, I had to readjust to the fluorescent lights, which overexposed the filthy, tiled bathroom. On the very first of a row of unpartitioned toilet bowls an old black guy was making miserable sounds as he tried to shit. I held to the wall, squinted at the floor, and limped over toward the farthest bowl. The floor tiles were cracked. The opposite side of the room was lined with marble urinals. I went to the last where I was about to pee when suddenly my stomach started kicking. Barely had I turned around when my face started spilling gunk. I almost fell head first into the crapper. For several minutes I was stuck there in spasms, as all, dating back to those ledge sandwiches, vomited up. "Whoo wee, I remember gettin' dat sick once," I heard someone behind me say. After finishing, I turned to a gathering of derelicts who were watching.

Slowly I got to my feet and could feel my bloated bladder bursting free. Turning around, I just made it in time for the high arc of urine to hit the marble urinal. In spite of all the agony, all the aches, in spite of the hangover that made my eyes feel like they were spilling out of my head, the transparent piss that was racing out of me brought me to new heights of glory and ecstasy.

"Did they start serving yet?" the black guy at the end shitter asked the exiting spectators.

"Not yet, but yous better hurry. Ernie already turned on the lights."

"That Ernie's a scoundrel!" laughed the old guy, as he tugged up his trousers.

I hobbled over to one of a line of sinks. The damned sink only had a single faucet; a cold water faucet that had one of those fucking overwound springs that would snap off unless a hand actively applied a constant life-force to hold it open. I jerked with that fucking faucet, trying to wash my face and body, but it was no damned good. Finally I went over to the toilet and took a wad of coarse toilet paper and used it to plug up the drain. Then I filled the dirty basin with cold water and submerged my wounded face in it. When I finally took my face out of that icy water, I was still drowsy as hell so I gave the face a couple stinging slaps. After that, I stroked my fingers slowly over my stubbled and scabbed face, and looking at the blood on my fingertips, I realized that I had broken open a couple of scabs.

"They serving!" I heard someone yell outside. Because there were only those sanitary, "deodorizing" blow driers, I gently patted my face dry with the coarse toilet paper.

Outside the bathroom, a network of fluorescent lights revealed a large barracks-like room packed with men, mainly black and old. Many of the beds were already empty. I took a sheet off one and wrapped it around my naked body. Then I followed the others out to the stairwell. There was a long motionless line along the right banister. I got on the end of the line and waited, trying to hold that filthy sheet around me, toga style. It kept slipping off. Several times, I had to move up a step because the big guys were cutting in down in the front. Finally the line started moving, one step every minute or so.

"There's my main man."

"Shake my hand, Ernie."

"Go get 'em Ern."

"Hey Ernie, is you still datin' dat Loni Anderson girl?"

A fat middle-aged guy with apple cheeks, cauliflower ears, and a potato nose wore a fresh T-shirt and a white apron, and as he moseyed up along the procession of broken and dilapidated men, each one either offered a hand or a comment. I held the banister tight in one hand and the sheet tight in the other, and waited for Ernie.

"Where the hell are my clothes?"

"Well, would you looky here," Ernie said in a loud and humiliating volume and added, "New Jersey's awake."

"Huh?"

"What are you talking about?" I asked.

"This ain't Saint Patty's day and you ain't at McSorley's. I'm talking about how on every major weekend the cops dump me with you drunken Jersey boys. Do me a favor when you get home and tell your friends that before they pass out here, the least they can do is wear an ID tag. Even luggage has that much. Bed space is a hot commodity in these parts."

"Hold on." He talked too fast for my shaky comprehension.

"You hold on. When things calm down you can call Mommie and Daddy in my office—collect."

"No one I know would accept the charges," I replied drunkenly, but he didn't seem to hear. He just kept walking away down the stairs, and I stood there holding the banister.

Finally I could see the front of the line moving down the stairs. The men were disappearing into a doorway. When I went through the doorway, I first picked up a tray, then a bowl, mug, spoon, and napkin. Next, someone in white put a small carton of milk on the tray, and the next guy in white put a full ladle of oatmeal in the bowl, and another guy put an orange on the tray. The last guy filled the mug with coffee. Then I took a seat. There was no exchange of words. I had trouble doing this while holding the sheet around me. Men ate everything completely, but due to my sickness, I could only eat one or two bites of the oatmeal.

"You want the orange?" someone asked me, I shook my head no.

"Geez, let him have a chance to finish." Big Ernie appeared behind me.

"Da man say he didn't wan it."

"You can hold on to the orange until you get hungry," Ernie said to me.

"I got nowhere to put it," I replied, referring to my nakedness.

"Follow me, I guess it's time for that collect call."

"I got no one to call."

"What d'you mean?"

"I mean this is it." Ernie looked to the floor and was quiet for a moment. "You telling me you have no family?"

"Right."

"How 'bout friends?" I shook my head no. "You must be at least twenty-five."

"Twenty-three," I corrected.

"You seem like an intelligent, well-mannered white boy. Tell me how an intelligent white boy can live twenty-three years without a single friend? There must be someone."

"I ain't from here. I used to have friends, a lot of them. But..." My toga slipped, I caught it and tightened it around me again. He looked at me with pity and waved for me to follow. Leading me back up the stairs, he quickly took me to a dark and windowless side room. There, he flipped on a light revealing a mountain of old clothing.

"This is kinda the lost and found." He then paused and smiled and added, "Actually, it's more like the live and die. Take what you need. Winter ain't over yet."

"I know you don't have to do this. Thank you."

"If I let you go out like that," he said, "I'll have mini-cam crews down here doing their breaking story about how we set our boys naked to the streets."

He then left and I rummaged through the pile of old clothes, mainly rags. They were filthy and stinky and full of holes and fleas. I dressed in layers. The cleanest undergarment that I could locate was a pair of itchy wool plaid pants that had the seams sliced open. I put these on. Over them, I pulled on a pair of army khakis with a big shit-resembling tar stain over the ass. There were no finds in that pile. For an undershirt, I found a paint-speckled T-shirt that read, "I Survived The 1980 Transit Strike." Over that, I used a petroleum-based, fluorescent red short-sleeved shirt that felt carcinogenic. Over that, I put on first a sweater, then a jacket, then an overcoat. On my head, I placed a beanie. There were only two pairs of shoes that didn't have serious ruptures in them; a pair of hiking boots that smelled like something had died in them, and a clownishly floppy pair of white tennis shoes. There were no socks.

I left the sheet and walked back out to the auditorium. Ernie was nowhere to be seen. Some of the guys were filing out in small groups. Ernie had a point; there had to be someone out there. I had to sit awhile. Ever since that beating, my energy was depleted easily.

"Nice wardrobe." Ernie suddenly appeared.

"I'm sure I'll be laughing about it tonight and I'll make sure you're well compensated for your generosity."

"Are you going to be all right?"

"Oh sure, I must have someone out there. I mean, this is too absurd."

"Well, we're here if you need us."

"Thanks for last night, but there's no way I would've come in here of my own volition. I mean, my being here is an accident. I'm no...you know." He nodded and departed, so I followed a gob of men leaving. Out front, some men headed east, and some west, but most just hung out front. I walked over to the Bowery. Most of the guys were just standing around a big oil barrel with a fire in it. Some of the more industrious ones were washing the windshields of cars that had been trapped by the red light. I used to see them from inside cars and think they brought it on to themselves, and they probably did but now it didn't make a difference. I went over to the fire and warmed my hands with the group. I looked at their faces: idiots, criminals, retards, schizophrenics, paranoids, rejects, fuck-ups, broken-down failures. Alone, once children, never asked to be put on this earth, they ended up as jurors. Their lives were the verdict: the system, man, something had failed.

Heated, I walked away from the barrel and started walking west on Third as it turned into Great Jones. I passed the Bowery, passed Lafayette Street. On Broadway I vaguely recognized the restaurant on the corner with the big clean windows filled with yuppies, and then I remembered. I had eaten there with Ternevsky. It was Caramba.

Drifting up Broadway, past the youth industry, complete with all the latest fashion outposts, I was a ghost. I tried to look into eyes, but if anyone cast a fearful glance at me it was only so that they'd be sure they were avoiding me. I was no longer a member of the human club. But I had to get back in. I kept reassuring myself that if I thought hard enough I could find a solution. But I was working under a ruptured brain. Thoughts braced against the incomprehensible, straining to pick up a weight just an ounce too heavy for my thought muscles.

There had to be a way out. I had undaunting faith that by tonight I would be carefully bathed and then nestled away in a warm bed, a full meal, full in stomach. Someone would be comforting me.

When the dust settled, the most obvious choice emerged—Sarah. The circle seemed complete. She was the only possible person I could think of. A corner pay phone. I made a collect call.

I could hear her phone ringing and ringing until the operator finally asked me to call back later. I called another operator and again it rang repeatedly, and again the operator said call back. The operators were obviously screwing things up. I hung up and marched over to her apartment. When I finally found her building, I kept my finger on the door bell for about a half an hour, but got no answer. The front door was locked. I sat and waited on the chilly front stoop. Occasionally tenants passed by giving me the look—a filthy bum on their stoop.

Eventually as they passed I would rise, distancing them from the dreaded me. Finally as one old fellow was leaving I was able to catch the front door before it slammed shut. The doorbell had to be broken. I banged on Sarah's door for about five minutes. And then I just listened silently, not a creature was stirring, not even a cockroach.

Back on the front stoop, I thought about Sarah's phone ringing. Where the hell was the answering machine? Finally I went up to look at her mailbox. Her name was there, but tagged next to it was another name. She probably had adopted a new boyfriend. Quickly it neared five o'clock. People filled the streets streaming homeward. As Sarah's neighbors dashed back into the apartment, I noticed some of them mumbling between themselves. I could almost hear them, "Yeah, he's been hanging out here for hours."

As the street lights blinked on, I sat in front of Sarah's door and recalled how many times I had thoughtlessly strolled through this hallway on the way up to Sarah's apartment. Finally, despite or perhaps because of the cold, I started drifting to sleep.

Suddenly someone said, "Time to get up." A cop was standing over me with some lady behind him.

"No, officer." I rose to my feet. "I'm waiting for someone who lives here."

"Come on," the officer started swinging his night stick. "Get out."

"I'm waiting for Sarah Oleski in apartment five."

"She's no longer here," the lady standing behind the officer informed him.

"Where is she?"

"Hey, I'm not playing with you anymore," the officer said, and then he whacked me on the forearm; years before the Tompkins Square tumult.

"I just want to know where Sarah is. I was her boyfriend. I'm concerned." I was backing out of the building, cradling the forearm.

"She went off to school," the lady told the cop. School, she was going to graduate school. It all came back to me. And out in the cold I started walking. It was night now, and I had no idea what to do. I walked by the Zeus Theater. From across the street I watched guys enter and leave. Soon it was midnight. I started back to the Men's Shelter on Third Street. The big door was closed and locked. I knocked until someone answered. Quietly I was led into a room, where some guy asked some preliminary questions. I was required to take a shower. Then I put my clothes back on, as crappy as they were. They were all I had. I was assigned a bed, but I didn't sleep at all that night.

The next morning, I pissed and joined the line in the hall. When Ernie started walking up the stairs banging his ladle against the pot, I lowered my head so as not to be seen. My pride wasn't completely dead yet. I gulped breakfast down quickly and got a second helping. I then shoved my orange in my pocket and before Ernie could spot me I was out the door. I wasn't sure where I was going to spend the upcoming night, but felt there was no way I could return to that shelter. I spent the day walking around places I had known when I was alive. Even if I saw Glenn or someone, I wondered whether I would have the guts to approach them. That night I went over to the Path Train stop on Ninth Street and without paying I rode the train from terminus to terminus, over and over.

Back in the early eighties, the cash machine enclosures were not nearly as ubiquitous, so subways were the predominant sleeping sites. The Path was much cleaner than the New York subway, but it was also better policed. Several times I was thrown off the train. The next afternoon I was accompanied off the train at the Christopher Street station. The cop who escorted me had thrown me off the train earlier. He told me that if he found me sleeping in his train again, he would walk me into the tunnel and shoot me, and that in six months' time the rats would have completely devoured my body. I'm not sure if he was serious, but I admired his rich use of detail. I walked down Christopher to the river, where I envisioned old bodies floating on the surface. Manhattan on the Ganges. Some guy came up to me, and mumbled, "The Pier is closed at sunset."

I reentered the labyrinth of streets and started getting very hungry. Passing an outdoor Korean fruit stand, I carefully snuck up to the very edge and slowly put my hand on a cantaloupe. When I removed it, others came rolling down, and the cashier guy ran out at me with a big machete.

"I'm fucking hungry, asshole!"

"Fug yer!"

"My great great grandfather fought in the Civil War!" I yelled back before I limped away. He probably didn't even know about that war. Soon I spotted another street person holding shopping bags, an old ugly guy. With nothing else to do, I followed him. When he got to the corner, I watched him going through a garbage can. He ferreted out some kind of discarded food product, which he carefully scrutinized and then he only ate several bites. Fumbling through the garbage, he pulled out a couple beer cans, which he emptied and shoved in his shopping bag.

"How do you know you're not going to get sick eating that shit?" I stepped up and asked him. He only looked at me and then walked away; some were idiots, some were psychos, and some were just luckless.

Imposed distinctions started fading. Periodically I had to stand in a doorway or over a subway grating in order to thaw out a little. After that, I had about a fifteen minute duration before the cold started hurting again. Inspired by other foragers, I found a bag. I went from trash pile to trash pile rummaging for cans; I did this mainly because it was something to do. Only a couple of times did I actually cash in the cans for the nickel deposits. While working the can circuit down Greenwich Avenue, I looked in the window of the bookstore at Greenwich and Sixth Avenue and spotted the new issue of the *Harrington*. Leaving my bags outside, I went over to the magazine and flipped through the pages to my poem.

"Shoo! Out!" Looking up, I saw the cashier, a well-dressed guy with long wavy hair and wire-framed glasses.

"I wrote this poem. Want me to sign it?"

"No thanks," he replied, plucking the issue from out of my hand and escorting me out the door. It was then, while picking up my bag of cans, that I remembered. Owensfield was rich and he respected my talents. It didn't occur to me that he might feel screwed by the theater deal. I took the cans to a deli. The guy didn't want to cash them, but I started crying so he just handed me a quarter. I found a pay phone outside and got the number of the *Harrington* offices. Putting my quarter in the slot, I dialled for salvation. The receptionist answered.

"This is one of the contributors to the current issue," I said professionally. "I'd like to speak to Mister Owensfield."

"I'm sorry Mister Owensfield just left town."

"Left town!"

"I'm afraid so. He's on his first vacation in two years."

"When will he be back?"

"In about a month."

"A month!"

"The next issue doesn't come out for another three months. Rest assured, there's plenty of time for any submissions."

"No there isn't!" I groaned.

"Perhaps I can help you?"

"Listen," I said desperately, "I'm nothing, I'm a fucking street bum. I'm eating shit out of the garbage and I crap in doorways..." The phone went click. I had made a faulty approach.

Wandering, I begged, I looked for little bites here and there, for possible places to grab some shut-eye, for discarded garments that might come in handy. I addressed remote questions I never imagined I would have to consider: How badly does food have to be decomposed before it's no longer edible? How cold should I be before I need warmth? Shame diminished; I was becoming accustomed to expelling waste in public. Pain became a passive verb: I no longer hurt, I was just in pain. I hadn't really experienced hunger before, now it was a constant.

It was an interesting phenomenon to sit and watch streets flood with people, sidewalks that were bone dry just an hour earlier. Time, now, was something for those who could use it. At night, I would go through the exit door in the subways. Occasionally a cop would catch me. But they never arrested; sometimes they'd hit me. Usually they'd just throw me back out, a fish too small to keep. Then I'd just go to another subway station and go through. Now and then, at night, a cop would expel me from the train. Usually though, I'd awaken in a train packed with scrubbed, well-dressed people swarming around me. Instantly I'd know that I was heading toward the city and that there was daylight above the tunnel.

Slowly the world seemed to be curving around my view of it. I kept hearing people screaming my name, a name that had outlived its purpose since no one knew it. My identity was my experiences. Everyday sights were turning into aberrations of a past breaking through; garbage in front of a lamp post resembled my grandmother from a half block away. I could've sworn that a discarded pile of newspaper was my old dog.

SEVENTEEN

I avoided the cold, dark, and dangerous and adhered to the dry, warm, and lit. On the occasions when I misjudged the two I usually ended up incurring some form of pain. Even though diarrhea had set in and I'd gotten uncleanably filthy, the smell didn't affect me. Ever since Junior's pals had kicked my nose in, I barely smelled a thing. One night, though, I perceived this strange phantom odor of flesh decaying. I had a bad flea infestation and I had scratched my skin raw. Like a vegetable out of a fridge, I had started to rot. I had no preservatives, a poor shelf life. I was getting more sick, tired, dull, and pain was no longer even painful. Based on the fact that I didn't know how I was going to turn out, I should have been either helped or executed. Death is the final shield from life.

I was moving away from myself; silly ideas and images moved their way across the desert of my mind. I no longer had control; all I could do was watch them and react; sometimes I'd laugh, sometimes I'd cry. The great caravan of thoughts passed more and more rarely until soon there was just the great desert: tabula rasa.

Life became a brutal continuum. The chronic fragments—the streets, the garbage cans, the crowds, the subways, the police—were all indicative of a life closing, sealing like an old scab. All the fragments were piecing together for a final kill.

I clearly remember the morning that time resumed. Weeks, maybe months, had crumbled since that party at the *Harrington* offices. I was snoozing on a bench in Grand Central Station until I was awakened by a cop's night stick. The night stick wanted me to leave the terminal so I left and started walking westward.

Soon, I saw the great steps of the Public Library, and there I sat and watched the cars. I don't know why, but at one interval, when the lights turned green, I walked into the center of the street and looked down Fifth Avenue. I suppose I wanted to see where all the cars were going. That's when I saw the Washington Square Arch. As I watched cars speeding down Fifth Avenue, their roofs disappearing toward it, I realized that I was trying to picture the white hood of a car, a Mercedes! And that's when I saw it, the resurrection of the dead and the life of the world to come, Amen. After being on the brink for so long, after the bland and aching season of decay, in that distant arch I wiped my watery eyes and focused on the glimmer that wasn't death.

Moving more quickly and more determinedly than I had in weeks, I walked over to the IND station at Sixth and Forty-second Street, opened the exit gate, and entered. Soon an F train rolled in. I boarded and counted the stops: Thirty-fourth, Twenty-third, Fourteenth, West Fourth, Broadway-Lafayette, Second Avenue.... Here a cop boarded and looked at me. If he was a good cop he'd have tossed me off. I sat up stiff and formal trying to give the impression of having a destination. He got off at Jay Street and two stops later, at Carroll Street, before the train came to a halt I got up.

My feet were numb as I walked down that platform, but I couldn't stop the smile from my lips. For the first time in weeks, even years, every step had a meaning. Time and space were now finite. I was walking the shortest distance between two points. When I got up the stairs, I could see it in the distance and I could feel the relief. Sensations were beginning to return. I thought about these last couple of years. I had washed ashore here, formed a tiny beachhead for myself, and for an instant felt like I had a shot at the big time: an opportunity to get published, a classy abode, even part ownership of my own business. But swifter than it came, it went. Like a cockroach on water, I had floated on my spindly arms and legs in the giant toilet bowl of New York.

I was only a block away now and I started chuckling. When I had parked the Mercedes there, it was the day after Helmsley's wake.

During his last few years, he moved away from literature and more and more toward history. When I asked him about this interest, he replied that when he got old and turned senile his memories might fuse with this vast bank of historical data and the history of the world would seem like his own personal past. I felt somewhat senile as I walked to my Mercedes. Glenn's son still wanted to mutilate me; Ox would probably toss me in the same jail cell with Miguel, if Miguel was in jail; Ternevsky would try to have me castrated.

I could see the car on the corner. Then I realized that I no longer had the key, but I knew how to hotwire engines.

And then like the Cheshire Cat the hope vaporized leaving only a mocking grin. I realized that this wasn't the car. I looked around and down the street. My last chance had vanished into itself like a snail coiling up into his shell.

Insidiously I had lost my grip, and now this was it. I thought all this without much emotion. I really didn't care anymore. I couldn't hang on anymore. I didn't have the guts to kill myself, but I didn't want it to continue. I walked a couple of blocks, empty, listless, and wished I could cry. I wandered through the neighborhood.

The religion of the car—the diabolic hope, the purposeful pulsing of blood, the flight into coherence—allowed for some rationalizing an afterlife. A new theology was evolving, one that had a faith-in-death clause. It was evolved when I kicked a dead waterbug on the pavement. It was dried out, hollowed, emptied, like some kind of shell. Maybe, I thought, its body is a shell, maybe all bodies are shells. We hatch and die. Our spirit or something like that is the yolk: it lives the real life, the true life. It wasn't comforting. The car would have been better.

"Spare any change?" I asked one guy who looked as if he could. He ignored me. I asked another guy, who walked by more quickly. And then another and another and another and so on.

"Get a fucking job, you bum," an apelike man said to me.

"I'm...not well," I replied meekly, unstably. But then some gear locked into place and I started yelling back, "I got nothing to lose. I could do anything I want to you, and the worst that you think you can do to me can only be better than what I'm going through now. I got nothing to lose, nothing..."

I walked some more, and I guess the light got dimmer, but it was still day; time wasn't going anywhere. I felt very tired and I went into a doorway and dropped to my knees and instinctively looked out for cops and foot-stomping kids. I saw cars and legs and sniffing dogs. My eyes trailed up a street pole. It was Sackett Street. What difference did it make? It could have been Mahoegushmoegel Street, and so what? And I laughed at that.

After some time, I started thinking. It would have been so good to see the Mercedes there. It would have meant there is a God and he's a good guy and he'll give you a break from time to time. I wondered what had happened to the last of Helmsley's books that were in the back seat of the car. If the car had been stolen, they probably would have been chucked; if the car had been impounded, they still probably would have been chucked. While I wandered around the neighborhood, I kept an eye out for them. But I saw no sign of them. The great sandcastle of literature that he had built for himself had completely vanished.

Before getting up to scrounge for food, I wondered if ever at any time anything—maybe a God or angels or some invisible force that watches everything—would know that I died, just know about it all. And then I thought. This has got to work itself out somehow. I wondered where I would be in a year. And then I realized that for the past couple of years, if asked where I would be in a year I'd probably have predicted that I'd find some meteoric, inexplicable success. For the first time, I realized that if I didn't die, I would probably just survive, and the next year I would just be grateful to have a place and maybe a couple of bucks in some savings account and a small TV or something, and that'd do fine. God was time, I remember thinking. Time was everything. God was the pace of time. I remember thinking about this magical unit of time, a year, just a small clip of God's pinky nail. I had faith in the duration. A year would come somehow and save me. At some point, I started repeating the phrase aloud, like a chant or a prayer. I remember that much, not because my prayers were answered, but because they got a response.

EIGHTEEN

"What the fuck are you mumbling?" A set of clothed knees were in front of me, glaring at me.

"Just a year," I replied and looked up meekly, and I recognized the face. "Your name is Bonnie, isn't it?"

"No, asshole; Angela, remember? What the fuck happened to you?"

"I got sick and..." I clucked my tongue and raised my eyebrows and asked for some money.

"What the fuck happened to you?"

Then I started crying because someone was actually asking me that, and I started begging her for some food or anything and said that I was in deep shit in a really bad way and needed help, and I knew that she didn't like me and could laugh at me and walk away, but please don't just leave me! I cried till I was exhausted. She just stood above me and looked down; her expression didn't change.

"You're right," she finally spoke. "I don't fucking like you at all. You're scum." And I thought she was going to spit at me, and she turned to go, and I swear I don't understand it, but she turned to me and said, "Follow a half a block behind me, you capisce?" I nodded. "I don't want anyone knowing you're with me, capisce?" I nodded.

She started walking down the street slowly, passing the OTB and saying hi to a couple of old guys. I followed slowly behind. I wasn't sure what the fuck it was going to lead to, but figured even if she was going to lock me in some room and beat the shit out of me, there was still some hope that maybe I could convince her to feed me, so I could feel the pain more acutely. There wasn't any more hope in that doorway.

I followed at a good distance. In case anyone was watching from a parallax angle, I deliberately walked this way and that—no one could have second-guessed my destination. I kept a tight line of sight on her. She was the only fish on my only hook, and I couldn't reel myself in until she was inside. Her door slammed shut halfway up the street, and I kept straggling this way and that, looking in garbages, keeping in character. Boy, was I hungry. In a moment I was in front of her house. I saw that the door was slightly ajar and I dashed in.

"Did you run right here?" she asked sharply as soon as I slammed the door behind me.

"I swear I didn't. I was real careful, I swear it."

"All right, come on then." She led me into the bathroom, put some clothes on a hook, and put a black garbage bag on the cover of the toilet. Before she left, she pulled the shower curtain aside and gave me some calamine lotion for the scabs and cuts.

"That goes," she said, pointing to my beard and handing me a razor. "Put your old clothes in the bag and seal it."

I towelled off, sheared the beard with scissors I got from the medicine cabinet, and shaved. I eagerly put the clothes on. Although they were not new and hung loosely from me, they were soft, well ironed, and smelled delicious: they seemed edible. When I looked in a full length mirror, I had this strange recognition and inspected the clothing carefully until I realized that I was wearing Helmsley's garments. I still had only my old shoes, and although I had these new clothes, I had no intention of throwing out my old clothes. There were still cold days ahead. At best this might be a comfort station, where I could get a meal, a shower, and a change of clothes. Then, perhaps, I might get some kind of job. At least I could sit in coffee shops without being thrown out immediately. I could shoplift without being an instant suspect.

"Hey, how did you get Helmsley's clothes?" I asked upon leaving the bathroom.

"He left a bunch here.... You can have them." She took the garbage bag and was about to take it out the door.

"Hey, I still need that stuff."

"Not in my house."

I remained silent as she threw the bag into a trash heap outside. Did she expect me to stay the night? Or perhaps just for dinner? If I asked her what exactly I could anticipate, I might make her nervous and panicky. I was in a very bad way and had little latitude. Like a fine tool or a dumb animal, she could be used and manipulated for one's benefit—or misused and made into a danger to everyone around her. Helmsley, in all his braininess, couldn't use this tool properly.

When she returned, she saw me standing in the middle of her living room floor, just standing there thinking.

"Well, sit down or something," she said as she walked off into another room.

I sat up against the wall and thought about how horrible the outside was. To be outside was terrifying to me; the security of being indoors was unbelievable. To have a place to come to of one's own design seemed unfathomable. An idea occurred to me: if I committed a crime, I'd go to prison. A place is an extension and confirmation of the identity, I thought. If you're neurotic or afraid or losing control, you might keep the place nunnery neat, with soups alphabetized in the cupboard or pillows on the couch arranged symmetrically. Strangely although I've always liked the idea of a clean place, I've always been a messy person. A place too clean and orderly makes me feel self-conscious. Angela's furniture, knickknacks, and such seemed to be watching me. No, more than just watching me, they seemed to demand, by example, a code of behavior. I had to remain within the protocol of the order of the place.

"What the fuck are you doing?"

"What did I do?" I asked, rising unsteadily.

"Why are you sitting on the floor?"

"What am I supposed to do, sit on the wall?" She pointed to a chair and started hollering about how it was the latest invention. I don't know why I didn't even consider the chair.

"I've sat in chairs before, okay?" I yelled back. "I had a good reason for sitting on the floor. Did that ever occur to you?"

"What reason?"

"'Cause I have an edema build-up in my knees, and I was trying to put some pressure on the area."

"What, you got water on the knee?"

"Yeah," I replied, rolling up my pants. Fortunately my knees were swollen so she bought it.

"Whatever suits you." She left the room. I sat in the chair. In a minute she returned, carrying some crumpled sheets.

"Well, what are you doing in a chair now?" she yelled.

"You made me feel uncomfortable sitting on the floor," I mumbled.

"Sit on the fucking floor if you want," she barked. And grabbing the back of the wooden chair, she yanked it so that I fell to the ground.

"My knees are fine now."

"I think you're a fucking liar about the knees."

"Why would I lie to you?"

"I don't know," she replied. I didn't say anything, and she walked out of the room. What was she doing in the other rooms? I crept to a doorway and peeked. She was making a bed. I moved silently back into the living room, went over to a bookcase, and surveyed its contents. There were a bunch of pastel-tone romances; the John Jakes historic novel series, named after frontier states and illustrated with covered wagons and cleavage; and glitzy soft-porn best-sellers with embossed red lettering. As my eyes travelled along the colorful, gumdrop-colored paperbacks, I suddenly spotted a dusty hardcover on an out-of-reach shelf: H. Lefebre's biography *Diderot*. I strained high to pick it off the shelf and, upon opening it, recognized Helmsley's Ex Libris mark—it was a first American edition printed in the 1930s. I quietly put it back, took my seat on the floor, pulled my knees up, placed my arms on my lap, and let my hands hang between my legs. I wished I thought of sitting on the chair from the start.

"Hey, hey!" I awoke from a deep sleep with her yelling and shaking me.

"Huh?" I jumped up nervously.

"This ain't a place to sleep, asshole." It was time to go.

"Okay," I said nervously and asked if I could use the bathroom.

"I don't give a shit," she said. I went to the bathroom and locked the door. I didn't have to do anything, but I didn't want to leave until I absolutely had to. I sat on the toilet seat and leaned back on the tank, drifting off.

"What the hell you doing in there?" she screamed while banging on the door.

"Nothing, nothing," I replied, opening the door.

"I thought you died in the bathtub or something."

"No, I'm okay," I replied, but used her idea. "Do you mind if I take a bath?"

"You just took a shower!" she hissed. But then, more gently, "I don't care, go ahead." She was about to close the door, but stopped and asked, "What were you doing in here all that time?"

"I guess I drifted off."

"Well, why don't you go to sleep?"

"I don't have anywhere to go," I confessed.

"Go to bed, asshole, in there." She led me to a room where she had made the bed earlier. I thanked her, and as soon as she left the room, I tiredly thanked the darkness, which seemed to embody a great presence, God maybe…. Sleep popped me down like a pill, producing a remarkably fulfilling emptiness.

"Are you hungry?" she screamed in at me. I sat up instantly. My mind raced, trying to bridge the gap between deep sleep and what seemed like an interrogation. She repeated, "Are you hungry?"

Instinctively I said no. If I say yes, I thought, she might interpret it as me trying to make her into a maid or expecting a service from her. I was surprised to see morning light streaming in through the windows.

"At least have coffee."

I got fully dressed, shoes and socks and all, and went into the kitchen, where I sat at a dinette table. She made herself a full breakfast—hash browns, eggs sunny-side up, three strips of perfectly crisp bacon, toast, and coffee. I longed for the smoothness of yolk, for the texture of salty bacon, and lightly done, buttery toasts. She chewed equinely. She might just as well had been chomping on oats and grain. When she had consumed barely a third of the plate, she tossed the meal into the garbage and then walked off into one of those rooms. I raced over to the trash can and scooped out a large splat of solidified egg white. But then I heard her coming and shoved the egg white deep between my sock and ankle, a cache to eat later.

She walked by the room. My God, she was dressing, probably going off to work, and that meant I'd have to leave at any moment. Angela glanced in.

"What the fuck is the matter with you?" she asked, noticing my peculiar expression as I felt the egg white slither into my instep.

"Nothing."

She then marched off, cursing. I shoved a catsup bottle down the front of my pants. I took some bread and shoved it into my shirt. I saw a can of string beans on the shelf and shoved it in my pocket. I took a spatula and before Angela returned I frantically bent it so that it slid along the leg of my pants. Angela returned, fully dressed in street garb.

"Here's the key to the place. Lock up and turn out the lights if you leave," she instructed and walked out. Just like that.

When she left, I took the egg white out of my sock and found a cellophane bag. I put it in the bag along with other little bits and pieces of food she had thrown out. I wrapped up the scraps of food, went back into the bedroom I'd spent the night in, and hid them under the mattress. I then looked through her cupboards and inspected her other foods. I poured out a half box of spaghetti, which I'd found can be eaten raw if you chew very little bits. I broke up the spaghetti into four peg-size parts, wrapped a rubberband around them, and put them behind the schlock in the bookcase. She had four cans of Del Monte Creamed Corn, so I took one and hid it in one of her winter boots in the hallway closet. I hid flat things like bologna and Swiss cheese under the living room rug. I took other small items, too, not even knowing what they all were. The biggest dilemma was deciding how much food I could take without its absence being noticed.

Something occurred to me. I collected all the hidden articles of food. I checked the lock on the door and made sure that she hadn't given me a decoy key—one that would give me confidence but not open the door after it shut. I didn't want to leave the house, but I had to for my backup plans. So I walked around the neighborhood and soon headed toward Park Slope by walking along President Street. Then I spotted the bushes bordering a little neighborhood park. I dodged into the shrubbery and, digging as furiously as a squirrel with a prized acorn, carefully buried the little packets of food.

I scurried directly back to Angela's house, this time passing the street Helmsley had lived on. I thought, if she's back at the house and has changed the lock I won't be able to get in anyway. I stood outside Helmsley's old house and looked at his old living room window where new Levolor blinds hung. I entered the building and knocked on his old door. A young guy opened and politely asked, "Can I help you?"

"I was just looking for an old friend."

"Well, I'm the only resident here."

"I know," I said. "My friend died, but he used to live here."

"Oh, was his name Helmsley?" I nodded.

"I keep getting his junk mail," the guy continued. "Here," he said and picked a letter out of a nearby wicker basket. He handed it to me. Its windowed envelope read, "Helmsley Micinski may have already won one million dollars..."

I stared at it a moment and finally said, "He committed suicide, and I'm living with the person that drove him to it."

"How 'bout that."

"I just wanted to see what became of his old place, you know, I lived here myself off and on." The guy didn't invite me in but he opened his door and let me peek in. It was yupped out—virtually a Conran's showroom—although the guy seemed nice enough.

"You would've liked Helmsley, but he wouldn't've liked you."

"I'm sorry he died."

"What I mean is, I'm not sure if he would've approved of you. But he always separated issues from individuals. He could disagree with you about something and still like you."

"Oh?"

"He lived here for years. What do you pay in rent, if you don't mind my asking?"

"What did Helmsley pay?"

"He paid something like sixty-two-fifty a month or something."

"Holy shit!" The guy finally woke up. "I pay more than ten times that."

"You should go to the Rent Stabilization Board. I don't think they can raise it that much."

"Thanks, I will," he said, shutting the door. Fuck him, that fucking yuppie living in Helmsley's house. I kicked his door with all my might and raced down the stairs and onto the street. I kept running until I reached Angela's house.

There, I opened the door with relief and disbelief. Clutching the key in my hand, I walked over the threshold, and then I locked the door behind me. Immediately I slipped the key back into my shirt pocket. I was behind a locked door with a key in my pocket. I felt comforted, happy, kingly. Next, I walked very quickly through each of her rooms and made sure the windows were locked and no one else was in the house. And then I returned to the kitchen and inspected the cupboards, making sure that everything was in place so that she wouldn't suspect I had rifled through them. I spaced cans evenly apart so that telltale gaps weren't apparent. I even spent some time thinking about topics I could talk about with her to subtly drain away the time. I tried to remember the names of popular television shows, but could only come up with "Starsky & Hutch," "Macmillan & Wife," "The Night Stalker," and other seventies stuff. So I decided that I would talk and try to guide conversation only if she initiated it. And then I sat down and tuned out awhile.

NINETEEN

Angela came home eventually, and we watched TV; there wasn't much conversation. She made us spaghetti, and then she went out. She came home late that night, loaded. I could hear a muffled sound coming from her room, and then I fell asleep. The next morning, she asked me if I wanted breakfast, and I said yes and ate everything and wondered if she was going to throw me out. Afterward, she asked me if I was thinking about getting a job (my reply was a grunt), and then she left the house.

It felt as if things stopped again when she left. I sat for a while, decided to steal some more food, went on a walk, hid the food in the bushes, and walked to another place where I thought I might have parked my Mercedes. It wasn't there. Then I walked a few blocks toward Brooklyn Heights, but I panicked and ran home. I put the police lock—the kind that you can't open from the outside—on the door. I got a piece of paper and made exact notes of the order of everything as I went through all her drawers. I took out her jeans and T-shirts and some of her underthings. In one drawer I even found a battery-operated massager with different attachments and smelled it. And then, exactly following the instructions I wrote, I put everything back in the correct order.

I moved on to some file cabinets that had records of utility bills and was amazed by how methodical she was. I found a copy of a very well-written letter responding to a phone bill for which she felt she was unjustly overcharged. I put back the files and went into a closet and took some cardboard boxes down from the top shelf. I went through old papers and found something that blew me away: her name written in Latin on a bachelor's degree from Sacred Heart College, on the bottom of which was written *cum laude.* She had a fucking B.A. in sociology with honors! I put everything back.

I watched TV until she came home that night. She made a dinner and ate it quietly. While she washed the dishes, I watched some TV. She came in with a six pack and handed me a beer.

"What you watching?"

"'Dallas.'"

"What do you do here during the day?" she asked out of the blue.

"I'm recuperating."

"Well, how much longer are you going to be recuperating?"

"I don't know. Why?"

"I think you ought to get a job and a place of your own." The idea seemed inconceivable and I told her so.

"Why were you like that, anyway?"

"Like what?"

"You were a bag man."

"Who?" I asked, feigning ignorance.

"How old are you?"

"Why?"

"In your early twenties or something?"

"Yeah, so?"

"Helmsley said he thought you were very intelligent."

"Yeah, so?"

"He said that you had some kind of fuck-up in life and you had to get back into the swing."

"What are you talking about?"

"He said that something happened back home.   Where you from, California or something?"

"Yeah, so?"

"I'm just trying to help. Helmsley and I used to talk about you a lot."

"You and Helmsley? You and Helmsley! You destroyed the man and you sit there calmly like you were talking with him a couple of hours ago."

"I was just trying to help you, asshole!"

"Where was all this help the night Helmsley stepped off the Brooklyn Bridge?"

She got up, left the room, and slammed the door behind her. It was only about ten o'clock at night, so I got dressed and went out for a walk.

I walked down Clinton Street to Pierrepont Street, to Glenn's house. It was a cold walk, but after living on the street I knew that it could never get too cold. Her house was a flicker of lights. Someone walked by the window, and then just as instantly was out of view. I wondered if she had reconciled with that guy, the fellow she caught cheating on her. It seemed like years had passed. I wondered about her kid, I wondered if she had gotten the Mercedes back. It was okay if she did. It served me right. I felt very sorry for her. And although I didn't really care for her, I was curious how it all turned out. Soon, when the cold got colder, I walked back to the house.

I locked the door, stripped down, and went to bed. As I lay in bed, I was able to just barely make out the sound of someone crying.

The next morning I awoke before her. Looking at the clock, I realized that it was well after nine, which was when she usually awoke me before going off to work. I thought that maybe to be tactful about using her, I should make her breakfast for a change. I gently knocked on her door. When I got no response, and since the door was slightly open, I pushed it open a bit more. She was sprawled out on the floor in a pool of what looked like blood. When I went over, I saw that it was vomit. There was an empty quartsize bottle of gin. I felt flustered and left the room, closing the door behind me. I quietly made myself some breakfast.

While eating, I thought about what to do. To me she was still the killer of Helmsley, and despite the charity I still didn't like her. I hated the fact that I needed her, and revenge was something I still desired. Opening a window, I noticed it was unusually warm out. On a shelf in the kitchen cabinet, I found a jar filled with coins. I extracted a bunch of quarters and left.

I went to the F train and lingered awhile looking at the posted subway map. When a Manhattan-bound train came into the station, I opened the gate, crossed the platform and boarded. The token clerk deliberately looked away; none of them cared anymore. I got off at the Second Avenue stop and walked northward. I reached Saint Mark's Place just as the police were arresting a group of street vendors. I saw Flowers, my old friend, standing across the street, looking sadly at his compatriots being ushered into police cars.

"What happened?" I asked him. "I never saw them arresting anyone before."

"I just got away in time," he said.

"You're lucky."

"Lucky, hell, they got my stuff," he said. "Four hundred dollars in leather jackets and clothing." I stood with him awhile and watched as they collected all the merchandise into plastic bags and loaded them into the trunk of their cars.

Looking up the block, I noticed something much sadder. On the marquee of the Saint Mark's Cinema black letters spelled out, "Closed for Renovation." Whoever Pepe was trying to fool, he didn't fool me. I remembered what Angel had said about the yuppie mall.

I walked up Second and stopped in at the Second Avenue Deli. I got a coffee and a homemade knish with sauerkraut and mustard to go. I paid for it in quarters. I walked over to Third Avenue and sat in front of Hudson's Army Surplus store, across the street from the Zeus, and ate my food. I watched the theater, hoping to see either Miguel or Ox, but neither appeared.

When I finished eating, I wondered what else to do. I considered going to the Strand Bookstore. I walked over to the Strand and looked at books until someone yelled out the name Kevin. I looked up and saw Kevin, an old friend of Helmsley's. I couldn't socialize. I snuck out so he wouldn't see me. Heading down Broadway, I walked slowly back toward Brooklyn. When I got to the base of the Brooklyn Bridge, I had to walk over some scaffolding; the bridge was undergoing a renovation. Stairs were being removed and the wooden slats were being replaced with a concrete walkway. The Statue of Liberty, too, was still under scaffolding. I lingered for a while on the bridge and wondered from which part Helmsley had taken his last step. I started feeling bad, so I jogged over the bridge, down Clinton Street, through the Heights, into Cobble Hill, finally reaching Angela's place.

I knocked first to give her warning. The door whipped open. Some middle-aged guy—a stocky, short, and close-to-the-earth type—looked me over. He wore a filthy white tank top T-shirt with suspenders pressing into his furry, fleshy shoulders.

"Who the hell are you?" said he.

"I'm a house guest of Angela's."

"She don't have no house guest. She's sick. Come back another day." He slammed the door on me. My heart was slammed in that door; it started palpitating wildly. I walked around a bit to calm down. The sound of change rattling around in my pocket offered some comfort. But the more I thought about living out on the street...sleeping in the subway...eating food out of garbage cans, I became aware that my reprieve was over. Maybe I could kill myself. After walking an hour or so, I thought for no good reason that maybe the gorilla had left her house. I finally became shackled to a reckless decision: a raid on her house in an attempt to salvage some supplies suddenly made sense. I returned to her door.

I pulled out my key and quietly slipped it into the cylinder. Softly I opened the door; I wanted at least to get some more of Helmsley's clothes. Maybe I could also steal some money. At least, I'd had the foresight to bury the food. I stepped into the living room and scanned for anything small of value. I spotted some knick-knacks—a polished stone egg standing upright in a holder, a small oriental style vase, a miniature glass bell—which I slipped into my pockets. Good folks love trinkets, I told myself, and slowly moved deeper into the house. I could hear them talking in her bedroom.

"Come on," I heard him say.

"No, I'm sick."

"What's it gonna hurt?"

"No," she said weakly.

I dropped a broom to the floor.

"Who the fuck is that?" she said, and the guy charged out at me. He threw me on the ground, pinning my arms down with his knees. I didn't resist.

"It's that guy who was here earlier," he yelled out to her in the next room, and then grabbing my throat between his thumb and forefinger he bellowed, "What the fuck's wrong with you?"

I didn't say anything. Then she was there, wrapped in a sheet, looking sweaty and white. She held the sheet in one hand and the wall in the other.

"Get off of him," she whispered hoarsely.

Punctuating each word with his hand on my face, the guy answered, "I"—slap—"told"—slap—"this"—slap—"guy"—slap—"earlier"—slap—"that..."

With mustered force, she kicked the guy hard in the ribs. He didn't budge. He looked up at her.

"Are you insane or what?" she croaked.

"Fuck you!" he roared. He got up and smacked her hard across the mouth. Her eyes squinted and rolled; he held her face tightly. I jumped on his shaggy back. He effortlessly tossed me off and was about to punch me in the face when she shrieked.

"For Chrissake, just leave the house! Please Dana!"

"You called me," he heaved. He stomped into the other room and emerged, heading toward the front door with his hat and coat. All the while he was talking at her, mimicking her voice, "I'm sick, Dana. I think I'm dying, please help. I rush right over, shower your own vomit offa you, get you chicken soup. And you treat me like this. Well, next time, have this clown come to your rescue. You fuckin' drunk." He slammed the door with a vibrating force. I was alone with her.

She collapsed into an upholstered chair and spoke in her hoarse whisper, "I got alcohol poisoning."

"I thought you just get drunk."

"No, you can poison yourself," she said. "I yelled for you for hours. Where the fuck did you go?"

"Just for a walk."

"Didn't you find it weird that I wasn't up?"

"I didn't think about it."

"Taking care of number one, is that it?" I didn't know what to say. I kept silently chanting, she killed Helmsley, right? But the hatred that was once hard and tangible was getting harder and harder to hold on to; it was melting in my hands. She rose and went to her bed. Not knowing what else to do, I followed her in.

"I need help," she said quite matter-of-factly. "Are you going to help me or do I have to find someone else?"

"I guess I'll help you," I replied.

"You guess?" she asked, and through squinted eyes she looked at me. "You ungrateful bastard. Just get your things and get out of here—I'll call back Dana."

"Fuck that!" I broke. I couldn't hold it anymore. "Helmsley killed himself because you dumped him. And you couldn't give two shits. Of course, I hate you!" She rolled over and looked up at me in surprise.

"That shouldn't come as a shock," I babbled. "I always hated you. And I'm not vain enough to believe that you love me, so what gives here? What the hell am I here for?"

In a very low, distant tone, and in a very slow cadence, she tried to explain: "I loved him. I really loved that man." Then she sobbed, "What the fuck did he see in me? Did he ever tell you what he saw in me?"

"Beats the shit out of me," I said sincerely; I certainly had never seen anything in her.

"Beats the shit out of me, too," she responded absently.

"You should have had more faith," I said to her.

"More faith!" she responded. "I remembered when I first met you, imitating the way I was talking, making fun of how stupid I was. I could only imagine what he must've thought."

That ensuing blank of silence filled me with self-disgust.

"I could love slobs and bastards," she continued. "I've had cripples and creeps in the sack, and I've bent over backwards for them. But for the first time, I meet a guy who really had it all. Good looking, brainy. The whole time I couldn't help thinking, What's the matter with this guy? When's he gonna dump me? He's not gonna keep a pig like me around, no way. I felt fucking anxious as hell, like he's going to get under my skin and bang, drop me from heaven. Well, I finally couldn't take it anymore. I told him I never wanted to see him again. He wouldn't leave it at that, so I damaged him and finally went off with another guy. The next day, when I heard he offed himself, I realized that he wasn't fucking around with me, that he really loved me." She started crying in a painful and frightening way.

"You know, you might have played a part in his suicide, but I don't think you were the total reason," I finally said. "He wasn't writing anymore. I think he was coming to terms with the fact that he couldn't be what he wanted to be."

"What was that?"

"Some kind of great towering thinker."

While she thought about this, her face seemed to brighten, like a dimmer inside was slowly turning up. The pores and lines seemed to vanish. I got up and buttoned the collar of my shirt, which I suppose she misunderstood as some gesture toward departing, because she said, "You don't have to leave. I owe you one."

"You owed him one. You don't owe me shit."

"Well, maybe not, but he used to talk about you. He used to say he wanted to help you."

"How?"

"He said that New York was your way of fluctuating yourself. No wait, he said you were flatualating yourself."

"Flatualating myself?"

"You know, when you hit yourself." She rolled her eyes. "And when I saw you sitting there in that doorway all zonked out, it was like Helmsley was right there saying, Help him."

"Did he mention why I was flagellating myself?"

"No."

I nodded and made a thank you expression. After a while, she asked for a glass of water. I got her a glass, which she drank slowly. Then she closed her eyes and lay back down. I sat on a chair near the bed and watched her sleeping. I was still shocked over how she felt about Helmsley. I had grazed along the surface of her actions and made deep judgments. Rejecting someone because you couldn't understand their love, that was a new one. The more I thought about it the longer the shadow of doubt stretched over all my conclusions. More often than not, things were as they seemed. But as I stared at her, she wasn't as bad looking as I had once thought. I realized how all this time I had seen her the wrong way, and how one's character affects one's appearance. Although she wasn't my type she was attractive. As I thought about her—the vulnerable intelligence, the violent honesty, and the fact that in the entire city she was the only one who took me in and fed me—she became more and more irresistible. Baited by an obscure beauty, trapped by an intense sorrow—all prior definitions had been overruled: this was love.

I must have fallen asleep because at one point I was aware of her stirring me. I climbed into bed with her, fully dressed. And she quickly fell back to sleep in my arms.

I've been living with her now for some years. I found a job in a chain bookstore and eventually became the manager. I've settled in, acquired new friends, people to console and to be consoled by. In Brooklyn I am content, the closest we can come to a sustained happiness.